Praise for *A Cliché Christmas*
by Nicole Deese

"A delightfully fun romance full of hope and healing that is sure to bring laughter, tears, and a reminder of the true meaning of Christmas."
—Tammy L. Gray, Kindle bestselling author

"It's impossible to read *A Cliché Christmas* without wishing for snow, thinking of mistletoe, and longing for small-town life. From tear-your-heart-out dialogue to heart-skipping romance, author Nicole Deese pens her stories in a way that will keep you turning pages and begging for more."
—Amy Matayo, author of *The Wedding Game*, *Love Gone Wild*, and *Sway*

"Nicole Deese won me over at fa-la-la-la. It isn't often that I laugh out loud when reading books. *A Cliché Christmas* was one of the rare few that earned that honor . . . and right from the beginning of the book. The character development and dialogue are always my main real considerations when I review books. Ms. Deese masters both of these with grace, wit, and a touch of sass. Needless to say, I simply loved this book and highly recommend it, not just for Christmas but at any time of the year."
—Sarah Price, bestselling author

"A Hallmark movie in the making, *A Cliché Christmas* is a magical love story that is anything but cliché, dazzling readers with a truly delightful plot and characters who shine more than the twinkle lights on a tree. One of my favorite holiday reads ever!"
—Julie Lessman, award-winning author of the *Daughters of Boston*, *Winds of Change*, and Heart of San Francisco series

A
Season
to LOVE

A Season to LOVE

Nicole Deese

Waterfall
PRESS

Text copyright © 2016 Nicole Deese

Published by Waterfall Press, Grand Haven, MI

www.brilliancepublishing.com

Amazon, the Amazon logo, and Waterfall Press are trademarks of Amazon.com, Inc., or its affiliates.

ISBN-13: 9781503950504
ISBN-10: 1503950506

Cover design by Jason Blackburn

Printed in the United States of America

To Tim.
For leading me to the mountain and loving me enough
to make me climb.

Chapter One

I could have promised my daughter anything—a pony, a princess, a rainbow in a bottle—but instead, I'd promised her something equally unattainable: my bravery.

Today my cancer-free seven-year-old was putting that promise to the test.

"Come on, Mommy!" Savannah tugged my hand, but my legs were stiff and sluggish.

"We have plenty of time. Slow down."

Slow down. Two words that had been on continuous repeat since she'd woken me, bouncing on my bed in her new sparkly red shoes— Uncle Weston's gift to feed her obsession for all things glitter.

She led our way through the parking lot, her energetic stride forcing her backpack into a bounce and me into a near jog. Pockets of people waited near the electronic signboard, with the scrolling FIRST DAY OF SCHOOL, but I knew better than to ask Savannah to stop for a picture. She had a goal, the same goal that had kept me awake at night for nearly a week.

The freshly painted double doors at the front of Lenox Elementary School were propped open to welcome the new year. Only, this pressure building inside my chest didn't exactly feel festive. We entered the lobby together, her thin fingers still curled around mine, my heart two strides slower than my feet. I willed it to catch up, to remember Savannah's countdown to this very moment—the scattering of purple *X*s on the bedroom calendar.

The smell of boxed crayons and pencil shavings filled the air, nostalgia painting a landscape from a lifetime ago—of a life that no longer felt like mine. The screech of sneakers against tired linoleum floors sang the anthem of reunited friends and faculty. But it wasn't my memories of attending this school as a child or even of teaching at this school as an adult that caused my spine to prickle with déjà vu.

Three turns and two hallways later, Savannah dropped my hand and studied the class list outside Mrs. Hudson's door.

"Alyssa's in my class!"

"That's great, honey." My words sounded as frozen as my smile.

Her dark-chocolate eyes took in the clusters of students, the maze of desks, the shelves upon endless shelves of books, puzzles, and crafts. Once inside the classroom, she found her laminated name tag quickly and waved me over. My fingers itched to reach into my purse and grab a handful of disinfectant wipes to saturate each and every surface of this room.

"Mommy—look, my very own desk." Savannah smoothed her hand over the top of the chipping varnish, her eyes alight, her voice the sound of childlike faith.

"Savannah!" Alyssa, Savannah's athletic redheaded friend, raced across the room.

A soft touch on my shoulder shifted my attention away from the giddy reunion. "She'll do great, Willa. I can see how excited she is to be in school. Oh, and I'll make sure to e-mail you the slots I have open for classroom volunteers."

Megan Hudson, Savannah's second-grade teacher, stood at my side. Since high school, our lives had paralleled each other: we both married our senior prom dates, we both graduated with honors, we both earned our master's in education.

Only, the sudden loss of my husband seven years ago had put an end to our shared life experiences.

"Thank you, Megan."

With a last gentle pat, Megan walked to the front of her classroom and pointed to the instructions on the whiteboard, reminding parents of pickup time and location.

The clock at the back of the room chimed a high-pitched ping, ping, ping, and a slow-snaking panic crept into my chest.

"Savannah—" My well-planned words were cut short. She sprang toward me and wrapped her arms around my waist. Her enthusiasm rocked me off center. "I *love* this day, but I love you most." Savannah tightened her arms above my hips, swaying us both as if in a dance.

I kissed the top of her head, her short, baby-fine hair a whisper of hope that tickled my lips. "Not possible."

Because it wasn't possible. She wasn't a mother. She hadn't counted the weeks of pregnancy, hadn't borne the pain of childbirth, hadn't felt the anguish of the six-letter word that could drown a parent in a pool of their own tears. *Cancer.*

She hopped away and waved. "See you after school."

With blurry, stinging eyes, I turned and exited her classroom, just like I had two years ago when I'd dropped my seemingly healthy daughter off for kindergarten only to admit her to the oncology floor at Children's Hospital a week later.

She's fine. I'm fine. Everything is going to be fine. The rapid fire of my pulse disagreed.

Pushing my way past a throng of happy families, I darted through the parking lot and shut myself inside my car. With my overactive imagination fully engaged, I fought against the quick, shallow breaths and answered the siren's call in my glove box.

A stashed package of red-and-white pinwheel mints.

Most people saw these candies as a way to freshen their breath; I saw them as a way to focus my mind. A method of coping I'd picked up in therapy years ago. Of course, not during one of my hour-long counseling sessions, but rather from my time sitting in the waiting room. Ironic how a little basket of mints had helped me more than my grief counselor.

I reached inside the bag, unwrapped the familiar, crinkly plastic, and popped a small disc into my mouth. Immediately, the smooth texture and taste of menthol worked its magic, knocking me down a few ladder rungs on my climb to an attack.

My head thumped against the back of the seat as I recalled the words I'd spoken to Savannah during her final round of inpatient treatment. I'd dabbed her forehead with a cool rag after she'd finished emptying the contents of her stomach, the color of her skin distressingly pale . . .

"You're so brave, baby."

She did little more than blink at my familiar words, her energy as absent as her smile. This oppressive weariness had shadowed her for days—a cloud cover to her sunshine personality.

I lifted the damp cloth from her temple and stared at my frail daughter—this child who'd given me a reason to hope time and time again. A sudden and desperate question pushed to the forefront of my mind.

Had I fought as hard for her as she had fought for me?

I touched her hand, wove her bony fingers through mine. "Things are going to be different when all this is over, Savannah—better."

She licked her chapped lips and I reached for her pink princess water bottle. "When all the cancer is gone?"

"Yes. Maintenance will be so much easier and then . . ." I bent the straw and slipped it into her mouth and waited for the slight shake of her head to indicate she was finished. "And then we'll be free to do all kinds of new things together, things we've never done before."

Her eyes shifted up to mine. "Like what?"

"Like . . . um . . . exploring new places and meeting new friends and trying some new hobbies and—"

She turned her head so that her cheek smashed into the folds of her pillow. "And going back to school?"

"Yes." Though the idea of her being outside my reach for an entire school day was hard to imagine after two years of homeschooling, a classroom was a far better alternative than a hospital room. "And then maybe—"

"Maybe you won't have to be afraid anymore?"

Tears gathered in my eyes as guilt pinched my heart. I'd tried to keep my fears hidden, tried to lock them away in some secret compartment, but my daughter was too perceptive to be kept in the dark. "Yes . . . Mommy will be braver."

"You promise?"

A hard swallow and then, "Yes, baby. I promise."

She closed her eyes and a soft smile graced her mouth. "We'll both be brave then."

With a jumbo bag of dinner mints splayed open on my lap, I pressed my forehead to the top of the steering wheel and wished I could ignore the glaringly obvious truth.

A promise was only as strong as the person who made it.

And my promise had become as empty as this school parking lot.

Four days and one finished book series later, I set my travel mug back into the cup holder and then lifted the newspaper from the passenger seat. Careful not to honk my horn, I smoothed the fold out of today's crossword and contemplated definitions to words I'd rarely spoken in any of my twenty-nine years.

No time like the present to brush up on my vocabulary.

Tap, tap, tap.

A not-so-gentle knuckle rap on my window nearly sent me into cardiac arrest.

Weston. My baby brother.

Suddenly I was sixteen again, sneaking out the back door to meet my boyfriend when Weston the Detective flicked on the lights.

Caught.

I blinked the memory away, the crossword crumpling onto my lap. I covered the recycled paper with my right hand, as if that gesture alone might save me from an explanation that sounded nothing less than certifiable.

"What's up, sis?" Weston's eyes had already spotted the incriminating evidence: the books, the coffee, and the little baggie of homemade granola I'd been munching on since midmorning. It was a perfect moment to use today's 10 down: *enmeshed.*

Sample sentence: Willa Hart is completely *enmeshed* in her own pitiful paranoia.

"I'm . . . I'm just . . ." *A horrible liar.*

Weston shook his head. "Nice try, but I've only got a few minutes left in my lunch period."

And yet, here he was. Lucky me.

As a high school shop teacher, Weston rarely left campus during school hours, which was likely why I hadn't calculated the odds of him seeing me. In the parking lot. A block from his workplace.

He disappeared from the window and came around to the passenger-side door. I popped the lock, though truth be told, locked or not, my brother would have found a way in.

With a sweep of his hand, he scattered my neatly stacked stash of parking lot supplies onto the floorboard and plopped down beside me.

"Staking out your daughter's school." He made a tsking sound. "You've taken helicopter mom to a whole new level. You know this isn't normal, right?"

I didn't answer. *Knowing* my actions teetered on the line of insanity wasn't really the problem.

"Listen, I didn't come to point out the obvious." He twisted in his seat and picked up my baggie of granola. "I found you a job."

Three deafening seconds ticked by as I stared at my brother. With everyone else he joked and pranked and goofed around. With me, he shot straight.

"What do you mean? I *have* a job."

"Working with Mom at the antique store is a sad excuse for a job. There's hardly enough work for her, much less you. Besides, you're too tied to them as it is."

"No, I'm *indebted* to them." My folks had done so much for me—and for Savannah especially. Aside from their active role in grandparenting, we lived in their guesthouse rent free. Their generosity had allowed me not only to homeschool Savannah during her treatments but to give 100 percent of my energy to her well-being. I couldn't have prayed for a greater blessing than what they'd been to me—even if their support felt overbearing at times.

Like usual, Weston ignored my comment. "And if you aren't willing to pursue teaching again, then—"

"I'm not." I cut him off, unwilling to hear the teaching lecture one more time: how I shouldn't waste my master's degree, how subbing would get my foot back in the door with the district, how setting a career goal would give me a sense of purpose. But I had a purpose. It just wasn't Weston-approved. "What job are you even talking about?"

"Parker Fitness Center." He reclined the seat and tossed a handful of crunchy oats into his mouth. "Sydney owes me a favor—actually she owes me about two million of them—and as you know, finding a *good* part-time job where they're willing to work around Savannah's school hours is next to impossible."

"I'm not interested. But please make sure to thank her for the offer." Adding another job and responsibility to the mix would mean more time away from what I *should* be doing: keeping the people I loved safe and healthy and whole. Distractions weren't the solution. They were the problem. "I'm working on a plan." And that was the truth, as long as the terms *working* and *plan* were relative.

Weston gave me his brother look—scrunched-in eyebrows, lowered chin, that annoying tilt of his head. "No, what you *have* is a promise you made to your daughter—to start living a *real* life. In the *real* world. And no, I don't count unpaid parking lot duty as a way to get over your life phobias."

Shame swirled in the pit of my stomach. "I'm trying."

He gestured to the school building. "It's September, Willa. She completed maintenance phase last month. The cancer is gone—it's *been* gone—so what are you waiting for now?" He exhaled, hard. "Taking this job could be a new start for you, a step forward. You'll be able to bank some extra cash *and* start saving up for a place of your own again—maybe even take that Disneyland trip Savannah put in her wish jar. You *need* this." I'd never heard pity in Weston's voice when he spoke to me, but this was close. "How do you expect to give her a 'better life after cancer' when you're too afraid to start a life of your own?"

Easy for him to say. In three months, he would be exchanging vows with his bride-to-be. His future was just beginning. But by the time I was Weston's age, I had buried my soul mate, had taught my then preschooler to read, and could hear my therapist's benediction to *create a new normal* in my sleep.

But that was the thing about "new normals." They, too, could change—in a single breath, or with a lost heartbeat, or even with a routine blood test.

He drummed a finger on his knee. "Besides, you need to make some friends."

"I have friends."

"No, you *had* friends. As in past tense. Don't get me wrong, any person in this town would give you the shirt off their back, but I bet you can't name a single time in the last year when you've done something for the sake of being social. Without Savannah."

I lifted my chin, a memory leaping to mind. "I went to coffee with Georgia."

"*Bzzzzzt!*" The irritating sound of a game show buzzer blurted from Weston's mouth.

"*What?* I did!"

"That was at the hospital's coffee shop. And Georgia is my fiancée. Doesn't count."

Using one of his favorite lines, I said, "A technicality you didn't specify."

Weston chewed on the side of his mouth to keep from laughing. He was better at masking his expressions than I was.

To be fair, he was better at most things than I was, including the best at getting under my skin.

"If you're gonna take the job, Sydney needs you Monday. It's front desk work—checking people in and whatnot. You can still drop Vannie off in the mornings and pick her up after school. She'll never know the difference. And better than that, *you'll* get socialized."

"I'm not an untrained puppy."

"Good, because I told Sydney you were housebroken. Wouldn't want to lose my reputation as an honest man."

I slugged him. Leave it to Weston to bring out the child in me. His laugh was as rich as it was deep, and I couldn't help but smile. He'd always been the happy type, but since Georgia had moved back to Lenox, his happiness could fill every floor of a Portland skyscraper.

"You're positive the position will be flexible around Savannah's school schedule?"

He narrowed his eyes. "Have I ever led you astray?"

No. A slow, deflated sigh slipped through my lips. Maybe he was right. Maybe taking this job would be the worry-free break my mind craved, at least while Savannah was in school.

Better yet, if this job could count as headway in the promise I made to my daughter, then . . .

"Fine. I'll talk to Sydney."

Weston lifted the newspaper from my lap and tapped the crossword puzzle. "Five across. *Victory.*"

Chapter Two

I'd never been one to hate Mondays.

Contrary to popular opinion, Mondays were just another day—a neutral day that neither gave nor took. But Thursdays, Thursdays were my nemesis. It was an early Thursday morning that took Chad from me by way of a cerebral aneurysm. And it was a late Thursday evening, huddled in a cold waiting room corner, when I learned of Savannah's cancer diagnosis. So it was no wonder that the day my daughter showed her first sign of sickness—a runny nose and a barking cough—happened on a Thursday.

"But Mommy, I really want to go to school today. It's Art Day." Savannah wiped her wet nose across the sleeve of her Dora the Explorer nightgown, her whine as pathetic sounding as the whine of the dog circling her feet. Savannah scooped Prince Pickles up in her arms, and he licked the underside of her chin.

Her laugh quickly broke into a coughing fit.

"No. I already called in to work." And I fully anticipated that by the day's end I'd be submitting my notice and committing to homeschooling for life. Sure, the staff at my new job was friendly and the building nice, but a paycheck and shallow social interaction weren't worth the risks. Weston was wrong. Taking this stupid job wasn't a baby step, it was a leap to the moon. Losing focus on what was important always ended in regret. I'd learned that life lesson too many times.

I grabbed a pair of her jeans and a red sweatshirt from her drawer and then proceeded to pull her nightgown over her head while she shifted her dog from one arm to the other. "But where are we going?"

"To the doctor."

"But you said—"

I winced at the confusion in her tone. "Savannah, honey, we're not going to the children's hospital, we're just going to visit Dr. McCade down the road. He needs to check your cough."

He was quite possibly the only doctor who could keep me from jumping to the worst possible conclusions.

I slipped a mint from my pocket, unwrapped it, and popped it in my mouth.

Dr. Ivar McCade had been Savannah's primary care doctor since she was a toddler. His practice was busy, but he'd always made Savannah a priority. It was because of his keen eye and attention to detail that Savannah had gone for more testing two years ago.

His early detection had quite possibly saved her life.

I took Prince Pickles from her arms and sat him on the ground. I wasn't certain whose whimper was louder, Savannah's or her dog's.

"Let's go, kiddo." I pointed down the hallway.

She pouted as she turned in the direction of the front door, but not before she let out a confirming sneeze.

She needed to see a doctor.

Today.

McCade Medical Clinic resided in the heart of Lenox. Sandwiched between the library and Jonny's Pizza, the small brick building with the

Scottish tartan sign hadn't changed much since the McCades moved to town five years ago from Portland, Oregon.

Doc Ivar McCade and his wife had fallen in love with the white-capped mountains and small-town feel of Lenox, and since moving here they'd become an active part of our community.

The bells on the clinic door chimed our entrance.

Marsha sat at the check-in desk, phone to ear, and motioned for Savannah to have a seat in the waiting room.

I approached the counter.

"I'll check you in," Marsha whispered, covering the receiver with one hand. "Sorry, on hold with insurance." She rolled her eyes and then slid the symptom sheet toward me. I quickly checked the necessary boxes and handed it back to her.

With the good fortune of a near-empty waiting room, we were called back to the yellow exam room just five minutes later.

As I gripped Savannah's waist to hoist her onto the padded table, my eyes caught on a blur of color next to the door. Hanging on the wall above the light switches was a framed landscape, a forest full of slender white pine trees, all frosted and wintry and beautiful. Yet it was the sunset beyond the timberland that captured my attention. A fireball of glowing oranges, brilliant reds, and radiant yellows spliced through the sleek tree trunks like a prisoner longing for escape.

The feeling was as familiar as the photograph.

A quick tap and the door opened. "Morning. I'm Dr. McCade."

Only he wasn't.

This man wasn't even old enough to doctor Savannah's My Little Ponies.

He stretched out a hand to me as I read—and then reread—the name stitched onto his white coat.

Dr. Patrick McCade.

"Hey! You're not Dr. McCade," Savannah said, stealing the words straight from my head.

He dropped his extended hand and turned to face my daughter, hands on his hips. "Oh yeah, why not?"

"You don't have white hair. Or bushy eyebrows. Or a potato nose—"

"Savannah." My whispered reprimand was ignored by both parties.

"And I don't speak like this either." The man straightened and cleared his throat. "You have a bit of a cold, do ya, lassie? Well, let's get you fixed up straight away so you can get back to playing on the school yard." The deep Scottish brogue was identical to Doc Ivar's.

Savannah clapped. "You grew young again!"

The doctor laughed while he washed his hands at the sink and then pulled out the rolling stool from underneath the cabinet. Hands flat on the seat, he drew it back as if getting ready to race a matchbox car. One lunge, one hop, and two tight spins later, he slammed on the brakes. An inch shy of colliding with Savannah's kneecaps. "Nah, little lassie. I'm the old doc's son." He said the last sentence without the slightest hint of an accent—as if he could turn it on or off like tap water.

Savannah's widening eyes were a telltale sign that her curiosity was about to show itself in the form of a thousand uninvited questions . . . if I didn't intervene first.

I stepped toward the energetic duo and cleared my throat. "I wasn't aware that your father wouldn't be seeing her today."

The impostor rotated in his seat, his sky-blue eyes finding mine just as an unruly lock of russet-brown hair curled into a half-moon near his temple. He looked more like the cover model for one of those health magazines set on waiting room tables than a physician.

"A letter was sent out six weeks ago to explain my father's leave of absence."

"Leave of absence?" My hand hovered above my heart. "Is he . . . okay?"

A slight hesitation—as if I'd been the only patient who dared to ask such a personal question. But surely that wasn't the case. Everyone in this town loved Ivar McCade, including me. "He's in Scotland with my mother, visiting my grandmother for the next few months."

"The next few months?" How had I missed this news? And why hadn't I received the letter? "But—"

"Where'd you get that scar?" Savannah pointed to a spot I couldn't see on the right side of his face.

I opened my mouth, ready to scold her bluntness, but the young doctor twisted away from me and pulled up his coat sleeves to uncover the taut, tanned flesh of his forearms. "The one on my face I got from hang gliding in New Zealand. But this one here"—he displayed a jagged iridescent scar that stretched from wrist to elbow—"I got from bungee jumping off a bridge in South Africa. Swung a little too close to the rocks. It's a good thing I think scars are pretty cool, huh?"

"I have one, too. See?" Savannah yanked down the collar of her red sweatshirt, exposing tender healed skin, her closed chemo port on the right side of her chest.

The man lifted his palm and high-fived my daughter.

A prickly heat filled my chest, my skin suddenly much too tight for comfort. This wasn't a show-and-tell visit. And if this stranger had any clue what she'd been through over the last two years—the hospital stays, the spinal taps, the hair loss and drug side effects—he wouldn't be playing a game of Map My Scars. Or high-fiving.

He might be the son of one of the best doctors I'd ever known, but he certainly hadn't fallen close to the tree.

"You know, on second thought, I think we'll just go ahead and check ourselves out with Marsha. Sorry about the mix-up."

"But Mommy—" Savannah's words broke into a fit of coughs, and my frustration surged. I'd have to take her to Bend and try to get an appointment with a real doctor before the end of the day.

"Ms. Hart." He swiveled on his toy stool. "May I have a word with you in the hallway, please?"

Savannah had stopped coughing and now she sat quietly, watching me. Reluctantly, I nodded.

He handed her a tissue and then led me to the door. I glanced again at the picture of the sunset before following him out into the hallway.

My arms were crossed over my chest, my mind spinning in circles. Confrontation wasn't in my genetic makeup, yet where Savannah was concerned I'd managed to find my voice.

"Is there a problem?" He leaned a shoulder against the doorjamb, but even slouched he had to be close to six foot two. The same height as Chad.

Everything about this man was just too . . . *too much*.

Amusement lurked in his gaze as he waited for me to answer.

I lifted my chin and straightened my spine. "I've been coming here with my daughter since she was barely two, and I've never once questioned the practices of your father."

He arched an eyebrow. "But you question mine?"

His nonchalance was irritating. "I question everything when it comes to Savannah."

"Seemed to me like she was having a good time." He shrugged as if this were some kind of casual interaction between old friends.

I blew out a long breath, willing myself to speak far more calmly than I felt. "Last time I checked, this isn't a circus. It's a clinic. And if you cared half as much about her health history as you do about making her laugh, then you'd know—"

"Savannah Hart. Had her seventh birthday this past June. Saw my father just over two years ago for fatigue and a complaint of a sore leg. After testing positive for anemia, my father referred her to Doernbecher Children's Hospital in Portland for further testing. She was diagnosed with standard-risk acute lymphoblastic leukemia. Her cancer went into remission after just one round of induction chemotherapy and if what I read is accurate, then she's likely finished the last of her outpatient visits for maintenance phase—to which you're both owed a huge congratulations. Would that be the history you're referring to?"

Numbly, I stared. I might have blinked or nodded. But I couldn't be positive about either of those.

"Now, if you'll allow me to check her congestion and cough, I'd like to make sure my suspicion is correct."

With that single phrase, my throat dried out. "Your suspicion . . . ?" My pseudostrength wilted into a lifeless pile of doubt.

I felt for a peppermint in my jeans pocket.

"Yes," he answered. "My suspicion that she has a cold."

He touched my shoulder and squeezed it gently before walking back into the exam room. In an instant, the two extroverts were engaged in a riveting conversation about winter snowfall and skiing on the slopes.

Silently, I slipped inside the room, careful not to meet the doctor's gaze as he finished the exam. All interaction between us had ceased, and it was Savannah who held out her hand to take the pamphlet of do's and don'ts for the common cold. He explained that as long as she didn't develop a fever, and as long as her symptoms didn't worsen, then she shouldn't have to miss school. Savannah beamed all the way out to the car.

Proverbial tail between my legs, I slinked into the driver's seat and listened for the click of Savannah's seat belt. She prattled on and on between coughs about how nice and funny and kind this doctor had been. How he was her "absolute favorite doctor of all time" and how she hoped that the old Dr. McCade wouldn't get his feelings hurt if he ever found out.

But as I drove away from the clinic, passing Jonny's Pizza and my mom's antique store located on the corner of Main and Pickett, I couldn't concentrate on anything other than the replay of the hallway scene.

Regret weighed heavy on my heart—made me tired and weak where I had felt justified and strong only moments before. I'd never treated anyone so unpleasantly, never judged a stranger so critically.

What a way to welcome the son of the man who had saved my daughter's life. *What had come over me?*

Warmth climbed my neck and ignited my cheeks. Unlike the flash of heat lit from anger, the heat of humiliation lingered. And burned.

Maybe my concern for his youth, his inexperience, and his lack of white-coat professionalism was all a front for a deeper issue. There was something about his flawless magnetism, something about his easy way of conversing, something about his smiling eyes that reminded me of a simpler time—of a simpler young woman. A woman who didn't wake up each morning and anticipate life's worst-case scenario.

A woman who didn't believe that love and loss were synonymous.

I coasted into the driveway that separated my tiny house from my parents' and put the gearshift into park. As I rested my head against the back of my seat, Savannah popped her chin over my shoulder and dropped a small piece of paper onto my lap.

"This is for you, Mommy."

I stared down at the prescription and blinked twice. She was right. My name was scribbled in the blank patient box at the top. Beneath it were the words:

Take a break from worry. You deserve one.

Chapter Three

Without a single glance up from her flavor checklist, Georgia slid the crystal cake platter out of Weston's reach.

I pursed my lips and waited for the next round of prenuptial battles to begin. They'd been at each other for the last thirty minutes, which in wedding planning time could be considered a millennium.

"Hey! What'd you do that for?"

"This is a cake *tasting*, Weston, not an all-you-can-eat dessert buffet. You've eaten all of your samples *and* mine." Georgia's gaze swung from Weston to me, pleading for female backup. I nodded my agreement while Savannah sat giggling at her uncle's fake pout.

"Do you see why I asked you to meet us here now, Willa? Weston's said yes to every flavor he's tried so far. All thirteen of them."

Weston pointed to an orange-yellow square of cake perched on the edge of the sparkling platter. Apparently, it was the outcast. "That's not true. I said that one tasted like citrus-scented toilet cleaner."

Georgia lifted one perfectly arched eyebrow. "And since mango isn't exactly a December wedding favorite, that particular feedback wasn't considered to be helpful."

Weston locked eyes with his soon-to-be bride, their wordless exchange lasting only a few seconds before Georgia's lips twitched.

"You lost," Weston whispered to her, leaning forward to kiss the tip of her nose.

"And you're hopeless."

Weston winked and slapped a hand over his heart. "Only when it comes to you, babe."

His chair screeched as he slid it back from the porcelain-topped table. He tapped a finger to my daughter's head. "Know what time it is, Vannie?"

Savannah hopped in place, and I gave my brother the where-do-you-think-you're-going look.

"Ooh! Is it pizza time?" she asked.

"You obviously got your smarts from your mother." With arms bent like a bulldozer scoop, he swept a squealing Savannah into the air, gave me a wink, and carried her toward the shop's exit before letting her slide back down to her feet.

I bit the inside of my cheek to keep from calling them back or offering to tag along. Restraint was not my greatest strength.

For the last two weeks, Weston had backed off from his little-brother patrols, believing I'd made good headway in all the areas of life he'd claimed I'd stalled out on—which were most of them. But denying him a pizza date with my daughter because I was simply too afraid to let her out of my sight for a second longer than necessary would pique his suspicions that I wasn't, in fact, quite as okay as I seemed.

"Um . . . Wes? Aren't you forgetting your little bet?" Georgia's sing-song voice halted his steps toward the door.

"Bet?" I asked, momentarily distracted.

Her eyes widened. "Wait—he hasn't told you about his new *bromance?*"

Georgia's excitement grew tenfold as she read the confusion on my face.

"*Bromance*, really, Georgia?" Weston repeated in a tone that could dry paint.

"About a month ago Weston went to play basketball at the gym and every morning since has set his alarm to play one-on-one with this guy who apparently should be the world's next Discovery Channel superstar. All I've heard about for days is Ricky said this, Ricky did this, Ricky wants to do this. But a-n-y-w-a-y"—she stretched the word out as if to derail any more potential protests from my brother—"they made this stupid bet that if Weston didn't lose twenty pounds by our wedding day—well, let's just say he won't be in charge of picking his wardrobe for the rehearsal dinner."

"Wait," I said. "You have a bet to lose weight? When have you ever cared about losing weight?" I eyed my never-out-of-shape brother carefully, noticing for the first time the extra padding around his midsection.

"Since Nan's cooking," he said, patting his belly and glaring at his fiancée in jest. Nan was Georgia's beloved grandma and the town's most acclaimed cook. "I've got three months to get back down to my college weight. Not gonna be a problem."

And with that, Savannah and Weston were headed down the block to Jonny's Pizza. I couldn't blame him for wanting to leave the frills of this feminine pastry shop. A high-end bakery covered in paisley wallpaper wasn't exactly the most fitting establishment for my brother. He was better suited for restaurants that catered to rowdy groups of children and served soft drinks in foam cups rather than tea in fine china. As Lenox's most adored high school teacher, he'd likely know two-thirds of tonight's patrons.

Georgia's lovesick gaze lingered out the shop's picture window, even after the chimes on the door had stopped tinkling. Their relationship had always been full of teasing and banter, their childhood competitiveness a legend in our small northwest town. But truly, there was no woman better suited for my brother. He'd pined over her when she'd left Lenox for the bright lights of L.A. and compared every available woman he encountered to the impossible standard of the one and only Georgia Cole.

After seven years of distance, he'd finally won her heart. For the second time.

Georgia blinked hard, blushing when her gaze found mine. "He's such a little boy sometimes."

I couldn't agree more. "How's everything coming together for the wedding?" The teal-and-white wedding binder took up half the antique table.

"Let's just say, trying to plan a wedding near Christmas while scripting for the spring production has been less than ideal."

Georgia hadn't owned the community theater for long, but her vision to give the youth of Lenox and surrounding areas a place to belong was beyond admirable.

"Oh, that's right." I'd forgotten about the script she'd been working on, just like I'd forgotten the details of so many other things over the last year. In some ways, Savannah's cancer clearance was like a green light on a busy highway. I'd simply forgotten how to merge into traffic.

Weston's challenge from Savannah's school parking lot replayed in my mind. *I bet you can't name a single time in the last year when you've done something for the sake of being social. Without Savannah.* Suddenly this moment felt a little less like pure spontaneity, and a little more like a setup, courtesy of Weston.

Georgia waved her hand as if to clear the cobwebs of my relational neglect. "But we don't need to talk about wedding details or the fact that I'm in over my head trying to direct a show I haven't even finished scripting yet. Tell me about the new job?"

The new job. *My* new job. "It's going pretty well." I took a sip of my tea to avoid the inevitable hard swallow that was my signature lie buster.

"You've adjusted well, then? To Savannah being in school and you working part-time? That's a big change."

Understatement of the world.

I nodded.

If lunch-break school drive-bys and daily check-ins with the school secretary could be considered adjusting well to Savannah's absence, then, yes, I was doing exceptionally well at my new job. And in life.

"Good. Weston was pretty happy when he told me about the position. It's hard to find something that will allow for a school schedule. I'm not the biggest Sydney Parker fan around, but I have to admit her fitness center is pretty remarkable. Especially for a town the size of Lenox."

True, the building had every possible upgrade—a piece of architectural art on the east border of town. Weston had drawn up the original design plans for the building.

I dragged the end of my pointer finger along the rim of my rose petal teacup. "He's a good brother. And I'm confident he'll be an even better husband to you."

The dark-haired beauty beamed at my words and then deflated with a long, drawn-out exhale. "The next three and a half months are going to be the longest months of my life."

I laughed at that—her innocence, her ability to dream of a future with such tangible desire and reverence. I'd been the same way in the months leading up to my wedding day. I had graduated from high school just weeks before I'd walked down that church aisle and pledged my future to Chad. A decision I'd remake in a heartbeat if given the opportunity to go back in time. Even though our years were limited, our love was real. I'd probably worn the same doe-eyed expression that Georgia was wearing now.

I cleared my throat. "Let me help you with anything you're willing to delegate. I'm not very crafty, but what I lack in creativity I make up for in my ability to follow step-by-step directions."

"Deal." Flipping her wedding planner open by way of the multi-color tabs and labels, Georgia slid her finger across the gridded page to an open Friday on her calendar. "Actually, I've been wanting to plan a night to work on wedding favors. And since I only have two local brides-maids, I would love your help. You can bring Savannah, of course."

The date was only two weeks away, but it had been so long since I'd planned anything that far out, unrelated to treatments or trips to Portland.

"Count us in."

"Great! Nan's been begging me to invite you over. She'll be thrilled to cook for you and Savannah, plus she's looking forward to teaching her piano again." She shut her planner with a satisfied grin. "Now, let's get out of here and get some real food. I'm starved."

Maybe I'd been starved, too—for friendship.

Chapter Four

The timer on my phone counted down the twenty-eight minutes and forty-seven seconds remaining on my lunch break. The nagging reminder of new member registrations and return-call memos tugged me toward the front desk in the lobby. But it was the car keys in my pocket that took priority.

Seven minutes later, I pulled into the deserted side lot at the elementary school. The playground was hidden from oncoming traffic, which meant it was also hidden from a certain high school teacher who might or might not be taking an off-campus lunch break.

The fall breeze whipped my hair into my eyes. I gathered the unruly golden strands into a makeshift ponytail at the base of my neck and held the bundle together at my shoulder.

Certain I was being watched, I glanced behind me. But unless that empty black sedan had suddenly grown eyes, there was no one around. Quickening my steps, I focused on the happy sounds of carefree children. Giggles, squeals, and delighted screams lured me up a mound of fresh bark. I wedged myself between a large thorny rosebush and a metal fencepost.

Savannah's hot-pink thermal was easy to spot. She'd worn her favorite top twice over the past week—a small battle I'd let her win.

The glee on her face shot an arrow of joy through my heart. She pushed her friend on the swings, her head tilted back, a wide laughing smile on her mouth.

A throat cleared behind me. "Ms. Hart?"

I whirled around and my balance faltered. My arms flung wide and the sleeves of my gray hoodie snagged on the thorny branches behind me. An arsenal of spears dug into my flesh.

"H-hi." With my hair whipping a wild mane around my face, I blinked down at the only McCade currently in town.

Wrestling against the snare, I yanked my arm away from the bush, the effort fruitless. His puzzled gaze ran the length of me, landing on my bark-covered shoes.

The doctor cocked his head to the side, a mischievous gleam in his eye. "Are you some sort of secret arborist?"

More like a modern-day scarecrow.

"No," I said, the thorns working their way into the back of my thighs with every tug. "I just . . ." *What?* There was nothing I could say to explain this away. Just like there was nothing I could do to tone down the heat in my cheeks.

Without another word, Dr. Patrick McCade set his leather satchel on the pavement and strode up the bark hill. This would be the perfect time for him to unleash some payback for my unkind words to him at his office last week. I wouldn't blame him a bit for leaving me confined to this prison of nature.

Placing a hand at the center of my back, he unclawed the spiky branches from my legs, arms, and hair. I winced, the burn in my face graduating from a smolder to a raging fire.

How many bad first impressions could I make with the same person?

"There," he said, as if he'd just rescued a wild animal from a big-game trap. "You're free."

After a single leap to the blacktop below, he turned to offer his hand to me. Only my hands were too busy shaking to be held. Along with the rest of me.

I declined the polite gesture and inched my way down the shifting bark until I reached solid ground.

"Some of the kids I had in the vaccination clinic this morning would have run out the door screaming if they saw that." He pointed to my hand, where two droplets of blood were rolling down my fingers.

"Oh . . . um?" My ability to speak in a comprehensive language had completely vanished. I curled my hand into a fist and pulled the cuff of my sleeve over my knuckles. "Thanks for . . . your help." *Your help untangling me from my own stupidity.*

And then I bolted to my car.

"Wait—hold up!"

I could only handle so much embarrassment with the same person in the same ten minutes.

But he was at my side in a heartbeat. I glanced around the parking lot again, the black sedan still the only car in the lot besides mine. And he had just blazed right past it.

"Let me look at your hand."

"That's okay, really. I'll wash it up at work." I didn't pause my stride, didn't turn my head. Even still, I could feel his stare on the side of my face.

"The gym, right? You work at Parker Fitness?"

I stopped in front of my car door, ready to ask him how he knew where I worked, when he dropped his knee to the ground and rifled through his bag.

"What are you doing?" I asked.

His thick, ruddy hair ruffled in the breeze, and strangely, I had an urge to reach out and feel the texture of it. I clenched my noninjured hand tighter while he rolled the sleeves of his white dress shirt to his elbows, exposing the jagged scar he'd shown Savannah at the clinic.

"Here we go." Pinched between his fingers was a blue Superman Band-Aid and an alcohol wipe. "Sorry, I ran out of Hello Kitty and Dora."

My gaze followed him as he stood to full height and the inside of my mouth went chalk-dry. *He wants to doctor me?*

"It will just take a second." He gestured for my hand and I shook my head. "Come on, I should have known better than to startle a mother spying on her kid."

"Oh, I wasn't spy—"

"And it'd be a shame to ruin such a pretty sweater." The side of his mouth ticked up.

Reluctantly, I gave him my hand.

His gentle clasp on my wrist made my breath catch. He worked the fabric of my sweater to the middle of my forearm, my skin tingling with awareness.

Though his hands looked callused and scarred, his fingertips felt as soft as velvet. With calculated pressure, he wiped the two puncture wounds clean and then tore open the bandage. He pressed each end to the inside of my palm.

I could have sworn the knock in my chest was louder than the ring of the school bell.

Recess was over. And so was doctor time.

"All better now." He dropped my hand and took a step back before bending to grab the handle of his bag.

Forcing a swallow, I met his gaze. "Thank you, Dr. McCade."

Kindness was such a rare commodity, and he'd just given it away freely. With a Superman Band-Aid.

"Oh, wait." He dug in his shirt pocket and pulled out a round red sticker. "I have something else for you. And it's Patrick."

I took it and laughed. *Way to be brave!* was printed on the sticker.

"From the vaccination clinic," he said.

I bit my bottom lip and rolled it between my teeth, searching for the right words to convey my horrible misjudgment. Searching for a way to tell him that his fake prescription had meant something to me—how I'd kept it in my car.

How I'd read it daily.

Instead I gave him the best compliment I could think of. "You're a lot like him."

"Who?"

"Your father."

Patrick's smile crinkled the corners of his eyes. "I'll see you around, Willa."

He remembered my name?

With a quick wave, he walked away, headed in the direction of the black sedan.

Sleep and I hadn't been on the same team in many years.

I'd never been one to remember my dreams, but you didn't have to remember a nightmare to know you'd just had one. The impression it left was enough—a sticky residue that wouldn't easily rinse away.

More often than not, the hours between midnight and three were reserved for household chores.

I lifted a basket of Savannah's freshly laundered clothes, and my elbow bumped the bookshelf behind me. A small four-by-six-inch frame clattered to the floor. It was the same picture Savannah propped beside her on the arm of the couch while she read her favorite bedtime stories.

I set the basket down again and bent to retrieve the photograph I'd memorized. Deep brown eyes, hands stuffed in his pockets, a lighthearted grin on his lips. It was taken just a week before his funeral. Nearly seven and a half years ago.

A familiar sadness pressed against my chest as I ran my thumb over the edge of the tarnished silver. There were hundreds of quotes dedicated to time and grief, dozens of books and pamphlets on heartache and loss, yet I didn't always want to remember those words and phrases. Sometimes I just wanted to remember him—the way he'd laughed, the way he'd felt, the way he'd loved me so completely. I'd prayed for years that God would take away the ache, numb my wounded heart, so I could focus solely on raising my daughter. And though the pain attached to his death *had* lessened over time, my soul-deep longing for companionship had not.

As I placed the frame back onto the wooden shelf, the Superman Band-Aid stuck to the heel of my palm snagged against the sanded edge.

This time the memory that surfaced was much fresher—as was the zing it ignited in the pit of my stomach. Patrick's tender touch, playful voice, and winsome smile.

Abandoning the laundry basket, I flicked off the living room light and decided to try my luck with insomnia.

·

Chapter Five

I had whiplash from the volume of phone calls I'd answered today, triggered by the 50-percent-off coupon for personal training listed in the *Lenox Tribune*. And I still had two hours until I picked Savannah up from school. Studio Two opened and an army of sweaty bodies flooded the lobby. The attendance for midday yoga classes had skyrocketed, with people willing to drive upward of forty-five minutes to attend.

". . . Patrick McCade . . . a traveling doctor . . . hotter than hot." Two brunettes stood near the staircase, chugging back their waters, yoga mats slung over their shoulders.

The phone buzzed again, but hearing his name had slowed my reaction time.

"I heard he's only here until the end of the year," Sports Bra Girl said. "Maybe someone can tame his wild side enough to keep him around."

"I'd like to give it—or him—a try," her friend replied with a shrill laugh.

"You gonna get that, Willa?" Sydney Parker, my boss, wearing her favorite snakeskin stilettos, had stopped in front of my desk and was pointing to the phone.

"Yes, of course." I lifted the phone to my ear and stumbled over the standard greeting while she tapped her long acrylic nails on the countertop. As if she were typing up a thesis on my job performance.

I hadn't even hung up when Sydney launched into her second sentence, speaking in her signature staccato—as signature as her too-tight blond bun and ruby-red fashion glasses. The woman was walking intimidation.

Sydney was two years younger than me, but her business age could account for an extra three decades. Maybe four.

". . . received your request for Tuesday mornings off. Fine. Just find someone to cover for you." She slapped the counter and then turned away.

"Oh . . . uh, I will. Thank you." I'd asked to come in two hours late on Tuesdays so I could volunteer in Savannah's classroom.

Two strides away from my desk, she pivoted on her heels to face me again. "And thanks. For creating that new member profile system. It's far more efficient. I'll be sending my new hires for you to train next week."

With a bob of her head, she was off again.

At least my administration skills were being put to use.

Too bad my front desk responsibilities didn't include peppering those annoying vixens with a box of protein bars and telling them to keep their claws out of Patrick McCade.

As soon as I thought it, I slumped back in my chair and tried to pretend it had never entered my mind.

On the way home from school, we stopped in at my mom's store, Antiques Plus. My parents inherited the store when I was only two and Weston was just a colicky newborn. They'd threatened to sell for years, claiming their only profit came between May and September, but obligation was often associated with the family business, and neither of my parents was ready to let the place go. No matter how heavy the burden.

The smell of dusty books, polished wood, and fanciful soaps overwhelmed us as Savannah pushed the door open. When she skipped inside, I realized I hadn't heard a single cough today. The dry bark had vanished. Just like Dr. Patrick had predicted.

The Superman bandage had fallen off after a couple of hand washings, but I found myself brushing my fingers over the pin-tip scabs on my palm.

"Mom?" I called, searching the dimly lit open space. She was likely in the back, working on a new project. The woman was a wonder when it came to refurbishing. She could take the old, the ugly, and the lifeless and transform them into something worthy of putting on display.

"Willa? I'm in the back. Just a minute!"

Mom pushed a red velvet curtain to the side of the doorway at the back of the store. Her blond hair was freshly dyed and twisted into an easy updo, her makeup flawlessly applied, but it was her eyes that spoke the truth of her age. They were underlined by a bluish tint of worry that no primer could erase.

She kissed Savannah's forehead and then fished in the front pocket of her jeans. An old garnet ring appeared in her hand. The kind Savannah loved to collect. Huge and gaudy, and in desperate need of costume jewelry cleaner.

"Is it for me, Grandma?"

"Of course it's for you."

Savannah turned to me. "Can I find a box for it, Mommy?"

I reminded her where the jewelry boxes were kept at the far side of the store and she walked down the aisle, a bounce in her step.

My mom sighed contentedly. "She looks so vibrant, doesn't she?"

"She really does." A statement I'd yearned to say for far too long.

"But you look tired." Mom's eyes drifted over my face.

Usually this was her opening line. Perhaps I should feel grateful for taking second place on her worry list today?

She touched my cheeks and assessed the pallor of my skin. "Are you sleeping well at night?"

"Yes." If sleeping well meant waking up several times clutching my chest and reaching for the peppermints I kept in my nightstand.

She dropped her hands, a temporary white flag raised between us. "How's the job going?"

If she was still hurt that I hadn't asked her about working more hours at her store before accepting the job at the fitness center, her tone didn't indicate it. She knew as well as I did that she didn't have the work to give me. Weston was right. Living in their guesthouse these last few years was enough intermingling of finances and schedules.

"It's a good fit for me," I said evenly. "The staff's friendly, and the work keeps me busy until it's time to pick up Savannah. I've been able to save some, too." I picked up a porcelain doll from the counter, touched the stiff braided hair and then the barely visible scar on the doll's hand where my mother had patched her up. "Really, I have nothing to complain about." My smile was so plastic *I* could have been put on display.

She studied me, as if searching for a new way to say the same old statement, a statement I'd heard more times in the seven years since losing Chad than most people would in a lifetime.

"Dad and I are concerned about you, Willa."

Yep. There it was.

She continued without missing a beat. "It's just a lot at once—Savannah back in school and you working again. We don't want you to have a setback." She eyed the doll in my hands. "It's fine to take your time getting settled back into life with Savannah. There's no rush."

There's no rush. But there was a lingering promise to expand my daughter's world, to give her back the time she'd lost. To be the mom she deserved me to be. The mom I'd been too afraid to be for far too long.

"Everything's fine, really." It sounded convincing enough, yet the crease in her brow remained.

"You know, Davis stopped by the shop yesterday. Said he's left a couple of messages for you." She swiped a rag from behind the counter. My fake smile faltered.

She spritzed the display case with streak-free window cleaner, wiping away smudges no eye could detect. "That man is mad about you, Willa. And he has the patience of a saint. You two could be a good match if you just agreed to go out with him—gave him a chance to be something more."

Because to my mother, the pairing up of a widow and a widower was a formula destined for eternal happiness and bliss.

"He's a good friend." I respected him, admired him, cared for him, but—

"A good friend who would propose to you in a heartbeat if you showed him the least bit of romantic interest. He has so much to offer you: a steady career, a nice home, a faithful, God-loving family. A good helpmate is hard to come by these days."

Helpmate. The word bucked against my heart.

Davis Carter had never spoken to me as frankly as my mother just had, but I knew she wasn't wrong. I knew his feelings ran deeper than the friendship boundaries I had set long ago, which was precisely why I hadn't picked up the phone to return his calls. Calling him would mean agreeing to a conversation. And agreeing to a conversation would mean being asked to make a commitment I was in no way ready to make.

And *no choice* was always better than making the wrong choice.

I set the doll back in place and she slumped onto her side, unable to sit upright without assistance. *Was that how the people in my life saw me, too?*

A bitter taste filled my mouth. If there was a reason to pretend to be stronger, braver, bolder than I was, it was for them.

Unlike this store, I refused to become another life-sucking burden on my family.

Chapter Six

Fall was most people's favorite time of year in Oregon, and I could understand why. The mix of deciduous and conifer trees offered vibrant patches of orange, yellow, and red against a backdrop of Crayola green— a stunningly artful combination.

Yet as gorgeous as fall was, winter had always been my season of choice. It was a season I'd been taught to prepare for even as a young girl. To chop extra wood for the woodpile, buy extra food for the pantry, gather extra blankets for storage under beds and in hallway closets. I appreciated its routine and predictability. I'd survived whiteouts, blizzards, and power outages—all because I'd learned how to properly plan. To never be caught unprepared.

If only this rule applied to life and not just to the changing of seasons.

Nan's cottage, which Georgia would share for only a couple more months, sat on the south edge of Lenox, across from the community park. Sparse branches clapped in the breeze, a few golden maple leaves spiraling to the ground below. I exhaled and rolled the tension from my shoulders as I pulled up to the cute little white house. Nan's presence— and her home-cooked meals—had a way of making weariness disappear.

Savannah was already halfway up the porch steps and knocking on Nan's front door when I popped my trunk to retrieve a store-bought pie. Before Savannah's diagnosis, I baked a lot, my weekly contribution to the hospitality table on Sunday mornings at church. But that particular hobby had been buried under immune-boosting recipes and organic supplements. And despite my brother's many invitations to join him and Georgia, my church attendance had become as sporadic as the use of my oven mitts.

"There's my little superstar pianist! When are we gonna start up lessons again?" Nan's voice was an unmistakable mix of sugary sweet and savory sass.

Savannah hugged the short, spry woman who pecked kisses all over her face. "Tonight?"

"I think that can be arranged," Nan laughed.

Savannah scurried off inside the house to find her uncle.

Nan greeted me with a warm embrace. "It's so lovely to see you, Willa." As her gaze shifted to my store-bought dessert, it was easy to see that she didn't feel quite the same way about my pie.

"Here, let me take that for you." She took the tin from my hand, then wrapped her free arm around my waist.

"Georgia tells me you're working at that fancy fitness club of Sydney Parker's."

"Yes, I am." I planted my feet on the top porch step. "It's been a good place to work. A nice flexible schedule." I was so used to rehearsing those lines that they almost felt natural now, as if my life's ambition were to scan memberships and answer questions about personal training. As if I didn't still picture myself in a classroom full of young, smiling faces.

Nan patted my cheek in her grandmotherly way. I braced for a comment about my tired eyes or my too-thin frame, or any of the million other remarks I'd heard from my family. But instead she simply said,

"You're a beautiful young woman, Willa—inside and out. Savannah's one very blessed girl to have you as her mother."

My eyes flooded unexpectedly and the wrinkle lines around her mouth stretched into a dozen happy parentheses. She gave me another side squeeze and then patted my hip. "Come on, let's get inside. Georgia and her beau are doing my prep work for dinner tonight. If I don't oversee them, I may not have a house by night's end."

I laughed and swiped at a rogue tear. "Sounds good to me. We came hungry."

Nan's cottage had the same comforting scent no matter what time of year you entered her home: a blend of nutmeg, cinnamon, and clove. Two steps inside the living room, I saw my daughter sitting atop her uncle's shoulders in the kitchen while he swayed side to side, slicing an apple. He glanced up from the cutting board, wiped his juicy fingers on Savannah's jeans to make her squeal and kick, and then crossed the room.

"Hey," Weston said, lowering Savannah to the ground. He knew how I despised heights, and yet he paraded her around on his shoulders every time we were together.

Savannah meandered toward the dining room.

"I've asked you not to do that with her, Weston." I kept my voice quiet enough not be overheard by Nan or Georgia.

"Sorry." He offered me a throwaway shrug. "But she loves it."

"She would love eating candy for breakfast, lunch, and dinner, too. But we're the adults in her life."

"Who said I was ready to be an adult?" Weston clamped his hands on my shoulders and waited for eye contact, ready to engage in a child-ish game of Who Can Blink First.

I lost.

"Maybe next time, sis." Weston patted me on the back and then strolled back to his post at the cutting board.

If I didn't love him so much . . .

"Willa, I'm back here if you need a break from your brother," Georgia called from the dining room. "And Nan, could you please check on the enchiladas? I forgot to set a timer."

I unzipped my jacket and slipped it over the back of a dining room chair, saying hello to my soon-to-be sister-in-law. I reached for the pile of silverware at the center of the table. "I can finish this up if there's something else you need to do in the kitchen." I counted the place settings twice. There was an extra. "Was Misty able to come tonight after all? I thought you said she was out of town this weekend."

Misty, Georgia's assistant at the theater, was a genius crafter and Georgia's only other local bridesmaid. Her maid of honor lived in L.A. and wouldn't be coming to Lenox until the week of the wedding.

Georgia flashed me a look I couldn't quite interpret and shook her head sharply, as if trying to get my attention without having to verbalize it.

My hands stilled and I mouthed, "What's wrong?"

"Nope," she said loudly, flashing the mystery face at me again. "Misty's still out of town."

"Hey—" Weston yelled from the kitchen. "Don't you dare ruin the surprise!"

"What surprise?"

Georgia wasn't one to appear nervous—never the biting-her-nails type of gal. She was confident, self-assured, and very vocal about her opinions, so when her eyes shifted to the front door and back . . . I was utterly lost.

"Make way for one steaming-hot enchilada tray." Weston carried the hot pan and set it on the table between Georgia and me. Savannah followed, carrying a large bowl of tortilla chips.

I looked at my brother, who stared unblinking at his soon-to-be bride.

"Okay, what is going on here?" I asked again.

Georgia raised her hands in the air, palms turned upright. "I just want to say this was all Weston's idea."

"Whoa." He held out his own palms. "You were ninety percent in agreement just thirty minutes ago."

"What? *I was not!*" She picked up a fork and shot it at him like a javelin. She missed and Savannah busted into a fit of giggles. "You need to march yourself down to church right now and repent for such a bald-faced lie." Georgia swung back to face me. "I swear this was a hundred percent Weston."

My blood pressure climbed so high it was practically pumping out of my eardrums.

"Weston," Nan announced to the house. "Your friend's here."

Surprises were not my thing—not in any size, shape, or color.

Weston knew this better than anyone on the planet.

Savannah followed him into the living room.

"Who's here?" I stared Georgia down, my mom eyes fully engaged.

"His friend Ricky—from the gym," Georgia said at the same time as I heard Weston's greeting from the other room.

I tried to gather the pieces, to make sense of the trail of clues she'd dropped. There was only one reason I could imagine as to why Georgia would be so apologetic about a surprise dinner guest. A male dinner guest. Tonight was a setup: my brother's new pal and his widowed sister.

My cheeks were so hot they could have cooked a second dinner.

"Weston asked him to dinner because he thought—" Georgia's words stopped short as Weston rounded the corner with my daughter and his friend.

"Mommy, look, it's the funny doctor! He's here to have dinner with us!"

Chapter Seven

Apparently, my brother had several nicknames for Patrick McCade. None of which were his actual name.

"Can you pass the salad?" Weston asked Nan, the only two adults at the table who dared to speak over the awkward glances and mindless water sipping.

Blissfully unaware of my brother's matchmaking scheme, Nan passed the bowl of leafy greens and filled us in on her plans to expand her garden next spring.

After two minuscule bites, Savannah pushed her plate away and asked to be excused so she could play Nan's piano.

"You need to take at least three more bites, please, Savannah," I said.

"But, Mommy, Dr. Patrick said I needed to leave room for the dessert he brought."

Patrick tried to hide his laugh with a cough before glancing away.

"Well, I'm sure he didn't mean that you should skip your dinner."

Patrick caught my gaze and shook his head dutifully. His smile seemed to stretch across the table, and I couldn't help but reply with a smile of my own.

"Not at all, I simply meant you shouldn't eat this entire tray of enchiladas," Patrick added while every eye at the table ping-ponged between us.

"That's just silly. I couldn't eat all of those!" Savannah pointed to the tray.

"Are you sure about that? I heard you had a pretty huge appetite. Isn't that what you told me, Wes? That she could out-eat you?"

I could only imagine what else my lovely brother had shared with his new buddy, "Ricky."

Weston played along, making up ridiculous tales about Savannah's insatiable appetite. In truth, she was small for her age, and for her wit. Yet she was completely enamored with these two men, giggling between every coaxed bite of her enchilada.

While the men were entertaining, Georgia scrunched up her shoulders and shot me a please-don't-hate-me look that quickly morphed into a please-don't-murder-my-fiancé plea—her fiancé who was currently using his fork and knife as horns to imitate a mountain goat.

"Have you seen a real-life zebra, Dr. Patrick?"

Patrick leaned forward in his seat and mimicked her rounded eyes. "Just once."

Savannah gasped and then furrowed her brows. "Wait—it doesn't count if you were at the zoo. I've seen one there, too."

Everyone laughed and Nan patted my daughter's hand. "You're too smart, darling."

"You are smart," Patrick replied. "But no, I wasn't at the zoo when I saw the zebra. I was on a safari, in Zimbabwe."

"Zimb—what way?"

"It's in Africa," I said, allowing Patrick a few extra seconds to recover before Savannah's next round of questioning could begin.

I pushed out my chair, but before I could stand, Patrick was on his feet, asking if he could help me clear the table.

A half-dozen pairs of eyes were focused on us now, waiting for my response, as if accepting help with dishes were the same as accepting a marriage proposal.

"Oh, I can handle it, you don't have to help—" I began.

"Neither of you have to help. Guests don't wash dishes. It's my house rule," Nan declared, saving the night.

Patrick remained standing, the look on his face indecipherable.

Wait—did he think I had a part to play in this whole matchmaking ploy of Weston's? If the gossip around the fitness center held any credence, women were practically lining up to date this ruggedly handsome bachelor. Did he think I was one of them? Did he think I'd asked my brother to bring him? My face flushed at the thought.

Nan took my plate. "Georgia, could you come help me with something in the kitchen for a minute? And Weston, would you mind getting Savannah the box of piano books from the top of my closet?"

In a matter of five seconds, Nan had revoked her previous offer of salvation. And no matter which name I called him—Ricky or Patrick or Dr. McCade—the result was the same. We were alone.

"So," he started, still standing and holding the back of his chair with one hand and pulling on his neck with the other. "How's the palm?"

I played with the hem of my sleeve, tugging it over the scabbed thorn wounds. "Better, thanks to Superman."

His laugh was bold and bright. It plucked at the tight strings around my chest, one by one. "Superman always gets the credit—especially where beautiful women are concerned."

The room pulsed and I wasn't sure where to look, let alone what to say.

Again with the neck tug. "Your brother's a fun guy."

True, but I wasn't exactly in the mood to talk about my brother, at least not about his good qualities. However, this was probably the best time to clear up my involvement in tonight's awkward dinner experience.

"Listen, Patrick, um, I'm not exactly sure what Weston may have implied, but I wanted to—well, if he asked you to—"

"Oh, it's fine." Patrick shook his head dismissively. "It's not like it's the first time I've been asked."

"Not the first time?" It was easy to imagine that Patrick had been set up a million times over, charming women worldwide with scar stories and safari tales, but the thought of him thinking I was one of those women was nothing short of mortifying.

"No, but it's the first time I've said yes, so I think that should count for something."

"Oh . . ." *Was that supposed to be flattering?*

I didn't have to wonder for long. "He can be pretty persuasive." Patrick's chuckle felt like a pinprick to my diaphragm, my oxygen level running dangerously low. I was too stunned to speak, too shocked to blink.

This seemed like a whole new low for Weston—bribing a friend to spend time with his sister?

"I'm sorry." I shook my head. "But what exactly did he persuade you *with*?"

Patrick pointed to the table. "Weekly dinners. I'd do almost anything for a good meal." Each word was a swing of a rubber mallet to my chest. I tried and failed to swallow my hurt.

Something shifted on his face and I could almost hear the backpedal cranking away in his mind, as if looking for a way to further explain. Only he really shouldn't have. "He's been a good friend to me since I arrived in town. I was glad for the opportunity to return the favor."

Forget the rubber mallet, Patrick had just plunged an ice pick straight into my chest and gouged out my heart.

A cold knot formed in my gut.

Return the favor?

So he'd agreed to spend time with me out of loyalty to his new friend—with a bonus of weekly dinners—while Weston got the satisfaction of watching his sister interact with a man he'd approved.

I stood up from the table, stiffened my shoulders, and forced a tight smile. It was time I struck a deal of my own with this man. "How about I don't tell Weston about this conversation, if you don't mention anything to him about the other day."

A crease formed between his brows. "You mean at Savannah's school?"

"What happened at Vannie's school?" Weston sauntered into the room, looking between the two of us, a goofy grin spread wide across his face.

I stared at Patrick, willing him to keep my lunch break stalking a secret.

He gave a half shrug. "Nothing. I helped with a vaccine clinic there last Wednesday, is all."

Please don't say anything more, my eyes pleaded.

"And you were there, too?" Weston's disbelief masked his usual cool-guy tone.

"Um . . ."

"No, I just saw her in passing. In the parking lot."

I held my breath, hoping my brother wouldn't ask for details. Lying by omission was so much easier than lying outright.

Patrick continued to stare at me, as if I were an equation he couldn't solve. Which just might make him the smartest guy in the room.

"Ah, okay." Weston nodded, yet I could tell the wheels of curiosity were still turning. Savannah often wore the same look. "Well, when Ricky here mentioned he'd met you, I figured it was only right to invite him over—encourage everyone to get better acquainted." Weston winked at me and then slapped Patrick on the back. "Hey, ya know, maybe we could make these dinner dates a regular thing? Like once a week?"

Because that idea hadn't already been thoroughly fleshed out between the two of them.

"I think I'll pass. Please, excuse me." Without a second glance back at either of them, I pushed in my chair and exited the room in search of Georgia.

I'd been in Georgia's bedroom with her for nearly an hour, thumbing through bridal magazines and adding to-do notes in her wedding planner. Nan and Savannah were busy plunking away on piano keys, and from what I could hear, Patrick was regaling Weston with yet another riveting high-stakes story about that time when he sailed across the Atlantic, or maybe it was the Greek isles. Was there anything the man hadn't done?

Whatever the answer, my hope to outlast him was fading faster than my resolve to stay.

"Are you really okay? We don't have to do this tonight." Georgia set her planner on her bedspread.

"Of course we do. You marked it down in your planner, remember?" I said, trying my best to ignore the male voices from two rooms over. I pointed at a picture of a white baggie filled to the brim with custom chocolate kisses. "What about something like this?"

"We already talked about that one."

Oh. I pursed my lips, my crossed leg bouncing furiously fast.

She took the magazine from my hand. "I told Weston it was a bad idea to invite him without asking you first, but I won't pretend I don't know why he did it."

I stared at the giant daisy pillow on her bed.

"Willa, your brother just wants you to be happy."

"His version of happy, maybe."

She sighed and brought her knees to her chest. "Would it be so bad . . . to put yourself out there? Date a bit?"

This conversation was as comfortable as hives. "I haven't even—"

"Don't try and tell me that you haven't even thought about it. I know men have asked you out." We both knew she was referring to Davis, though she didn't speak his name. "You're gorgeous and sweet and one of the most compassionate people I've ever known. I used to want to *be* you in high school."

Now that made me laugh.

"I'm serious. Do you know how much people pay for your natural hair color in Hollywood? Not to mention your figure." I rolled my eyes and she tossed the flower pillow at me. "What kind of brother would Weston be if he didn't want to see his sister in a healthy, loving relationship?"

"The kind of brother who minded his own business?"

"Well, that's never gonna happen."

"Just like his matchmaking connections."

"Touché." She waved me up out of the chair, propped open her door, and waited for me to pass. "Now, let's go get dessert."

But even after her pep talk, my interest in dessert paled in comparison to my interest in getting the heck out of this house and away from a certain world traveler and his sidekick.

I took a deep breath. Two steps into the living room, I spotted Savannah. I made sure my gaze stayed focused only on her. "It's time for us to go, sweetie. Make sure you tell Nan thank you and give her a hug good night."

"But I didn't get my pie yet. And I ate all my enchilada."

And this was exactly why you shouldn't make deals with children. "Maybe we can take a piece to go and you can eat at home?"

"Let me get you both a slice." Patrick's arm brushed mine as he passed me. I tried not to inhale his woodsy scent, but that proved an impossible feat.

I waited by the door while Patrick sliced his obviously homemade pie, which sat right next to my fake apple reject.

Patrick served everyone, ignoring my impatient stance. Fine, I'd take one bite of his stupid pie and then we'd leave. Unfortunately, that single bite tasted like heaven on my tongue. Whatever this butterscotch-cinnamon-apple goodness was, it was definitely unique.

"Oh my! What is this, Patrick? It's delightful!" Nan said, her mouth full.

"It's my mum's favorite Scottish recipe." He caught my eye. "Afraid I can't take baking credit, though. She left it in the deep freezer for me and all I did was follow the heating instructions."

"Well, you tell your mum that I'll be knocking on her door come bake sale time," Nan continued.

Patrick laughed. "I'll do that."

Georgia sat on Weston's lap, feeding him a small bite of her pie, even though he'd polished off a slice of his own. My brother murmured something to her and she giggled. Their romantic display captured the attention of everyone in the room—which was the perfect opportunity for me to reach for Savannah's hand and walk out that door. "Thanks again for dinner, Nan. Good night, everyone." It was a statement that ended with the close of the front door while Savannah still chewed her final bite of pie.

Savannah buckled herself into the backseat, her favorite book already secured on her lap. The drive would be short, but I could tell by her eyes that she'd likely fall asleep before I even made it back to our driveway. I'd just opened my car door, the dull overhead light illuminating the interior, when Patrick jogged down the front porch steps with my jacket draped over his forearm.

Just let me leave.

"You forgot this," he said, although he made no effort to hand the jacket to me.

Even in the shadows, his ocean-blue eyes were luminous.

I held out my hand, and slowly he offered me the captive piece of clothing. Leaning forward, he peered at something inside my car. All at once, my organs crystalized.

The prescription.

He shifted his gaze back to me. "You kept it?"

Like a fool.

Because the man who wrote me that note, the man who doctored me in a school parking lot, could not possibly be the same man I'd spoken to tonight. Had my brother sent him running after me, too? When would this nightmare end?

"The way that appointment went, I wasn't sure you'd accept anything from me that day," he said.

I turned my face away, my throat scratchy and tight. "I really should get Savannah home."

He gripped the top of my door. "You know, I have the distinct feeling that I've done something wrong, and that usually means I have."

"I think you and I have different definitions of wrong."

His smile faltered. "How do you mean?"

"Your little agreement with my brother."

"You think I should have told him no?"

"I think *returning a favor*," I said using air quotes, "should be kept to dog sitting and airport pickups. Not agreeing to a pity date with your friend's sister. Even if you get a weekly dinner out of the deal."

Patrick's grip of the door frame slackened. "What? How does agreeing to be a groomsman in your brother's wedding make you my pity date?"

Air whooshed from my lungs and all I could do was blink.

"Wait—you thought, you thought I came here tonight because Weston persuaded me to . . ." He scrubbed a hand down his face as if replaying our conversation from earlier. "And then with the weekly dinners . . . oh, wow—"

"A groomsman?" My voice was a tiny squeak.

We stared at each other, each lost in our own world of humiliation. I, for one, couldn't handle one more moment of embarrassment with this person.

"I'm so sorry . . . I don't know what's wrong with me lately." I slumped into my seat. "Please, just forget this whole night—better yet, forget me." I yanked my door closed, started the engine, and pulled out of Nan's driveway.

I'd made it halfway down the road before I glanced in my rearview mirror. Patrick was still there, still staring after me.

With shaky fingers, I crumpled the prescription and tossed it to the floorboard. Then I popped a much-needed peppermint into my mouth.

If only this little fix could cure a case of chronic humiliation.

Chapter Eight

In a small town like Lenox, it was nearly impossible to avoid someone. Especially when that someone was Patrick McCade. He'd managed to invade my whole world the way a patch of thistles could overtake a hillside. I passed his car on random side streets, saw his name on gym sign-ups, and overheard stories of how he'd waived co-pays for several low-income families in our community.

And now he was in my brother's wedding.

I clicked into his membership profile for the second time today, his picture creating a flurry of unwanted emotion. And just like the first time, I analyzed how different his picture was from real life. The camera had failed to capture all seventeen shades of Caribbean blue that swirled in his irises, just like it had failed to capture the unique quality in his smile, the one that could make a person feel interesting—even special—when it was directed at them.

Pretending to feel indifference for the town's favorite philanthropist was almost harder than pretending to ignore him.

"Willa, can you come into my office for a moment, please?" Sydney's voice crackled through the phone intercom at the front desk, and my pulse rate tripled.

I clicked out of the membership site, kicked my purse farther underneath the front desk, and then took the elevator up to the third floor.

I'd been called obsessive-compulsive a few times in my life, but walking into Sydney's office was like walking into the headquarters for OCD. There wasn't a speck of dust in sight—not a chair or notepad or pen out of place. She sat at her desk, posture perfect, her navy pantsuit a contrast to the ruby frames of her glasses.

They also highlighted her red-rimmed eyes.

"Please, have a seat."

I sat in the fancy chair opposite her. I guessed it had cost more than my entire sofa set.

Sydney stared past me. "I need your help."

"You do?" My reply was throaty and rough.

"Yes. I need you to oversee the health assessment workshop on the last Saturday of the month. I'd ask one of the college-age newbies to do it, but I'd be better off hiring children from the local preschool." Sydney rubbed at the single crease in the center of her eyebrows. "I'll be out of town that weekend and the date has already been advertised." Her eyes shifted to a framed photograph on her desk, but all I could see was the glare off the glass.

There was something about the expression on Sydney's face and the uncertainty of her voice that made her seem strangely vulnerable.

"I'll pay you double time, even pay for a sitter if you need one."

My mind skipped ahead to that weekend. "I think I can help out."

Her shoulders relaxed, her model-thin body slouching ever so slightly against the back of her leather chair. "Thank you."

I stared at her. The words were barely audible, muffled as if she were speaking into a blanket—very un-Sydney-like. We'd never been friends, but you didn't have to be someone's friend to recognize pain.

She rotated her chair, angling her face away from me. "I'll e-mail you the details."

Then silence.

"Sydney?"

More silence.

There was no response except for the swift movement of her hand swiping her cheek.

I took a half step forward and said gently, "If you need someone to talk to . . . I'm here."

A single nod and then she reached for her phone and pressed it to her ear.

Discussion over.

Weston's garage was like a mini version of Home Depot. He was always building, always fixing, always imagining a solution to a problem. Which was why he circled me like a hawk.

"Consider it a peace offering." Weston said, as we watched Savannah ooh and ahh over a new hand-carved dining room set for the dollhouse he'd made her last Christmas.

I shot him my best sisterly glare, and he bumped my shoulder. "Come on, you can't stay mad at me forever. Inviting a single guy to dinner without checking with you isn't a crime."

"But the reason you didn't check with me was because you knew I'd say no."

"Exactly."

"Wes." I kneaded my temples and released a tension-filled sigh. This particular conversation had no end, a Ferris wheel we'd already hopped on many times over during the last week. I didn't have the energy to discuss Patrick one more time. "Let's just drop it, okay?"

"Dropped."

He strode toward my daughter, who sat on a red rocking chair. It was the first piece of furniture Weston ever made for Savannah and she'd opted to keep it in his shop, so she'd always have somewhere to watch him create. They chatted about the tiny chairs and table set he'd created, and my heart warmed. I could fault Weston for being an overbearing brother at times, but I could never fault him for the way he loved his niece.

"I'm gonna grab a drink inside," I said, leaving the two of them to plan the next dollhouse addition.

I flicked the light on in Weston's kitchen. He ate with Georgia and Nan most nights, so the few coffee mugs in the sink and practically bare pantry didn't surprise me. But the neon-yellow flyer on his fridge did.

Lenox Little Kicks Soccer

My eyes struggled to make sense of the list of names.

Weston—head coach. And then several players underneath his name was my daughter's.

I slipped the paper from the magnet adhering it to the fridge and read it over for a second time, as if I'd missed a simple word or phrase or perhaps a much-needed parent signature.

A hard knock on the front door was followed by a twist of the knob and—"Hey, Wes?"

Patrick.

I knew his voice even before I saw his face—probably because I'd replayed our last conversation every night before giving in to the pull of sleep, wishing I could take a step back through time and erase my hasty accusation.

The instant Patrick saw me standing in Weston's kitchen, his footsteps halted. We stared at each other, a silent game of Who Will Speak First playing out between us.

He won—or maybe he lost. I wasn't quite sure of the rules.

"Hi," he said, his chest heaving, hands squared on his hips. "I didn't know you'd be here."

Code for *I wouldn't have stopped by if I had.*

He lifted the hem of his damp T-shirt and wiped his brow, flashing a set of abs that made my throat feel two sizes too small.

"Hi. Yeah, I was just . . ." What was I even saying? He didn't care what I was doing. I'd given him every reason to believe I was an emotionally disturbed woman. "I'll grab Weston for you."

I reached for the door handle that led to the garage, and he moved toward me.

"Wait."

I froze under his quiet command.

"I'm sorry, Willa."

His words shook something loose inside my chest. "No . . . I'm the one who should be apologizing to you. You did nothing wrong."

Like usual, I'd jumped to the worst-case scenario and created a familiar chasm of doubt and fear that couldn't be bridged.

He continued into the kitchen, the overhead lighting illuminating the copper undertones in his hair. He wore black mesh shorts, a gray cotton shirt, and running shoes. Obviously the man didn't believe in taking a breather after office hours.

"That's not the way apologies are supposed to work." Patrick's gaze held steady. "I say, 'I'm sorry,' and then you're supposed to say, 'Apology accepted.'"

"But honestly, there's nothing to accept. I was the one who—"

He cocked his head to the side and gave me a look that said he wasn't going to change his mind.

"Okay," I said on a sigh. "I'll accept your apology as long as you accept mine."

"Deal." He stretched his hand out and my fingers tingled.

When our palms touched in a warm clasp, goose bumps traveled down my arm.

The door to the garage burst open. Savannah's giggles and Weston's teasing tenor entered the room before they did. I pulled my hand away from Patrick's.

"Oh, hey," Weston said, eyeing us both.

"Hey yourself. So much for taking that five-mile run you bragged about this morning, huh?" Patrick asked him.

Weston patted his barely-there gut. "I'm already down eight and still have plenty of time."

Ah yes, the bet to lose twenty pounds by December 20—Wedding Day.

"So, you'd say your diet is going well, then?" I asked facetiously, as I'd just watched Weston inhale a double bacon cheeseburger and fries an hour ago.

"I'd say it's going *fine*." He stretched the word out, as if lengthening it might burn a few extra calories.

"And what happens if he loses?"

Patrick stepped up to the plate. "He wears a kilt to his rehearsal dinner."

Weston gave a hearty one-ha laugh. "You'll be the one in a kilt, pal. Twelve pounds is nothing."

Savannah rose up on her tiptoes, her hand reaching for the neon flyer I'd set on the counter. My stomach nose-dived. That was the last discussion I needed to have right now. In front of Patrick. Hadn't we aired enough family drama in front of him?

I tried to pluck the paper from her hand, but she was already reading it aloud for all of us to hear.

"Oh, good! I meant to tell you about that." Weston's tone was casual, as if he hadn't trumped my parental power by adding my daughter to his soccer team. "I'm gonna coach Little Kicks soccer. Practice starts next week and runs for eight, ends just shy of the wedding. Worked out perfectly."

"I get to play soccer? But Mommy said I couldn't because—"

Weston squeezed her to his side. "Because she didn't know that *I* was gonna coach you."

Savannah's confusion lifted and she smiled brightly. "Wait till I tell Alyssa! Is she on the team, too, Uncle Wes?" She searched for her friend's name and then yelped when she found it. "Yes!"

Weston chuckled, amused by her delight. I wasn't nearly as amused. The last thing I wanted was for Savannah to overexert herself. Wasn't going to school six hours a day enough of a change?

"We'll need to discuss this later, Savannah." As in, *not in the presence of your substitute doctor.*

"That always means no. You *always* say no even though you promised to start saying yes." Savannah's pout was evidence of an oncoming emotional storm.

And this was what Weston did best: work her up, commit her to things he couldn't deliver, and then leave me to deal with the consequences.

Painfully aware of our captive audience, I chose my next words carefully. "That's not true."

Her eyebrows shot up. "So I can play, then?"

Weston's puppy-dog eyes grew rounder as the twosome waited for an answer. As if my answer should require no thought at all. As if I had nothing to consider but his overzealous desire to please her. Sometimes it felt like I had more than just one seven-year-old to parent.

The hollowed-out ache in my chest radiated when I spoke. "You can play." But the thought of her breaking a bone or getting a concussion or needing IV fluids for dehydration was enough to make me want to throw my glass of water at Weston's skull.

"Do you have a soccer ball here, Uncle Wes?"

"Sure do. Follow me, kiddo."

She followed him down the hallway as I gripped the counter behind me with slick palms. Patrick leaned against the opposite wall.

"You don't think she should play."

His statement distracted me from the mental clutches of my increasing anxiety. "Apparently what I think doesn't matter."

And there I went again, airing the family drama—parents who pulled me back, a brother who pushed too far. I lifted my head and—wait . . . maybe . . . maybe what I needed was standing right in front of me. A third-party opinion from a medical professional.

I straightened my spine.

If Patrick agreed with me, then wouldn't Weston be forced to see reason as well? "You know her medical history. Do *you* think she's ready to be thrown out into the world, allowed to do all the normal kid stuff that Weston thinks she can do?"

He pushed away from the wall, watching me. "I'm not sure that's the right question."

With a single exhale, hope rushed from my lungs. My whole world revolved around that question—around keeping her well and happy and whole. And if that wasn't the right question, then—

"What about asking yourself if *you're* ready?"

My eyes snapped to his face. "To give my brother free rein over her childhood? To let him risk her health for the sake of momentary happiness? No, I'm not ready for that."

Patrick widened his eyes as if to indicate that I'd missed his point.

Sucking in my bottom lip, I rethought his question.

And then I reconsidered *him*. This man who'd bungee jumped off bridges and safaried with zoo animals. Perhaps I hadn't asked the wrong question; perhaps I'd asked the wrong person.

Patrick was risk in its most concentrated form.

I folded my arms over my chest. "Are you about to tell me the answer is to swim with sharks or hike Mount Everest or—"

His laugh was deep and even. "No. That's not what I'm suggesting at all."

My pulse beat hard against my throat, fear mounting in the pit of my belly. Yet the part of me that wanted Patrick's advice was bigger than the part of me that wanted to pretend I didn't. "Okay?"

"We take risks every day. The key is to make the ones you take count."

A soccer ball rolled down the hall and into the kitchen. Before I could blink, Patrick had trapped the ball underfoot and then proceeded to bounce it from heel to toe.

With a light tap, he popped it into the air.

I caught it with both hands.

"Your turn."

Chapter Nine

I'd organized every closet, matched every single pair of Savannah's socks, sorted all the Tupperware bowls and lids, and still had three and a half hours until Savannah came home. Her paternal grandparents were in town for the day and had asked to take her out to lunch and to the latest animated movie. And for the first time since her diagnosis, I'd allowed her to leave with them. Alone.

Sure, I'd eaten a quarter of a bag of my mint candies, but still this had to count as a medal-worthy leap forward.

And Weston wasn't even here to see it. Because Weston was off rock climbing with his add-on groomsman.

I slumped against the sofa and reread Georgia's invitation to join them, to eat a picnic lunch and enjoy one of the last days of sunshine before winter.

And then I reread my immediate decline.

My leg bounced to the cadence of my internal debate. *Should I go? No. I should definitely not go.*

Patrick's face floated to the forefront of my mind again: a set of piercing eyes, a jaw edged in day-old stubble, an Olympian's smile and build. I should really stop being so ridiculous. *Think of something else.*

Anything else. Like the grime on the bottom of the oven or the dust on the living room shelf . . .

But none of my mental scolding worked.

Less than five minutes later, I locked my front door and headed to Cougar Mountain.

"Willa!" Georgia waved me over to the covered pavilion at the base of the mountain. A row of empty picnic tables lined the inside of the old wooden structure.

"Hey." A quick glance at the rocky peak was all it took for my head to feel woozy.

"So glad you changed your mind! The guys should be down any minute for lunch." She pointed to the assembly of sandwiches, chips, and fruit. "They'll be happy to see you."

I wasn't as sure. Although my last interaction with Patrick had felt . . . well, like the beginning of an understanding, that didn't mean I had the right to spoil his day off with my adventure-phobic self.

"Oh! I could use your help, actually." She slid her iPad from her bag and tapped on the photo icon. "Will you help me choose an engagement pic for our invitation? They're due to the printer on Tuesday."

Georgia's enthusiasm washed away my insecurities about showing up unannounced, and I smiled as I took the iPad from her.

"These are gorgeous. Wow." I clicked through the pictures, each one exquisite. The shots were taken several months ago, up at our family cabin near the Cascades. My thumb paused, hovering over the arrow. A picture of Weston and Georgia, foreheads pressed together, eyes closed in peaceful reverence, was centered on the screen.

She stared at the image. "That's my favorite, I think."

My heart squeezed, remembering my favorite wedding picture of Chad and me. It was strikingly similar to this shot. "It's gorgeous."

"Do you think it's right for the invitation?"

I glanced up from the screen. "I think it's perfect."

Her smile was contagious. "I hoped you'd say that. Weston says he loves them all, and Nan is no help when it comes to this kind of thing, and my . . ."

She stopped herself from saying more, but I could guess her next words. Georgia's mom had never been very involved in her life, and the wedding had proved no different.

I placed my hand on her shoulder. "All these details will come together. You've already figured out the most important part of that day."

"You're right. I would marry Weston in a back alley if it meant spending the rest of my life with him."

The hope in her voice warmed me. I wanted nothing less than forever for them.

We heard their voices long before we could make out their words. Patrick and Weston were headed our way. Hiking gear circled their waists and they had climbing shoes on their feet.

All girl talk ceased the moment they entered the pavilion, and I became absorbed in the stacking of paper plates.

"No way! Is Willa really here or am I suffering from altitude hallucinations?" Weston clamped a hand to my arm and then searched the perimeter. "And without Vannie? Where's the cake? We need to commemorate this event."

Any sort of triumph I'd felt earlier had completely diminished under his sarcasm.

I put on my good-sport smile and set the napkins on the table, splaying them into something that looked like a warped seashell. It was also a safe place to stare as Patrick moved closer to me.

"Hey." His voice was like a lightning rod through my nervous system. "That's some fancy napkin art you've got going on there."

Warily, I peeked up at him through my eyelashes. "I try."

Georgia looped her arms around Weston's neck. "So how was the climb?"

"Incredible." Weston held her waist. "You have to go up with me after lunch. The view is unreal." And then he kissed her, as if Patrick and I weren't standing two feet from them listening to their smooching lip noises.

Patrick hitched his thumb at the couple and rolled his eyes. I choked out a laugh—not sure which was funnier, a grown man's eye roll over a kiss or our shared discomfort playing the third wheel.

With one giant side step, we left the lovebirds to do what they did best.

I held out a plate to him. "You must be starving."

He took the plate but didn't attempt to fill it. "Not quite yet, actually. My adrenaline is still pumping."

"Ah." Though I couldn't relate to the kind of adventure-adrenaline Patrick thrived on, I'd spent many a night watching monitor screens and listening for the sound of a sick child. My adrenal glands hadn't quite recovered.

"You ever rock climb?" Patrick asked me.

"Willa—rock climb?" Weston decided this was the perfect moment to join the conversation. He laughed and straddled the bench seat. "Never. I broke my leg the summer of my sophomore year and had to bribe her with twenty bucks to get my sketch pad from my top bunk."

Patrick looked at me. "Please tell me you did it."

I gave a sassy shrug. "I needed the money."

Patrick's laugh made my cheeks tingle. "Good girl."

Something about those two words, his praise for something as ridiculous as climbing a five-rung ladder, made me wish I could hear them again.

"Well," Weston continued. "She hasn't climbed anything that high since. Her fear of heights has definitely increased with age."

I tossed a chip at him, and Georgia laughed as she handed out the sandwiches.

For the next hour, we talked and laughed like old friends. Like a group of high school seniors who had skipped seventh period to go to the park.

When all the lunch trash was cleared away, Georgia announced she was ready to see the view. Patrick stood, unclipped his harness, and handed it off to her. She stepped into the leg holes, tightened the cinches, and then secured the waistband around her hips. Weston double-checked the hold.

A cold rush of blood drained from my head and filled my belly. Just watching the preparation made me queasy.

Hand in hand, they set off for the rock face.

Patrick plunked down on top of an empty picnic table across from me while I took my time rolling up the chip bag and tucking it inside the basket.

"So, we've established that you hate heights." He clasped his hands loosely in between his knees.

"Ha. Yes. Thanks to Weston."

Patrick laughed. "So what do you love?"

My hand paused on the edge of the wicker basket. "My daughter."

"That's like saying 'God is love' for every answer in Sunday school class. I mean, what do you love to do—for fun?"

I wiped my palms on the back of my jeans and made my way to the splintery table opposite Patrick. Following his lead, I sat on the tabletop and planted my feet on the bench.

"Hmm. For fun." The words sat heavy on my tongue.

"There's no wrong answer," he teased.

"Maybe not *wrong*, but I guarantee my answers will pale in comparison to yours." I gestured toward him.

One lone dimple dented his left cheek. "Wasn't aware this was a competition."

"I doubt you want to discuss my affection for label makers or my affinity for Post-it Notes? My fun list isn't exactly a walk on the wild side." I scraped the soles of my shoes against the wood grain.

"If I wanted to discuss sharpshooting or fire breathing, I would have opened with that." He fixed his gaze on mine. "I was simply hoping to learn something about you. And actually"—his smile grew wide—"since you mentioned it, I'm on the hunt for a good label maker."

I laughed. "You are a terrible liar."

Patrick drew an *X* over his chest with his pointer finger and switched his Scottish brogue to on. "I not be telling ye an untruth, lass."

The rich sound of his accent made my heart swell. "Well, feel free to peruse my collection any time."

He tipped his chin. "An invitation I'll accept as long as you don't leave me to fend for myself."

Was he flirting with me? Was I flirting with him?

"Okay." I pursed my lips and watched a family of ants gather around the crumbs next to the garbage can. "What about you? Were you born with adventure on the brain? Did you always know you wanted to travel the world?"

"Not even close."

"When then? In high school?"

"My parents moved to Portland from Aberdeen, Scotland, in their midtwenties with big dreams and four young sons. My mum homeschooled each of us until the age of sixteen." Patrick's voice was reminiscent as he spoke. "Our father loves to joke that his love for medicine must have been a dominant gene, since each of us graduated college early and took our MCAT before our twentieth birthday—went to the same med school our father did, Oregon Health and Science University." He shook his head, his laugh light, as if his prodigy-esque family were some kind of everyday normal.

My brain was in search of some sort of reply that didn't leave me sounding like a complete moron. "That's so . . ." *Incredible? Amazing? Unreal?*

"Insane," he volunteered.

"Not at all what I was thinking."

He leaned back and rested his weight against his palms and stretched out his legs. "It's the truth . . . and part of the reason why I left it all behind."

"What do you mean you *left it all behind*? You became a doctor."

"Yes, but not the kind I thought I'd be. I was all about chasing the big fellowships and subspecialties, lured by prestige and salary and reputation . . ." A self-deprecating laugh and then, "Thankfully, God has a way of trumping our plans with his timing."

I chose to ignore the last part of his statement. *God's timing* wasn't exactly my favorite subject matter. "So, what happened, what changed your course?"

"Rex." One word, yet there was something profound in the way he spoke it. Like he was sharing the coordinates to a secret treasure. "He was a patient of mine during my third year of residency." He paused, cleared his throat. "He didn't just change my career track; he taught me how to live—how to partner my passions with my profession."

The back of my throat tingled, but I didn't dare interrupt. Whatever Patrick wanted to share, I wanted to hear.

"Rex Porter was ninety-two when he died of kidney failure—he'd gone blind and nearly deaf, but his mind was still razor sharp." Patrick was looking off in the distance now, visualizing something I wished I could see, too. "He was a renowned photojournalist, had traveled everywhere, met thousands of people, and had a profound faith in God. And he kept this . . . this travel journal full of notes and pictures and randomness." Patrick held his hands in the shape of a book. "Most of the pages were so beat up it was hard to turn them; a few had even been taped back together. Every week he asked me to flip to a new page—remind him of his adventures. And then we'd talk."

I pressed my hand to my chest.

"So I did. I read a page and then the next week I'd read him another one. Stories of his adventures—the highlights, the low points, the absolutely insane risks he took to document a story. All of it was in there." He paused and blinked me back into focus. "He gave me the journal a month before he passed, and by the end of that year, I registered with a reputable locum tenens agency and went on my first short-term assignment to New Zealand. I was hooked after that."

"Locum tenens?"

"Yes, it literally means 'placeholder.' The agency specializes in contracting physicians for short-term projects worldwide. It's allowed me complete autonomy over my schedule. Been with them for three years now. I choose which assignments to accept and which to pass. The flexibility has not only allowed me time to explore and travel, but also to partner with some amazing nonprofit organizations during natural disasters and epidemic outbreaks, too."

"Plus, it gave you the ability to help your father out when he was needed back in Scotland."

Despite Patrick's impressive resume, I hadn't detected a trace of arrogance in his voice or on his face. Instead I'd heard humility and gratitude. "Exactly."

I did a rough calculation, adding up all the figures he'd thrown out over the course of our conversation. If my math was correct, then Patrick registered with the locum tenens agency at age twenty-seven, which would make him thirty. Only one year older than me. While I'd burrowed away in my small town, Patrick had traveled the world.

Without a doubt, he'd experienced more life than any person I knew.

"Wow." I released a slow breath at the realization.

"Sometimes it takes seeing the world through someone else's eyes to realize where you fit inside it, you know?"

Not at all. But I nodded anyway.

My mind wandered as I searched the trees beyond the pavilion—recalled the promise I'd made to my daughter to live without fear. How might my life be different if I could conquer the very things that held me back: the panic that kept me up at night, the worry that never let me go? I wondered how different my life would be if I approached it with the same zest and zeal that Patrick did.

"You have a very pensive-slash-panicked look on your face right now. Like I just threw down an organic chemistry quiz and gave you three minutes to complete it."

I cleared my throat and rubbed my palms on my thighs. "Oh . . . sorry. Just thinking."

His eyebrows rose in a silent would-you-like-to-share-your-thoughts-with-the-class? look.

I wouldn't. "Um . . . it's just that I admire that."

"What?"

"Your attitude about life." I studied a bluebird that swooped through the pavilion before returning to the skies beyond. "I wish bravery could be taught."

Wait—did I just say that out loud?

Patrick shifted, his elbows planted firmly against his knees. "Who says it can't be?"

My honesty trance was suddenly cured. "I didn't actually mean that."

"Sounded to me like you did."

"Well . . ." I gave a stiff shrug. It wasn't like I could blame the slip on my habit of blurting without thinking. He was smarter than that. I wasn't a blurter, although I wasn't usually much of a sharer either.

"What does living brave look like to you?" he asked.

"Probably something very different than what it looks like to you."

He pointed at me. "There you go with the comparisons again."

Something told me that even the most skilled diversion tactic couldn't get me out of answering him. "I guess it would look like . . . trying new things, changing up my routine, stepping out of my comfort zone a bit more." *Keeping the promise I made to my daughter.*

"Then let's do it."

"Let's?" I repeated the word, certain he'd meant to say something very different than the contraction that meant he and me—as in he and I together.

"Sure. I happen to run the best Camp Courage around."

I stared at him, unblinking.

"I'm kidding."

My nerves uncoiled. "Oh."

"But only about the camp part." He hopped off the table and stepped toward me. "Here's how I see it, Willa. Fear is learned the same way bravery is learned. Over time."

My heartbeat stuttered against my rib cage. "Okay . . ."

"So if you want to be braver . . . then you have to take some chances. Learn by experience."

"Okay?"

"So what if I could help you? Give you a few of the life tips Rex gave to me."

Everything about him now seemed serious. There was no laughter in his voice or teasing in his eyes. So why did I keep waiting for him to pull the rug out from under me. Tell me this was nothing more than a prank arranged by my meddling brother. Only I knew it wasn't. Weston hated my phobias even more than I did.

"Why would you do that?" I asked.

"Are you always so untrusting?"

Before I could fully register the impact of his candor, he lifted his palm apologetically. "I shouldn't have said that. Forgive me?"

"Yes." This entire day was like some kind of backward reality show.

"Okay."

"No." I shook my head. "I mean, yes . . . I'm always this untrusting."

He considered me then for several silent seconds. "What if I gave you a timeline? I leave for a job in the Pacific Islands in twelve weeks."

His meaning went without further need of explanation. Somehow he'd figured me out. In order for me to accept his offer, I'd require a finish date, and he'd just given me one.

Twelve weeks. The span of a single season.

"And before you ask me what I'm hoping to get out of this," he continued, "it's simple. I get the satisfaction of passing on the wisdom of a legacy. A man who meant as much to me as my own father does. That's more than worth it for me."

I bit the inside of my cheeks and then repeated—out loud—what he was suggesting. Just in case one of us was missing something. "You want to show me what you learned from Rex and his journal? Help me learn to live bravely?"

A single nod and another shuffle forward. "If you're willing."

Patrick stood smack-dab in the center of the chasm between our picnic tables.

My heartbeat quickened, a booming bass inside my ears. "But how will this even work? You're at the clinic full-time and—"

"I'm resourceful." Patrick's lopsided grin made my stomach flip.

That he was.

I wrung my hands, the pad of my thumb pushing against the two healed puncture wounds on my palm, and weighed the risks.

He dipped his chin to catch my eye again. "What do you say, Willa?"

I slid my feet off the bench but didn't leave the safety of the table. "I say okay."

"I think you can do a lot better than 'okay.'"

"Were you hoping for a blood oath?"

"Not quite," he said with a laugh. "Just a commitment."

I pictured my daughter's face and replayed my empty vow for the thousandth time. *"Mommy will be braver . . . I promise."*

It was time to keep my promise.

One deep breath, two quick strides, and three thunderous heartbeats later, I extended my hand.

"I'm committed."

Chapter Ten

For some, second-guessing a decision might take the better part of a year. Others, a few weeks. For me, it only took a weekend.

To further amplify my apprehension, I hadn't seen or heard from Patrick since our handshake two days ago.

Maybe he had forgotten about the whole thing. Or maybe he made deals with lots of pitiable females in picnic pavilions. Whatever the case, Patrick was a physician, not a psychologist.

Not a magician.

Scribbles about courage from some old travel journal could not eradicate my fear, just like they couldn't eradicate the past.

I pulled open the glass door into the lobby of Parker Fitness with the plan to leave a message for Patrick as soon as I got through the Monday morning pile of pink sign-up sheets. Only there was more than a stack of paper sitting on my desk. There was a girl. A girl with short spiky blue hair, a black leather jacket, and a well-used pair of combat boots. My eyes scanned the exposed skin at her neck in search of a skull and crossbones. Shockingly, it wasn't there.

"You Willa?" The girl smacked on a wad of pink gum.

"Yes, and you are . . . ?"

"Alex." Her focus on me was brief. She was too busy transforming a mound of paper clips into a motorcycle. "Syd said you'd train me."

Syd? I couldn't imagine anyone referring to Sydney Parker by a nickname. Especially a new employee.

"She did?" She told me she was hiring some new staff members, but given how Sydney had expressed her dissatisfaction over the "college-age newbies" from her last hiring—and firing—I couldn't quite grasp how Alex fit into Sydney's high standard of professionalism. The girl didn't look old enough to hold a full-time job, let alone work with the public.

I took a cautious step toward the staircase. "Well, maybe I'll go double-check with Sydney on what exactly she'd like me to—"

"She's not here."

I stopped midstride. "What do you mean she's not here?" Sydney was *always* here, before I clocked in and after I clocked out. It wouldn't surprise me in the least if Sydney slept in her office.

"She dropped me off and then left. Told me you'd be here to help out soon enough." She pointed to the second floor. "Along with the other gym rat employees."

The other gym rat employees. As if I were one of them. Truth be told, I hadn't worked out in a decade. Worse than that, I had no plans to start. "Okay, then. First, let's get you a Parker Fitness T-shirt, and then I'll give you a quick tour before the morning classes let out."

She hopped off my desk and gave me a mini salute. "Lead on."

Alex followed me into the locker room, her black boots beating against the concrete floor. Maybe Alex was hired off a phone interview? It was the only explanation I could muster.

"Will a small work okay?" I stood on my tiptoes, reaching toward the back of the storage closet.

"Large."

I rocked back on my heels and glanced at her again. The only way this girl would fit into a size large was if she put it over her leather jacket, and even then she would need to stuff it. My fingers skimmed over the piles of shirts, hesitating on the smalls and grabbing a medium. "Here. Why don't you try a medium. They run pretty big."

"Fine."

Fuchsia shirt in hand, I pivoted to face her when something she'd said earlier looped though my brain. "Wait—did you say Sydney *dropped you off* here?"

"Yep." Alex swung her leg and rested her boot on one of the locker room benches. Several dirt clods crumbled to the cement floor. "She's got a nice rig."

What is happening here? Sydney wasn't known for her philanthropy. She fired the majority of people she hired without thought to their needs or life circumstances. Every decision was calculated and motivated by business success.

I tried not to show the confusion churning inside me. Sure, this girl wore cargo pants and biker boots. Sure, she had a bleeding heart tattoo on her right forearm. Sure, she had Kool-Aid-blue hair. But none of that meant she was incompetent or that she wouldn't be a loyal employee. Maybe Sydney had made a decision with her heart and not her—

Alex yanked the T-shirt from my hand, her mouth a grim line. "Let me put you out of your misery. She's my half."

Alex tugged the T-shirt over a black tank top.

I stared at her. "Your half?"

"Sister. Syd's my uptight half sister and I'm stuck here in this uptight joint because our mom's in jail."

Not only was Sydney a no-show for the rest of the day, but the employee scheduled to work the desk during the evening shift called in sick.

After I'd spent an hour looking for a replacement, my only viable option—outside of leaving the front desk to Alex—was to ask someone to pick Savannah up from school. Thankfully, Weston's work hours were almost identical to Savannah's school hours.

I stood in the break room, waiting for his text to come through.

WESTON: No prob, I can pick Vannie up. U still helping with auction tonight?

ME: Thanks. Yes. Does that still work for you and Georgia? Pls call if anything comes up.

Savannah's teacher had asked if I'd be willing to help out at the school's biggest annual fund-raiser. I couldn't possibly say no, although trusting Savannah to Weston's care for the evening would prove interesting. At least I knew Georgia would make sure she ate more than cookies and ice cream for dinner.

WESTON: Stop worrying. She'll be fine.

My fingers hovered over the text screen, itching to ask him for Patrick's number. But even if he gave it to me, what would I say to him?

Before I could slide my phone back into my pocket, it vibrated again—this time with a text from one of the more responsible employees. Toby would be here at five to cover the desk, which was exactly when I needed to leave for the benefit. *Thank goodness.*

I reached for a bottle of water in the mini fridge. Though in truth, water wouldn't offer me the kind of strength needed to get through the rest of the day with Alex. The girl had to be the least customer-service-oriented person on the planet. I'd spent the majority of the morning keeping her from insulting clients.

As I rounded the corner, I saw that the lobby had swelled with arrivals and departures. Even though I couldn't have been away from the desk for longer than ten minutes, Alex was in another confrontation.

"You haven't paid. That's why your ID card isn't working," she said to Preston Wilkerson, a high school senior who came to the gym every day after school to lift weights.

"I'm on auto draft." Preston said, staring at the bleeding heart tattoo on Alex's right arm. "I paid."

Alex slid his card away from the computer with a single finger. "Sorry. No pay, no pass."

Preston's cheeks were a blossom of red.

I quickened my steps. "Actually, we had a bit of a glitch in the system update last night. You can go on up, Preston. I'll adjust your account manually."

His eyes flicked from Alex back to me. "Okay. Thanks, Willa."

Hiking his gym bag higher onto his shoulder, he walked away without another word.

Alex crossed her arms over her chest. "I hate jocks. They think they can have anything they want—whenever they want it."

"Well, he's a member of this gym," I said, keeping my tone light. "It's our job to solve member issues as they arise."

"Fine." She slumped back into the chair, and it bumped against the wall.

Volunteering at the auction tonight was starting to look better and better.

Two more hours to go.

"Oh, I forgot." Alex used the heels of her boots to walk the chair closer to me, stopping just shy of my toes. "Your boyfriend called. He sounds hot."

The quick twist of my neck released a loud popping sound. "What did you say?"

"Your boyfriend. He. Sounds. Hot." She pushed a yellow phone memo toward me.

Scribbled on the piece of paper was a time and a place: *6:00. Lenox Elementary.*

I held it up. "Who's it from?"

"Figured you would know your boyfriend's name. Didn't think I needed to write it down for you"—she held out her arms as if to indicate the room—"unless that's another rule I'm supposed to remember. This place has more rules than a military academy."

My blood pressure was climbing, skipping by multiples of ten. "I don't have a boyfriend, Alex."

She furrowed her eyebrows. "You don't? Weird."

I closed my eyes and took a deep breath. "I have no clue who this note is from—or what it's supposed to mean."

She tucked a stray piece of bright-blue hair behind her ear. "I guess you'll find out at six, then. Think of it as a mystery."

If there was one thing I disliked more than a surprise, it was a mystery.

Chapter Eleven

As the clock struck six, the refreshment tables looked like a fast-food restaurant at lunch hour. Parents and faculty swarmed around the finger foods, but I was less interested in bean dip and mixed nuts than I was in the entrance doors. In the last twenty minutes, I had greeted no fewer than one hundred Lenox residents, pointed to the beverage table, and instructed each patron on how to sign in with the auction manager before being seated.

Sipping on a full glass of watered-down strawberry lemonade, I searched the far corner of the room again.

"I'm afraid I have a bad habit of running late."

I spun around, clutching my drink. "Patrick." His name sailed from my lips without thought.

That smile, and then, "I hoped I'd find you here. I left a message for you with a girl at the center, but she seemed . . . interesting." That one word could replace a paragraph of adjectives for Alex.

"Yes, well, it was an *interesting* sort of day." I met his eyes and wondered if there was a name for that shade of blue. If there wasn't, there should be.

"Maybe we should compare notes." He pointed toward the stage. "After we find our seats."

The tingling sensation at the back of my neck was slowly subsiding. Maybe he'd forgotten about our little deal. Maybe this was his way of letting me off the hook so I didn't have to back out. Maybe—

He pulled a small piece of white paper from the breast pocket of his dress shirt. "Your first Rex Lesson."

Trying to conjure up a reason to reject whatever was written on that piece of paper, I set my slippery plastic cup on the edge of the refreshment table. Unfortunately, it didn't stay there.

Patrick grabbed my shoulders and pushed me to the side. Pink liquid splattered to the ground, spotting our shoes with sugary food coloring. I grappled for a stack of napkins and immediately bent to wipe the mess from Patrick's leather shoes.

He bent down, too.

The blush creeping up my neck was likely ten shades darker than the liquid I smeared with these useless recycled napkins.

"I'm so sorry," I said, making another swipe at his shoe with a clean napkin. He stilled my hand, plucked the wet wad from my fingers, and pitched it into the trash can. Naturally, he made a basket.

"Willa, this is the least toxic substance I've had splashed on these shoes today. It's fine, really."

Pulling me up by the arm, he smiled, and something inside me smiled back.

"Ladies and gentlemen, please take your seats. The twenty-second annual auction is about to begin."

"Shall we?" Eyebrow raised, he motioned for me to join him.

The note, still pinched between his forefinger and thumb, was like the silent tick of a bomb as we passed row after row of chairs.

He stopped at the end of an aisle and waited for me to take the seat beside him. The inside seat. I released a deep breath, felt for a peppermint in my pocket, and inched my way past him—all while debating how I might go about asking him to switch places. How might I explain my I-have-to-sit-on-the-aisle neurosis? I could have avoided this entire evening if a certain new employee had taken a proper phone message.

I sat and popped the peppermint in my mouth, which dulled my anxiety but not the weight of Patrick's stare.

"Willa, dear?" That crackly voice could only belong to one person.

Mrs. Carter—Davis Carter's grandmother—waddled toward me, cane in hand.

"Good evening, Mrs. Carter," I said, pushing the mint to the side of my cheek.

The woman was a full foot shorter than me, but what she lacked in height she made up for in volume. Hair like fluffed black cotton and lips a year-round shade of CoverGirl coral, Dolores Carter was the queen of Lenox town gossip.

She craned her neck to scope out exhibit A.

He offered her his hand. "Hello. I'm Patrick McCade. I don't believe we've met. Mrs. Carter, is it?"

"Yes. A pleasure." She eyed him, her smile as phony as her pleasantries. "I doubt there's a soul left in Lenox who doesn't know who you are—Dr. Ivar's *traveling* son."

Her eyes skimmed the length of him again before squeezing past us to her seat—just two chairs down from mine.

"My grandson says you're a difficult gal to get hold of these days."

As much as I wanted to avoid this conversation, I was even more certain I didn't want to invite Patrick into it. I twisted in my seat to block him from view. "It's been a busy few months."

She reached over and patted my knee. "Sure, sure. He told me you took a job at that fancy gym on the east side of town."

This conversation was the definition of "small town." Every decision, every job change, every intimate detail of a person's life was like a publicly traded commodity.

"Yes, working and mothering are two full-time jobs." I smiled in hopes she would take my subtle hint and drop the subject.

Instead she leaned in closer, flicking her gaze at Patrick before adding, "And making new friends, it would seem."

Another reason I avoided the inside seat: meddling women determined to matchmake their sons, or in this case, their grandsons.

"Davis tells me Savannah's in class with Brandon this year. I was thrilled to think of those two little sweethearts playing tag together on the playground. I'm sure your mother told you, but Savannah's been on our prayer chain since her diagnosis. I doubt there was a group in Lenox happier to hear about her clear scans. I'll never forget the day Davis called us after talking to your mother." She patted me again. "Maybe now you can finally move on."

I stiffened, my gut clenching. *Move on . . .* it was difficult to find two words in the English language that repelled me more. A young widow was a magnet for well-intentioned advice. Yet nothing about that phrase felt constructive. Or compassionate.

Patrick cleared his throat beside me. "We should probably discuss the auction items." He nodded to Mrs. Carter, then handed me the program.

I didn't miss the way Mrs. Carter narrowed her eyes, or the way she tilted her head to listen for my response.

"Oh, right." I opened the itemized ballot, and the piece of white scrap paper was pressed into the fold.

Place a bet you know you can win. It makes the bets you lose a lot less defeating.

Patrick kept his voice low. "See? Painless. I told you we'd start easy."

I glanced up at him. He wanted me to bid? But I hadn't registered as a bidder. I was a refreshment table volunteer.

Moving his Rex quote aside, I skimmed the list printed in the program, searching for something as small as a pack of gum, or maybe a pair of Nan's knitted mittens. Something I had a chance at being able to afford.

He plucked the program from my hand and set it on the floor. "Relax. A bid you can't lose means I'm paying. You just get to decide what we're bidding on."

This was insane. Did he hear himself?

As quietly as I could without alerting the grandmother who had scooted one chair closer, I said, "I can't do that." High-pressure events weren't my forte. No matter how insignificant the risk.

"You can. This is the only thing you need." He dropped a red paddle into my lap. "Just remember, it's for the kids."

He winked and turned his gaze back to the stage.

I nudged his elbow. He ignored me.

I knocked my knee against his. He ignored me.

I opened my mouth to protest, but Patrick simply shook his head.

I was pinned between two seemingly impossible options: I either gave in to Patrick and spent his money, or I risked making a scene by refusing to participate in this strange game—which of course would allow Mrs. Carter to go back to the gossiping geese she called the town's prayer chain.

Out of the two choices, I'd choose Patrick's challenge any day of the week.

I gripped the paddle and straightened my back.

Patrick's low chuckle was like a gentle tickle to the back of my neck. Slightly irritating, yet still managing to make me smile.

"Tonight's first item up for bid—a year of lawn care by Willie and Sons," the auctioneer said into the microphone.

Patrick glanced at me and I shook my head, whispering, "Willie isn't the most reliable—especially after his bar-hopping weekends." I scrunched my nose and Patrick laughed.

"This is like insider trading."

Three people raised their paddles, bidding against one another until it was down to just one. The lawn service went for 150 dollars.

The next two items were easy to pass up, too: an annual membership to Parker Fitness Center—I knew Patrick's membership was paid through to the end of the year—and a family pass to the Oregon Zoo. Couldn't really see a man who traveled the world needing six passes to the zoo.

"Next up for grabs is a guided tour down the Rogue River." Now this seemed like something Patrick would love. I twisted in my seat to ask him, but he refused to meet my gaze.

"Wait—don't you like white-water rafting? It seems so very Patrick-like."

The corner of his mouth twitched. "I said *you* choose, Willa. I'm not giving any hints." He leaned back in the stiff plastic chair and crossed his ankles, his right heel resting on the corner of the blue program.

Several paddles shot up around me.

My mind went fuzzy as I tried to recall a single item coming up in the auction—or even the total number of items listed. What if this was the best option, the one best suited for a guy like Patrick? What if I passed it up only to be left with crocheted hats and ice scrapers? What if I spent his money on something he would never use?

Quick decisions were my nemesis. I needed time to research, time to weigh the pros and cons, time to consider every possible option. Twice.

Patrick's note had distracted me from the program. A quick refresher, just one quick glance-over would be more than enough. I bent to grab the program from under Patrick's foot. But he was faster.

Patrick kicked it from my reach. "No cheating. Just make a decision."

Argh!

It was down to just two paddles now—a bidding war between Al Rogers and J. R. Peterson. Adrenaline pumped through my veins; my legs bounced and my fingers twitched.

I didn't want to make a mistake. I didn't want to choose poorly. I didn't want—

"Going once, going twice . . ."

I shot my arm up, heart pounding in rhythm with my headache.

The auctioneer acknowledged me with a nod—as did the two men.

The bidding went higher. I raised my paddle again.

Higher and higher the number soared and still Patrick's stony face held strong.

I raised my paddle again and it was this time that won Patrick his trip down the river.

My lungs pumped air in and out as if I'd just run around the building and not simply lifted a paper paddle.

Patrick leaned in close, his woodsy scent causing my brain fog to dissipate.

"Good choice. That's been on my list since I got to town. Rex would be proud."

I wanted to punch him and hug him all at the same time. Pride climbed in step with my hope. If I could conquer the first of Patrick's little tests, then maybe I could conquer them all. Maybe courage really did start this small.

I closed my eyes and breathed deep, my tension releasing through each exhale.

Several more items came up for grabs, all of them unlikely to be desirable for a man like Patrick: custom tailoring, a family photo shoot, a dozen cupcakes from the Frosting Palace.

None of them compared to what I'd won him.

". . . a stunning shot of the valley at sunset." I sat up straighter, my ears suddenly attuned to the auctioneer's voice. A rush of air escaped my throat as he unveiled the enlarged canvas photograph. It was Lenox, draped in the golden hue of a setting sun. I had never seen my town from this angle—a bird's-eye view.

People all around us murmured as the auctioneer continued. I leaned forward, straining to hear him. "One of a kind, folks. A gorgeous representation of our town."

Three dozen paddles flew into the air as I studied the piece. Though I hadn't seen this exact picture before, it spoke to me . . .

"Bid." Patrick's voice made me jump.

"What? Why?" *What would Patrick do with a canvas this size?* "You don't even own a wall of your own to hang it on."

Lip curled upward, he shook his head at my joke. "Just bid, will ya?"

I raised my paddle.

Ten paddles were left in play, the bidding war climbing well into the thousand-dollar range. I glanced at him again, waiting for him to pull the plug.

Patrick bumped my shoulder. "What? Don't start acting shy now."

Suddenly I understood.

In the same way I would know my favorite author's writing, I'd recognized my favorite photographer's work. Dr. Ivar's youngest son—Patrick's brother—was the eye behind the camera lens of this picture. I was sure of it. His talent was not only on display in his father's clinic, but in my home as well, thanks to a gift from Dr. Ivar in one of the scariest seasons of my life.

I held my paddle up with pride, realizing for the umpteenth time how generous this family was to our community. If Patrick's brother had donated the sunset photograph for the auction, perhaps Patrick's form of generosity was to see that it sold for top dollar. Because just like he'd reminded me earlier, *it was for the kids.*

"That's the biggest smile I've seen on your face to date," Patrick said. "I'm storing this moment away for future reference. Want to see Willa smile? Just hand her a credit card."

"Very funny." My grin did feel outrageously large, but I couldn't help it. The McCade family was quickly becoming my favorite family of all time. "It's a gift for your father, isn't it?"

Patrick winked in confirmation.

Something close to giddiness pushed its way up my throat. "There's a perfect spot for it in the waiting room at the clinic—just to the right of the front desk."

Amused, he nodded, then gestured toward the last bidder standing, Mr. Hayes, the vice president of our local credit union.

Mr. Hayes lost.

Patrick tipped his imaginary hat to me, and my appreciation for him grew tenfold. A son who would do something this kind, this big-hearted for his father was the kind of man I wanted Savannah to marry one day.

The auction ended with a round of applause for the school and instructions on how to pick up the night's winnings.

I stood and handed the paddle back to Patrick, practically tripping over his feet so I could avoid another run-in with Grandma Carter.

"So I passed?" I asked him, not really sure what to call tonight—a lesson, a test, a bravery trial?

"I would hope so. You just spent all my money."

"What? But you said—"

He threw his head back and laughed.

I swatted his arm. "That was so not funny."

"Oh, that was more than funny. Your face—" He couldn't catch his breath.

"You're mean." I smashed my lips together.

"And you're gullible."

I swung my purse over my shoulder, making sure it grazed his arm. "*Gullible* is pretty low on my Worst Personality Traits list."

His eyebrows shot up. "Oh, please tell me you have this list written down somewhere—perhaps on a colorful Post-it Note?"

I ticked my finger at him. "Never underestimate the power of a Post-it Note."

"Spoken like a true office supply junkie."

"That's right."

"You hungry?" he asked.

"A little." I pointed to the very picked-over refreshments table. "Looks like there's some bean dip left. Or maybe that's chocolate pudding. Hard to tell."

"I meant for actual food. I haven't had dinner. We could go grab something, celebrate your big win?"

My stomach rumbled at the offer, but the clock above the exit doors made the decision easy. "I really should head home. I haven't seen Savannah since school drop-off this morning."

Several beats of silence and then, "You're a good mom."

Warmth blossomed in my chest. "She's easy to love."

The smile in his eyes lingered as he reached into his pocket and pulled out a crinkled piece of paper. "You should keep this. You earned it." He deposited tonight's completed challenge into my palm and pressed my fingers around it.

I lifted my eyes from our connected hands. "Thank you, Patrick." *For teaching me that not every decision has to be charted, weighed, and pie-graphed.*

By the look on his face, he knew I was a Camp Courage convert.

Chapter Twelve

"You earned it."

Patrick's words from the auction had flitted through my head at random since I woke up. They kept me sane while training Alex, kept me patient while Sydney stayed locked in her office, kept me calm while my chair legs sank into the soggy soccer field.

"Hey, Mommy!" Savannah waved from the field, her cheeks as bright as the neon-pink jersey she wore.

Weston and Georgia had taken her shopping last night. New cleats, socks, and shin guards had likely cost them a small fortune, but any attempts to pay them back would be waved off. Like they were every single time I tried.

I twisted in the canvas seat and zipped my too-thin jacket to my chin. I didn't know how the kids were weathering the chill this afternoon but guessed Weston's warm-up drill had something to do with it. He tooted that whistle about every three seconds. Another few minutes of shivering and I was considering joining them for a round of jumping jacks.

"Here, this might help." A wool blanket dropped onto my lap. Unfortunately, the face behind the gesture didn't match the man I'd been thinking about all day.

"Hey, Davis." I unfolded the blanket and tucked it under my thighs. "Thanks for this."

The flash of his straight white teeth and his clean-shaven face remained a stark contrast to his short ebony hair. "Glad I had it in my trunk. I could see you shivering from the parking lot."

That was Davis in a nutshell: considerate, kind, always planning for the future. A future I hoped we could avoid discussing for a while longer.

"I was surprised to see your brother as head coach when I signed Brandon up." He nodded to the soccer field.

"Yes, I was surprised, too." The understatement sank in my belly like a boulder, but my smile stayed fastened on tight.

Weston and Davis had known each other since grade school, but not even time could blend their oil-and-water personalities. I tried to keep my commentary to a bare minimum when speaking to one about the other. It was better for everybody that way.

"My grandma said she sat with you at the auction last night." True to Davis, there wasn't an ounce of accusation in his tone. "Should I just go ahead and apologize now or after I hear what she said to you?"

"Ha." I twisted my hands together on top of the blanket. "Neither. She was fine."

"Or maybe you're too generous." His quick wink accentuated his long dark lashes.

With a polite smile, I shook my head and focused again on Savannah, who was sprinting down the field.

"It's awesome to see her like this," he said, shifting his gaze from the field back to me. "To see you both like this—settling back into life."

A hot ball of uncertainty swelled in the hollow of my belly as I studied the weave of the blanket on my lap. I picked at the minute pieces of lint, one by one.

The short blow of a whistle cut through the tension in my body, and a blur of motion at the edge of the field captured my attention.

In a moment I'd tossed the blanket aside and was running. My focus narrowed on the petite blonde cradling her knee near the orange cones. As I dropped beside her, cold wet mud seeped through my pants. I rested my hand at her back.

"What happened?" It was my question but Davis's voice.

He also knelt behind Savannah while Weston worked to pry her hands away from the wound.

Blood pulsed between her fingers and my world tipped on its side, my breath shallow and unsteady.

"Vannie, I need to see how deep it is." My brother's stern command was edged with an emotion that made my own blood run cold.

She whimpered and shook her head, her eyes meeting mine for the first time. Tears coursed down her dirt-smeared cheeks, and she pleaded for me to take her home.

My brother plucked a sharp-sided rock from the blades of grass at Savannah's feet. "How did this get on the field?"

But I was beyond caring about the *how*s and *why*s. I just knew that my daughter was hurting. Bleeding. Crying.

Davis scooped her up into his arms, his T-shirt pulling tight around flexed biceps. I got to my feet quickly and followed after them.

"What do you think you're doing?" Weston raced after us.

"Taking her to urgent care," Davis said without slowing his steps. "You have a practice to finish. I'll be back to pick Brandon up."

"Willa." Weston grabbed at my elbow, forcing me to a stop. "Let me take her."

I yanked out of his grasp, my silence saying more than my words ever could. *You've done enough.*

Savannah reached her free hand over Davis's shoulder as they crossed onto the blacktop. "Mommy."

I quickened my steps.

This time when Weston called my name, I didn't turn back.

Pressing one of Brandon's old T-shirts to her kneecap, Savannah sat in the backseat of Davis's car and leaned her head against my shoulder. She was a tough girl and rarely cried over the small stuff, not when a large portion of her childhood had already been spent enduring pokes and tests and drug side effects that could make a grown adult crumble.

"Take her to McCade Medical Clinic, please." It was Tuesday night—the clinic was open until seven.

Davis glanced at me through the rearview mirror. "Urgent care could be faster—"

"Please, Davis. Trust me." Because I trusted Patrick. More than any emergency care doctor in town. The realization sent a zing down my spine.

Davis didn't say another word until we pulled up to the clinic. He opened Savannah's door, then lifted her up into his arms again to carry her inside.

Marsha stood as she saw us come through the door. "Let me tell Dr. McCade you're here—he was just about to leave for the night."

Time is relative in a crisis, yet from the moment we entered the clinic we hadn't stopped moving. Nurse Lilly prepped a tray near the sink, Davis untied Savannah's mud-coated shoelaces, and I rubbed calming circles into her upper back.

And then Patrick opened the door and everything slowed to a standstill.

The sizing up between the two men seemed to last a year, the handshake and introduction formality as painful to watch as it was awkward to listen to.

Before I could gather my thoughts, Davis was halfway through the recap of today's soccer field trauma. During the entire exchange, Patrick glanced in my direction a total of one time—right before he made his way to the sink.

And that one look felt like a spur-kick to the gut.

Snapping on a pair of blue nitrile gloves, Patrick approached Savannah. "Might I take a look at your knee, lassie?" The Scottish brogue was back.

She shook her head, the bloody T-shirt still pressed to her wound. With the toe of his shoe, Patrick guided the rolling stool toward him. I took a step back to allow him space as he sat eye-to-eye with his young patient.

Accent switched off, he spoke again, "Did you know that during a blizzard some reindeer make a loud clicking sound with their knees?"

Savannah lifted her head and sniffled. "No."

"It's true. That way they can stay with their other reindeer pals. Never get lost."

She blinked.

"And did you know that a penguin—whose knees you can't even see—can jump six feet in the air?" He tucked the towels underneath her leg and then reached for the bottle on the tray marked *saline*.

She shook her head. "Uh-uh."

Holding Savannah's gaze, he slowly peeled away the cotton shirt from her kneecap to expose a slice in her flesh that made my own knees weak. I gripped the counter behind me and Davis clamped his hands onto my shoulders.

Patrick flooded the wound, and dirt, blood, and debris soaked into the towel. "So you probably didn't know that elephants are the only mammal on earth that can't jump at all. I kinda feel bad for those guys," Patrick said with an exaggerated sigh.

Savannah's lips parted, a slight lift to one side. "I kinda do, too."

"Yeah? That's because you're empathetic."

"What's empa—?"

"Empathetic. It means you feel something for the elephants that can't jump like the rest of the animal kingdom."

Patrick removed a large chunk of muck and Savannah yelped.

"But it would be kinda funny," he added.

"Hmm?" Her voice shook as she stared at her knee.

"To see an elephant jump."

Her eyes snapped back to Patrick, the panic on her face transforming into something unexpected. A smile.

"What do you think would happen if an elephant *could* jump?" He reached for a small square package at the end of the tray, never missing a beat.

"Um . . . an earthquake?"

Patrick laughed as he unwrapped a cleaning pad. "I think you might be right. Maybe that's why God didn't allow them to jump. Probably the wisest choice."

He held the pad out so she could see it. "Savannah, I'm going to use this to clean out the cut, but I need you to count to five, okay? You can yell out the numbers if you need to. I'll even do it with you. But if you can let me clean the rest of this yuck from your cut for five whole seconds, then I'll let you pick from my supersecret treasure box."

Her forehead creased as she looked from Patrick to me.

I nodded. "I'll count, too, baby."

"Me, too," Davis said, his thumbs kneading the muscles along my upper back.

"Good, see? We're all going to count with you," Patrick said.

Savannah pinched her eyes closed. "Okay."

It wasn't her style to scream or carry on. She would own this pain and power through it—I'd seen it too many times to count.

"One." Patrick started us off, his strokes with the pad against her knee as precise as they were quick. "Two, three . . ."

"Four," I chimed in.

The grimace on Savannah's face lightened. "Five!"

"Done." Patrick tossed the scrubber into the trash. "Well, the great news is you don't need sutures. Just Steri-Strips. You'll be jumping again in no time." He leaned in close and whispered, "Just don't tell the elephants."

Savannah covered her mouth and giggled.

Patrick rotated on the stool and stood, his feet just inches from mine. In the half second before he pointed to the cabinet and his eyes met mine—or rather met the hands that were still attached to my shoulders—I could have sworn I saw a flash of irritation on his face. *And maybe . . . disappointment?*

"I need to get in there," he said to me.

I stepped out of Davis's grasp to allow Patrick access to the shelf he needed and then hugged my arms to my chest, noting the clock on the wall.

"I don't want you to be late getting Brandon from practice, Davis. I'm sure my mom can come pick us up so you can take off."

He pulled his phone from his back pocket. "I don't mind waiting. I'll just arrange for one of the moms to watch him until we're done here."

Sliding my phone from the side pocket of my purse, I prepared for a texting battle. "No, really, I'll text my mom."

"I can drop you off. Savannah's my last patient of the day." Patrick's focus remained on Savannah's knee, his words a dangling carrot.

"How long are you in town for, doc?" The lighthearted Davis of moments ago was no more.

"Just till the end of the year," Patrick countered.

A fact I should write on the palm of my hand with permanent marker.

"It's your choice, Willa." Davis's words were weighted with meaning, but my mental pros-and-cons list would make my decision easy. Accepting a ride with the doctor would require far less energy than avoiding a badly timed let's-be-more-than-friends discussion with Davis.

Patrick's quick-working fingers stilled on Savannah's leg.

With the tip of my thumbnail, I pressed the peppermint candy in my pocket into my outer thigh. Maybe I could absorb its calming powers through osmosis. "Thank you for all your help tonight, but we'll catch a ride back with Patrick." The instant his first name passed over my lips, I knew I'd made a mistake. I should have called him Dr. McCade.

Davis studied me for two seconds too long. "I'll call you later." And then he exited the office.

He hadn't missed my verbal slip either.

Chapter Thirteen

Unlike Davis, Patrick didn't scoop Savannah into his arms and carry her when we arrived home. Instead, he became a human crutch, showing her how to bear the brunt of her weight on her good leg as she walked.

"Can I watch a show on your laptop, Mommy?" She plunked herself onto her bed and scooted back against the headrest. Immediately, Prince Pickles joined her, snuggling into her side and licking her cheek every few seconds.

Sometimes I wondered if that dog worried about her more than I did.

"I'll wait out here." Patrick exited the room as I set Savannah up with a movie in bed, propping her foot on a pillow. She gave me a thumbs-up, as if the events of this evening had been the same as every other Tuesday night.

My phone buzzed again in my pocket, and with a single press of my finger, I silenced it. Just like I had the other five times Weston had called since we'd left the clinic.

I pulled the door halfway closed behind me and wandered down the hallway in search of Patrick. I found him, standing near the bookshelf, a frame in his hand.

He set the picture back in place as I entered the room. "Hey."

"Hey." I gestured to the silver frame. "That was my husband, Chad." Even after seven years, the past tense of that sentence still stung to speak aloud.

He nodded slowly. "Savannah has his smile."

I stared past him at the man forever bound to memory. "Yes, she does."

"But she has your brown eyes."

Patrick's face captured my focus and for two, three, four heartbeats, the charge between our gazes felt as achingly familiar as it did increasingly uncertain. I blinked, and Patrick's open, unbuttoned shirt collar caught my attention. The crumpled, turned-up seam begged to be smoothed.

I took a step back and curled my fingers into a loose fist at my side, silencing the impulse to stretch out my hand and press the tips of my fingers to his neckline—

I shifted my weight and glanced away. "Thank you. For what you did tonight. I was panicked before you came in, but you were . . ." *Exactly what I needed.* "So great with her."

Patrick braced his hands against the back of the couch, his stance as casual as his tone. "Blood seems to do that to people."

"Not to you it doesn't."

"Doctors are a strange breed." Patrick's modesty was laughable.

"Well then, I wish I could be a little more strange and a lot less whatever it is I am," I said.

"You're a mom."

And a paranoid control freak. "That's one way to put it."

The amusement on his face dimmed. "A mother's intuition can't compete with a medical degree. You've done a whole lot right, Willa. Probably more than you give yourself credit for."

The sincerity on his face sent an electric current through my body. A tension settled in the space between us, the air thick and my breathing shallow. On unsteady legs, I wove a path around him—through the dining room and into the kitchen. The tiled breakfast bar had never served so great a purpose than it did currently: a physical barrier. A forced reality check. I pressed my palms flat onto the smooth surface and cleared my throat. "So . . . the aftercare instructions, for Savannah's knee? Is there anything I should know?"

"Oh, right." Patrick pushed off the back of the couch and patted his breast pocket for a pen. "Do you have something I can write on? I forgot to ask Marsha for the official handout before we left. Really, the most important thing is to keep the Steri-Strips dry for the first twenty-four hours. I can follow up with you in a couple days."

It would take a couple days to clear the fog in my head. "Sounds good."

I rummaged through the junk drawer I'd just reorganized, searching for my kitchen Post-it Notes, but turned up nothing. Unfortunately my daughter had an affinity for them, too.

"Let me check her art box, just a—"

Patrick strode past me into the dining room. He stopped at the head of the table, facing the far wall—where the photograph that had acted as a lifeline hung. Throughout Savannah's treatment it had been my visible hope.

"Did . . . did my father give this to you?"

I bumped the kitchen drawer closed with my hip. Careful to keep my distance, I joined him at the table. "He did." *At a time I needed it most.* "That one's my favorite."

Patrick's gaze swung from the art to me, his brow wrinkled. "Wait— how many do you have?"

I folded my arms around my middle. "Three. Two he took straight off his walls at the clinic. Your parents gave them to me the day Savannah's diagnosis was confirmed." I stared at the photograph of frosted trees, at the glow of the setting sun just beyond them. The slatted spaces of forest were alight with the kind of fire that could ignite even the most hopeless of hearts. "Somehow he knew this one was my favorite—probably because I'd commented on it several times during past visits. He enlarged it for me, said that even when we couldn't leave the house due to risk of infection, he wanted us to have a piece of God's creation in our home to admire." The moment was one I cherished, the same way I'd cherished this picture. "His love for sunsets has rubbed off on the whole community. Your younger brother is quite the photographer."

Patrick's blink was like a visual stutter. "What, uh, what did you do with the others he gave to you?"

"One is in my bedroom, and one I left at the family apartment we stayed in while Savannah received treatments in Portland."

"Why? I mean, why did you leave it behind?"

My reply was simple, an answer that hovered close to my heart. "So it could do for someone else what it had done for me." I looked back at the photograph. "Sunsets are a reminder that every day will come to an end. And no matter how hard, or how trying, or how all-consuming that twenty-four-hour period might feel . . . every day can be as different as every sunset."

I didn't have to turn my neck to feel Patrick's gaze on my face, or the spark of desire it ignited in my core.

I cleared my throat, hoping it would clear the hormone fog I must be under. "Which is your favorite of your father's collection?" Surely he had one; his brother's talent was the main décor of the medical clinic where he worked every day.

"I don't know if I have a favorite . . . the truth is, no matter how good the lens, it's hard to replace the memory of the real thing."

I twisted around and his grin exploded.

"Wait . . . you're the—?"

"Youngest McCade brother, yes."

I couldn't stop staring at him, my jaw completely unhinged. How had I missed that Patrick was the baby of the family?

"It's just a hobby," he said, as if to dismiss my starstruck reaction.

I tried to swallow away the sudden throb in my throat, but then the significance of this moment would hit me all over again. Patrick had captured *this* sunset. *Patrick.* There was no possible way for me to explain to him what his picture had done for me over the last year. How many times it had kept me from the clutches of an oncoming anxiety attack. How many prayers I had prayed beneath it for my sick child. *Patrick.* The same man standing in my dining room right now, downplaying his talent as "just a hobby."

"Honestly, learning how to take a decent picture seemed to be the easiest way I could share my life—my travels—with my family." He was still speaking as if his art were the work of a second grader. "I had no idea how much of a sunset enthusiast my father had become until the first time I walked into the clinic. I was shocked to see how he'd turned my pictures into canvas prints."

"Wait—so that picture, the one I bid on at the auction for you— you took that one? Of Lenox?"

"Yeah." His gaze strayed from my face. "Like you said, my father needed something to fill that blank wall in his lobby."

I had the strangest sensation to cry at his humble words. "You could have just given it to him . . ."

"It was a good cause."

I opened my mouth, hoping something coherent would come out, when my phone buzzed again from my pocket.

Patrick cleared his throat. "I should probably go so you can return your calls."

"Okay, right."

"Here." He pulled out his phone and opened to a new contact screen. "Why don't I text you the aftercare instructions for Savannah's knee; that way you don't have to hunt for a piece of paper." He winked as I took the device from him and entered my information.

I gave it back and he shot me a text, my pocket vibrating a second later.

"I skimmed through Rex's journal again last night, after the auction."

"Oh, yeah?" My voice sounded far from normal, but I hoped I was the only one to recognize that fact. "You figure out my next bravery lesson?"

A knock at my front door cut him off.

Patrick shot me a questioning look, but I had zero questions about who was behind that door.

"That would be my brother."

Patrick swiped his keys off the counter and followed me to the door. "I'll leave you to that, then."

"Thanks. You know, this may not be the only house call you make tonight." I rolled my eyes at Patrick. "My brother may be in need of your care after he leaves here."

I yanked the door open.

Weston stood on my front porch, hands shoved deep into his pockets. "Can I please see her?"

Patrick moved aside and allowed my brother to enter and then stepped onto the porch.

"You leaving?" Weston asked.

After slapping Weston on the back, he jogged down the porch steps. "I'll see you on the court at six."

"I'll be there."

Patrick offered me a simple wave. "My bet's on you."

I smiled down at the "secret hobbyist" and closed the door.

While Weston tucked his niece into bed, I waited for him in the living room. He was on the last stanza of the silly good-night song he'd made up for her years ago.

A minute later, he treaded down the hallway and stopped at the sofa.

He picked up a throw pillow and tossed it to the empty couch against the far wall. "Why do women always insist on filling their seating areas with these froufrou pillows? They aren't even comfortable."

"Weston."

"Nan and Georgia have these things everywhere in that tiny cottage—on rocking chairs, beds, sofas—"

"Weston." My patience was thinning.

With a forceful sigh, Weston sat and staked his elbows on his knees. "I'm sorry, okay?"

"For what?"

Weston never had a problem saying he was sorry, but I often wondered if the only reason he apologized was to avoid a fight. End a quarrel. Prevent an ongoing confrontation.

He lifted his head, his right dimple fully indented. "You don't know? I thought it was pretty obvious."

And this was how a serious discussion went with my brother: he says *sorry*, tells a stupid joke, makes me laugh, and then I forgive him.

Only this time I didn't want it to be that easy for him. He pushed me whenever he wanted to. But tonight it was my turn to push back.

I said nothing, using the same approach I had as a teacher. Sometimes silence was the best solution.

He tugged at the back of his neck. "I don't know who is more stubborn sometimes—you or Georgia." He shook his head as if reconsidering. "Nah, it's definitely Georgia."

I stood up from the chair, my patience gone. "If you want to play games, then you can leave."

"Willa." This was Weston's favorite tone—his younger-brother, you-can't-possibly-be-mad-at-me-forever tone.

I crossed my arms and he slumped deeper into my sofa.

"I'm not leaving."

"Then I'm going to bed." I started down the hall.

"Fine."

The change in his voice caused me to pivot.

There was no smile on his mouth, no humor left in his eyes. "I'm sorry for signing her up for soccer without asking you, and I'm sorry she fell and hurt her knee. But the real reason you're mad at me is because I'm forcing you to keep a promise you had no intention of keeping. If not for me, Savannah would be walking around this town in Bubble Wrap."

No. He wouldn't turn this around on me. Not tonight. "How do you know what I'm doing or not doing? I don't tell you every little thing that goes on in my life, and I shouldn't have to. Maybe you need to start trusting me to—"

"Why do you think I push you so hard, Willa? You think I enjoy it? I don't. I push you because *I know you*, and I know if I didn't push, then you'd never step out of your comfort zone. I'm not the bad guy here." The tremor in his voice cut me deep. "I came back to Lenox when you needed me most." He pointed down the hallway. "And I stayed because of her."

It was true. He'd given up an architecture scholarship in Boston to return to Oregon after Chad died. Because of his love for his family.

The rigidity in my shoulders relaxed. "I know you did, and I couldn't have made it through these last few years without you. But Weston . . . you have to let *me* be her mom."

He pushed a hand through his hair and stared at the floor for several seconds. "Okay."

"Okay?"

Silence, and then, "Yeah, okay, just as long as you never replace my best-uncle status."

His laugh was light as he pulled me into a hug, but my heart was not. Weston committing to let me play mom without interference was like me committing to conquer my fear of heights.

Great in theory yet far from reality.

Chapter Fourteen

One by one, I gathered the three opened—and very expensive—protein bars on my desk and held them up. "Um, Alex? Are these yours?"

This earned a single nod and a glance up from her paper clip art. "They're all gross, in case you were wondering—especially that brownie nut one. Whoever decided on *that* flavor has obviously never eaten dessert before."

I breathed through my nose and thought carefully about my next words. Alex was seventeen, but sometimes she seemed closer to seven. Other times closer to seventy. I still hadn't figured out why she wasn't enrolled at the high school like all the other kids her age. Every time I wanted to ask Sydney a question regarding Alex, she either avoided me or gave me the old "I have a meeting" line.

"You do know these cost money, right?"

"Yep. And so do groceries. But my *halfie* won't go shopping. She told me to just shop online." She shrugged. "Who does that—I mean, who buys their cereal online?"

Alex had made a similar comment last week. And it wasn't the first time, or even the fourth time, I'd seen her wearing the same pair of gray cargo pants since we'd met a week and a half ago. "Alex . . . do you need me to take you to the store? I have some time after work today if you don't mind my daughter tagging along."

Her large ebony eyes shifted to focus on something behind me—or someone. A throat cleared behind me.

Sydney.

"Did you get my e-mail regarding Saturday?"

The four-page e-mail with instructions on how to run the Fitness Day? Yes. I certainly had.

"Yes, and I was hoping we could discuss a few things? In private," I suggested as kindly as possible.

Sydney's granitelike stare chilled me. "I have five minutes before I have to be on a conference call. So if you need to ask a question, ask it now."

She knew I couldn't ask what I wanted to ask. Not in front of Alex.

My mind skipped ahead. "When do you leave?"

"Early Saturday morning."

Three days from now.

I glanced back at Alex, who was suddenly very occupied with a stack of my Post-it Notes.

"And which employees will be here that day?"

She didn't blink. "Toby and all three of the personal trainers."

"And me," Alex added, her tone so sharp it could cut glass.

Sydney frowned. "Alex."

"I won't go." She glared at Sydney. Apparently Sydney's cold stare was hereditary. In my opinion, she used it even better than Sydney.

"We aren't discussing this here."

"Well, you don't discuss anything with me anywhere else."

"We can talk at home."

"But you said your house was *not* my home, remember?"

Sydney tugged at the hem of her blazer as if to straighten an invisible wrinkle. "The appointment is set. It's the best thing for you."

The four-inch heels Sydney wore drilled into the floor as she marched away.

Slowly, I turned back to Alex whose face was as red as a vine-picked tomato. I waited. For what, I wasn't exactly sure.

"How would you know what's best for me? You don't even know me." Alex said to her back, her voice half the volume—and half the fury.

I waited for two older women wearing skirted bathing suits to pass us before speaking again.

"Where won't you go?"

"To some kind of boarding school up north. But I don't need that. I can homeschool myself if Syd would just give me a chance . . ." She stomped her boot on the ground and cursed.

There were so many unknowns, so many things I didn't understand about the complicated girl sitting in front of me, but I could read pain, the same way I could read grief.

I touched her shoulder. "What's the story with your parents, Alex?"

"I never met my dad, and my mom—*our* mom"—she glanced to the top of the stairs—"won't be up for parole for another three years. The court appointed Sydney as my guardian, but apparently she doesn't want the job."

The thought of such a young girl walking through life without the guidance of a stable parent . . . I clutched the edge of the desk to anchor the throb in my heart. Alex's idiosyncrasies were many, but shipping her off couldn't be the only solution.

"Can you come over for dinner tonight?" I said without thinking about the ramifications of my invitation—or about how Alex might behave in front of my seven-year old. But I knew this girl needed someone. I'd simply have to deal with her colorful vocabulary one word at a time.

Alex swallowed. "I know how to make lasagna."

I smiled at her offer. "Lasagna it is, then."

"You have blue hair," Savannah said as I helped her into the car at school pickup.

"And you have a busted-up knee," Alex pointed out.

"Savannah." I looked between the two of them. "This is my friend from work, Alex Reyes. She's gonna run some errands with us and then come over for dinner tonight."

"At our house?" Savannah asked, sitting up a little straighter. She waved at Alex from the backseat.

"Yes. At our house."

"But no one ever comes to our house for fancy dinners, Mommy. Not like at Nan's or Grandma's."

I slipped back into the driver's seat, then pulled out of the parking lot. "I *can* cook fancy dinners; I just haven't cooked one in a while."

Alex kicked her foot up on the dash. "So, what you're saying is that without my special lasagna recipe you two would starve tonight."

I gave her a sidelong glance. "Yes, Alex. We need you to survive."

"Thought so."

Savannah took up most of the space in the grocery cart, her knee propped on her backpack while she played a game on my phone. Together, the three of us entered the megastore, which would not only supply our grocery needs but some of Alex's personal needs as well.

"Let's start here." We stood under the banner of Personal Care.

Alex shot me a look.

"Are you stocked up on shampoo, deodorant, makeup?" *Hair color?*

Savannah looked up from her game. "I have some makeup. You can borrow it."

Alex patted her on the head. "Thanks, Busted Knee."

Alex touched the end cap of herbal hair products. "I could probably use a couple of those things."

"And maybe then you could help me in the clothing section, before we shop for tonight's dinner ingredients." I had no intention of buying new clothes, not for myself anyway. But Alex wasn't the type who would respond well to pity.

Two pairs of jeans and a pile of girly products later—all smell-tested and Savannah-approved—we left the valley of personal care and entered the land of produce.

Alex had grabbed several onions, a green pepper, and a handful of garlic and was on her way back to the cart when Savannah popped her hand up, my phone clutched in her grasp. "Mommy—you have a text."

PATRICK: I mopped the court with your brother this morning. You're welcome.

I laughed out loud and replied quickly.

ME: Ha. And my debt to you just keeps growing...

PATRICK: Consider it my act of community service for the week. Savannah's knee looking better?

I pushed the cart slowly, texting him as I steered.

ME: Yes, thanks to you.

Alex slammed into my side. "Texting in a grocery store is considered hazardous. Bad example for Miss Know-it-all here."

Savannah laughed. "Just because I knew avocados were a fruit and *you* didn't."

Alex studied me for all of two seconds before her face broke into an electric grin. "Oooh. Who's texting you? A man? Maybe even . . . your *mystery* man?"

I stuffed the phone into my pocket and shook my head, trying to kill the smile on my mouth. "No one." My pocket buzzed twice in a row.

"Who's a mystery man?" Savannah asked.

"Thanks, Alex," I chided.

She shrugged. "Your mommy has an admirer."

"That's enough."

I turned down the pasta aisle, allowing Alex her pick of lasagna noodles, and slipped my phone back out to sneak a peek.

PATRICK: Want your next Rex challenge?

PATRICK: Or maybe you've given up? Maybe the auction was too emotionally draining and you've lost all confidence in me.

I laughed and Alex whipped around, a box of noodles in her hand.

"Ya know, the Warden—my old guidance counselor—would confiscate our phones if we got caught laughing at a text. Or she would make us read them aloud."

"Neither of which are happening here." I rolled my eyes at her. "Let's head up to the registers. I'm getting hungry."

"Me, too!" Savannah piped in.

Alex shook her head and chuckled.

I shot back a text.

ME: Hardly. Send it over.

PATRICK: "The best way to kick your comfort is to invite diversity into your life."

I stopped the cart and looked over my shoulder. Could he see my little blue-haired friend? How could he know that tonight was the first time I'd invited someone to dinner since before Savannah's diagnosis?

ME: Are you stalking me?

PATRICK: ?

I paused to help Alex unload our groceries onto the conveyor belt and waited for my total to appear on the tiny screen. I texted Patrick back.

ME: I'm hosting a little dinner party at my house tonight. One very interesting teenager and one cute little blonde. Pretty diverse for me. I think it should count.

PATRICK: Hmmm . . . in order to get full credit, I will need to verify.

I put my phone down and looked at Alex.
"What?" she asked.
"How would you feel if I invited a friend over tonight, too?"
"Who—mystery man?"
Bad idea. "Never mind."
The cashier hit a button on the keyboard and then said the total. I swiped my card as Alex's face paled at the sight.
"Wait, I have Syd's credit card. You didn't have to pay—"
I shook my head. "I'm happy to pay, Alex."

She squished her mouth to one side and then looked down at Savannah. "Yes, invite him." She gave a firm nod. "I promise to be on my best behavior."

"No, really. We can just keep it to the three of us tonight. I don't want to make you uncomfortable."

"Willa, my middle name is *uncomfortable*. Invite him."

She tucked the grocery bags around Savannah's propped knee and grabbed the handle of the cart. Savannah laughed as Alex pretended to steer them into a tower of Diet Coke.

I lifted my phone again, finger suspended over the text box for a full five seconds. *Here goes another big leap in the span of just a few hours . . .*

ME: If you're feeling brave you can come join us for a night of lasagna and makeovers.

PATRICK: I'm always feeling brave.

Chapter Fifteen

Alex reached across the table and slapped another slice of extra-cheesy lasagna onto her plate. "Wait, go back. How the *heck*"—she emphasized the word for my benefit—"did you get out of that murky swamp with the broken-leg guy? What happened after the raft sprung a leak?" She shoved another forkful into her mouth and gawked at Patrick, who was, once again, owning his role as Captain Story.

"Well, since the water was up to our necks, we had to float him on our backs. The splint we rigged was out of tree bark, so it was very buoyant, but—"

"But helllllooo, the alligators!" Alex's hands flew up in the air. "Bet you and your doctor pal dropped more than a few f-bombs over that ordeal."

Patrick chuckled at her while I pinched my lips and hoped Savannah's next question wouldn't be about f-bombs. Fortunately, she was just as engrossed in Patrick's story as the rest of us.

"Did you see one—an alligator? Did it have a lot of ugly green warts?" Savannah asked.

"Yes, we saw several that night, actually. If not for the pickup truck waiting on shore, I don't know if we would've escaped. My friend nearly lost his hand."

The ping of Alex's fork dropping onto her plate made us all jump. She pushed her chair out and picked up her dishes and drinking glass. "Well, thanks for the nightmares. I'll be sure to send my therapy bill to your house. Or to your hut. Just leave your forwarding address with Willa."

Patrick and I both laughed. Alex went back and forth between the table and kitchen, clearing the plates and putting away all the extra platters and pans.

The girl was a puzzle of complications. Every time I pegged her as irresponsible or immature, she'd proved me wrong. She had made a full lasagna dinner from memory, cleared the table without being asked, and was about to let Savannah "paint her face" with a bunch of old makeup.

"Okay, kid, make sure whatever you do to my face, it doesn't clash with my hair," Alex deadpanned.

Savannah sat at the edge of the couch while Alex knelt in front of her on the floor.

"I like your hair." Savannah brushed it back with her fingers. "It looks like cotton candy. I got that once, at the hospital."

"Yeah?"

Savannah added a shade of taffy-pink blush to Alex's cheeks. "Yep. I had cancer. But not anymore. Now I just get to be a normal kid and have fun with my mommy and my uncle."

"That's cool."

I pressed my hand to the base of my throat. Savannah's resilience never failed to astound me—a trait I wished we shared.

A warm touch at my elbow caught my attention. Patrick's crystal-blue eyes met mine. He inclined his head toward the kitchen as the girls chatted about eye shadow and lip glosses.

Moving to the sink, I turned on the tap water and rinsed the last few serving utensils before adding them to the dishwasher.

He set a glass on the top rack, his voice quiet and close. "So, what's her story?"

It was a loaded question. "I don't know everything, but what I do know is . . . complicated."

Patrick closed the dishwasher and then leaned back against the counter. "I'm sure that's true, but I'm also sure that what you've done for her so far will leave a positive impact."

I wanted that to be true, but how much help could I really be if she was being shipped off in a few days?

"So . . ." Patrick's change in tone held an extra note of mischief. "I may have heard from a little birdie that you like to bake."

I huffed a short laugh. "Well that birdie is either four feet tall and insists that Cinderella should be a part of the Bible, or he's six feet tall and is often confused about the meaning of 'none of your business'—so which one is it?"

"The bigger of the two, I'm afraid."

Naturally. "I can only imagine what else he's told you about me."

"Afraid I can't divulge that information. What happens on the court . . ." He tilted his head to the side and I rolled my eyes.

"Maybe you should write a new clause into whatever basketball pact you two have going on—*eliminate* some topics of discussion." I pointed to myself. "Like me."

His smile widened. "Or you could just bake me something and I can judge his honesty for myself."

Bake him something?

"I don't have any ingredients for baking in the house." At least I hadn't used them in a very, very long time.

"Hmm." Patrick tapped his chin. "I'm trying to recall—yep, there's a very specific page in Rex's travel journal dedicated to baked goods."

"Liar." I swatted him with a kitchen towel. "I think I need to see this journal for myself."

"Anytime." Was that a challenge or an invitation?

The theme song for *101 Dalmatians* blared from the living room.

"Crap, that's my phone," Alex said.

When we stepped around the corner, I had to hold my hand to my mouth to keep from laughing out loud. Alex no longer looked like a tough biker chick. Instead, she looked as if she were about to interview for the circus.

She stood up from the floor and reached for her phone in her backpack. "Yep. Cruella just called."

"Who?" I asked.

"Syd."

Again, I stifled a laugh. "Does she need me to take you home? It's just around the corner, I'll grab my keys."

Alex texted her back. "Nope. Too late. She's on her way."

"Okay, well . . . you might want to take a look in the mirror."

"Doesn't she look so beautiful, Mommy?" Savannah sat up taller.

I kissed the top of Savannah's head. "She looks quite exotic. You have a gift, sweetie."

"Hey, can I take a look at your knee, Vannie?" Patrick asked, moving around the couch. The use of her nickname—a name used only by my brother—made my heart flip.

And then flop.

Because Patrick McCade wasn't staying in Lenox. His life was bigger than what our little town could contain. We were as temporary as his timeline.

The knock at the door was a welcome distraction from my conflicting emotions. Only, when I pulled it open the face that stared back at me did not belong to my boss.

It belonged to Davis.

The seconds seemed to stretch and pull like taffy the moment Davis stepped into my tiny house. The ceilings shrank, the walls narrowed, and the thrumming of my pulse intensified.

Davis held out a colorful bouquet, tethered with a giant smiley-face balloon. "These are for Savannah."

Patrick stood from his place next to Savannah as Davis approached the couch.

"It's not my birthday." Savannah peeked over the back of the sofa, clearly not understanding the concept of a get-well gift.

"No, sweetie. Mr. Davis brought these for you because of your hurt knee." I clasped my hands and wrung them. "Which was a very kind thing to do."

"But I'm better now. Dr. Patrick fixed me all up, see?" She pointed to her exposed knee, and to Patrick's handiwork.

"Yes. I see that," Davis said, eyeing Patrick the way one might eye a persistent weed in a garden bed.

Alex shuffled down the hallway from the bathroom, her fuchsia lips curved in a rueful grin. Apparently she had decided against washing off Savannah's artwork in favor of witnessing the scene in the living room.

"Well, *hellllooo*," Alex practically sang the word, her eyes darting between Patrick and Davis. The girl really did thrive in uncomfortable situations. "I'm Alex, Willa's friend." She looked at me and clucked her tongue. "And you said your hosting skills were rusty."

Davis shook her hand, his brows arched as if trying to figure out where this eccentric teenager fit into my life. I would have offered him an explanation if Sydney hadn't knocked on the door before I could.

I invited her to join the town meeting taking place in my living room.

Sydney's designer heels sank into my tan carpet. Her no-nonsense gaze swept across every face, stopping at last on Alex. "Why do you look like that?"

Alex squared her shoulders. "It's a new trend."

Sydney's lips thinned and before another battle could break out between the two of them, I intervened. "Savannah gave Alex a mini makeover tonight. Just for fun." The irony of my word choice rang in my ears. Fun was not exactly the atmosphere Sydney had just walked into. We'd transitioned from a dinner party to a testosterone competition.

"The car's running," she said. "Get your stuff."

Alex's eye roll could have been seen from heaven. Amazingly, though, she obeyed.

"See you later, squirt." Alex tapped Savannah on the head, gave me a quick nod, and then pushed her way out the front door.

Sydney exhaled and the rigidity in her body seemed to diminish by half. "Good night," she said, stepping onto the porch.

"Wait—Sydney?" I turned away from the alpha male stare-down happening in my living room. "If there's anything I can do—for Alex—I'd like to help—"

"You know, I never pegged you as the ask-forgiveness-before-permission type."

I rocked back on my heels.

"The next time you want to play Debbie Do-Gooder, you can do it with someone else. Alex needs structure, not sympathy."

"Yes, I agree that she would benefit from some structure, but perhaps there's a better way to—"

Her tight blond bun didn't budge when she shook her head and cut me off. "I'll see you at work."

The bang of the door seemed to reverberate in the deafening silence. As I swung back toward the living room, both men watched me with renewed interest.

Nothing like a good boss scolding to add to the pressure cooker of this house. I glanced at the clock on the microwave, looking for any possible excuse to end this evening. There wasn't a single diplomatic topic to be discussed between Davis, Patrick, and me. That, I knew. "Well . . . I should probably get Savannah to bed. It's a school night."

Savannah moaned and hobbled off the couch toward her bedroom.

Patrick touched my arm. "Thanks for dinner, Willa." Yet the way his hand lingered, the way his jaw pulsed, the way his eyes scanned my face, made me wonder if there was something else he wanted to say—or ask?

Davis stepped away from his place near the couch to stand beside me.

"You're welcome." My reply was as underwhelming as Patrick's nod.

He dropped his hand, grabbed his coat, and let himself out.

As I turned back to Davis, the hurt reflected in his deep brown eyes stole my next breath.

"Mommy . . . aren't you coming? I can't reach the toothpaste."

I pointed down the hall. "I . . . I need to—"

"I'll wait." Two words he'd spoken to me before.

After I'd switched off Savannah's bedroom light and cracked her door, I found Davis standing near the sofa. Right where I'd left him.

"I've never pressured you, Willa . . . and I don't intend to start pressuring you now, but I do need to know where we stand."

The words hung in the air, suspended between us—the same way this conversation had been suspended for months.

He wanted an answer; he *deserved* an answer.

Only I didn't have one—or maybe I just didn't have the one he wanted. I didn't know for sure.

Unlike Patrick's ruddy hair that curled over his ears and at the base of his neck, Davis's hair was cropped short, a dark espresso like his eyes. He wasn't a gym member, yet his athletic build could have fooled anyone. As a veterinarian he was as active as he was ambitious, making pet house calls, visiting rural farms, and building his clinic from the ground up.

Stable, secure, and safe. The very attributes that my husband had possessed in spades.

"Settling back into normal life has taken a lot more time and energy than I anticipated."

"And yet you've had time to make new friends."

Somehow, I doubted he was referring to the angsty teen he'd met earlier tonight. But Patrick wasn't a threat either, not when he came with an expiration date.

"He has nothing to do with this. With us."

"Us?" He tilted his head to the side. "I think that's the first time I've heard you refer to you and me as an *us*."

Probably because I never had. Relationship titles were just one of the many reasons I'd stayed clear of dating.

"Davis . . . you've been a good friend to me during a very difficult season. Visiting Savannah in the hospital, taking care of Prince Pickles when we stayed in Portland for treatments . . . even carrying her off the soccer field yesterday."

"You know I want to be more than your friend." The raw quality in his voice was like the snap of a rubber band against wet skin. Painfully loud. I didn't want to hurt him, but I also couldn't make a commitment I wasn't prepared to keep.

"I'm just not ready to be more."

He took a step toward me, his body so close that I could smell the scent of cinnamon on his breath. "I get it. I understand what losing a spouse before your twenty-fifth birthday feels like. I've been scared, too. But I'm not proposing marriage—not yet. I just want you to think about what life could be like. With me and Brandon. And Savannah. Together." He lifted his hand, his fingers skimming my cheek. "I would love her, Willa. I would treat her like my own—you know I would. She deserves a father, the same way you deserve a husband that will love and protect you."

The dizziness in my head rivaled the dizziness in my heart.

His thumb grazed my jawbone, the first intimate touch from a man in many, many years. "Just . . . promise me you'll think about us, okay?"

I swallowed the anxiety pounding in my throat. It would be so easy to slip into his arms, to bury my sorrows in his offer of steadfast comfort, to give my daughter the family life she desired. Yet, like always, something held me back. The same something that pulsed in the middle of my chest and reminded me with every beat that love should be more than a convenience.

Ignoring the burn in my lungs, I nodded. "Okay."

Davis leaned close and brushed a light kiss on my temple. "Thank you."

My phone vibrated on my nightstand, the glow illuminating the ceiling I'd been staring at for the last two hours. I rolled over and picked it up.

GEORGIA: Your brother is driving me crazy.

ME: Welcome to my life.

GEORGIA: Seriously, he's refusing dance lessons. I already PAID for them.

Only Georgia would be up texting me after one in the morning. Yet another quality we shared—chronic insomnia. Hers was mostly due to the stresses of script writing, while mine was due to something else entirely.

ME: Want me to beat him up?

GEORGIA: Already tried that . . . but I have a plan B.

ME: Good luck!

I sent her a smiley face and set my phone back down. It vibrated again a second later.

PATRICK: How do you feel about dancing?

I laughed out loud and then slapped my hand over my mouth, thankful that Savannah had stayed in her own bed tonight.

ME: I take it YOU are Georgia's plan B?

PATRICK: You're awake? Everything go OK after I left?

I rolled my bottom lip between my teeth and contemplated a dozen different replies to that one very loaded question, and chose to do what I did best, divert.

ME: Yes. I'm a night owl.

PATRICK: Does that mean you're in?
My fingers hesitated, unsure of what *in* meant.

ME: I don't really dance.

PATRICK: That's not what I've heard.

ME: Remember—never trust the big birdie.

PATRICK: Then prove him wrong.
Again, my stomach dipped. What was he asking?

ME: How . . . ?

PATRICK: If I go, Wes will go. And if I
go . . . I'm hoping you'll go, too.

Heat prickled in the center of my chest, but as fast as the fire came,
I doused it with a splash of cold reality.

Nothing about Patrick was long-term. Which, in a way, meant that
Patrick was safe. No matter how many times my stomach dipped and
pinged when he was near.

ME: When? (This is not a yes yet . . .)

PATRICK: Yet is always a yes . . . I'll
pick you up Fri at 6. (This will earn you
extra credit.)

I sucked in a breath and contemplated the words *extra credit* before
shooting back a simple *OK,* followed immediately by *Goodnight.* I set
the phone on my nightstand screen down, rolled onto my side, and
pinched my eyes closed.

Somehow the line separating life lessons from real life was being
crossed. One day, one conversation, one text at a time . . . and so far
neither of us had redrawn it.

Yet.

Chapter Sixteen

Since arriving at work I'd been asked on three separate occasions by three faithful water aerobics patrons why there was an extra bounce in my step. *Had I tried a new protein shake? Taken a new supplement? Pumped an extra shot of caffeine in my coffee?* Though I'd politely answered *no* to all of the above, the real reason was as simple as it was complicated.

I snuck another glance at my phone—at the text that had doubled as my morning wake-up alarm.

PATRICK: If your first thought this morning was about extra credit, you're in good company. See u Fri night.

Yet despite the boost in my own serotonin level, the tension between Sydney and Alex dampened it. Their drama could radiate through concrete walls.

Alex had declined all my efforts at social interaction, setting up camp in the break room, while Sydney had locked herself away in her office. I hadn't seen either of them for hours.

Which was probably in the best interest of our members.

A lull in lobby traffic inspired me to stretch my legs and peek in on a certain brooding blue-haired girl. The midday break in fitness classes was when Alex usually cleaned the locker room, picking up stray articles of clothing, mopping the floors, and double-checking the lost-and-found bin for personal items that should be held at the front desk: phones, keys, wallets.

Because she'd spent the morning boycotting life, I'd figured that had included boycotting her responsibilities, too. But once again, Alex surprised me. The orange CLOSED FOR CLEANING sign was propped in front of the locker room door.

Pressing my palm to the cool metal, I pushed the door open slowly. Immediately my jaw went slack.

I couldn't see her from where I stood, but I could hear her. Singing.

Not the kind of singing one does in the shower or while sitting at a stoplight or even while performing in the church choir. This was the kind of singing that could shatter a heart . . . only to stitch it back together again. The raw, youthful sound of her voice was infused with emotion, not just talent.

Not a note out of pitch, not a breath out of place.

I stood in the shadows, hidden behind a tower of lockers. My chest ached from the haunting melody, the lyrics like a sad, solemn lullaby.

> *"May you always sleep in peace*
> *And never wake up somber*
> *May you always find a path*
> *And never stray or wander."*

She held the last note for several seconds and my eyes pricked with tears, the chorus forcing them to spill.

> *"When you start to lose your way*
> *When you can't find words to pray*

Hope is just beyond the bend
Reaching out to lend a hand
Don't give up, you're almost there
God still hears unspoken prayers
God still hears unspoken prayers."

The pounding in my chest swelled to the booming beat of a bass line. I wasn't sure what I'd just experienced, but I knew that Alex's gift was as unique as it was unexpected. I didn't want the song to end, and yet it had. She'd gone quiet. The only sound in the room was the slosh of mop water against polished concrete.

I swiped at my damp cheeks. Just like the words in her lyrics, I understood the value of a silent prayer. In the deepest season of my grief, those wordless prayers had been all I had.

I wondered if they were all Alex believed she had, too.

I cleared my throat, doing my best not to startle her as I edged closer to the sink. My quiet approach backfired.

Alex whirled around and chucked the soggy mop at my feet, the long wooden handle clanging against the side of a metal bench.

Our eyes met. The flash of surprise quickly hardened into a defensive scowl, the line of her mouth angry and tight.

Still, I chose not to speak. Words are often the last thing a hurting person needs.

If Alex thought I'd come to scold her for sulking the day away, she was wrong. The girl in front of me didn't need to be punished. She needed to be loved.

Whatever she was expecting from me died the moment I opened my arms and extended an invitation I wasn't sure she'd accept.

Seconds passed; she didn't move. Neither did I.

The war within her was palpable, a struggle of trust and fear. A battle I knew well.

And then her bottom lip began to tremble, her nostrils twitched, her throat bobbed in a sequence of swallows.

Alex rushed forward.

She slammed against me, the force knocking me back several steps. She crumpled against my chest. Her soul-deep sobs were a crushing weight that made my eyes sting.

She was only in my arms for a few minutes, but the way Alex wept, I wondered if these tears weren't the first she'd cried in a very long time.

When her tears subsided into quiet hiccups, I lowered us to the bench.

Head cradled in her hands, she peeked at me though open fingers. "I haven't . . . it wasn't . . ." Another tearful shudder.

I waited.

"I tried . . . to take care of us both." Alex's tone was soft, breathy. "We had enough, you know? Enough to make it. She didn't need him."

"Who?"

"My mom's ex—the washed-up football player. He screwed us— just like I knew he would."

I held her closer. I didn't need to know the details, I just needed Alex to know that I was here for her. To listen to whatever she needed to process.

She was quiet for a few seconds.

"Syd says I can't stay here—that she doesn't know the first thing about taking care of a teenager." She lifted her head. "But I'll run away before I get into that car with her on Saturday."

"Let's try and take it one day at a time, okay?" Even as I said this, I knew I hadn't lived that way. I hadn't allowed my tomorrows to be lived without yesterday's baggage.

"What's the point? Sydney thinks I'm just some troubled punk kid with blue hair and a fetish for tattoos—even though I only have one. She won't listen to me."

Maybe she wouldn't listen to Alex, but maybe . . .

I patted her back one last time and stood up. "Why don't you finish up in here, okay? I need to get back to the front desk." *And find a certain half sister of yours.*

I was two steps away from her when I stopped midstride.

"And Alex?"

"Yeah?"

"You have the most beautiful voice I've ever heard."

I pushed through the door quickly, before she had a chance to tell me otherwise.

I rapped on Sydney's office door and then turned the knob without waiting for permission—or, presumably, a dismissal. Sydney sat perched in her black leather chair, peering at her computer screen.

She was alone and couldn't fake a meeting or a conference call this time. Surely she could stand to take a few minutes to hear me out.

A flash of surprise crossed her face. "Willa? Is there a problem downstairs?"

This would have to suffice as an invitation to enter. I closed the door behind me.

"Actually, yes. There is a problem. With Alex."

She sighed and returned to work. "This isn't the place to—"

Alex's confession fueled my determination as I approached Sydney's desk. "I know you're extremely busy and I don't want to pry into your personal life, but sending her off to boarding school isn't the answer."

"It's her best and only option."

"Not in her mind it isn't." A steady and quiet boldness rose in my abdomen.

She twisted in her chair, a silent exchange playing out between us.

"She's planning to run, Sydney. If you insist on taking her there, she'll leave."

Her eyebrows lowered. "She told you that?"

"Yes." Another pulse of courage. "Leaving Lenox is not what she wants, and I think with a little guidance she could—"

Sydney shook her head. "I don't have the time for guidance." She spread her arms as if to indicate her office. "What you see here is only a fraction of what goes on in my world. Alex needs more time than I can give her."

"Then let me help." The words flew out without thought or plan. "Let me help you with Alex."

Sydney snapped her mouth shut and pushed her back against her chair, confusion wrinkling her brow. "You haven't even known her for two weeks, how could you possibly help?"

"If you enroll her at the high school I could—"

"Her transcript is a mess. She's missing credits and has failed several classes due to lack of attendance." Sydney glanced at the picture on her desk.

"There's all kinds of options for seniors to make up missing credits, but she would have to get enrolled soon in order to have a chance to graduate with the senior class," I said. "The counselors can help her make a plan and I could tutor her in whatever subjects she's fallen behind in." I softened my voice. "She wants to stay with you, Sydney."

"She hates me." But the lack of conviction in Sydney's voice told me she didn't believe that. Not for a second.

"No, she *needs* you, in whatever capacity she can have you. Sending her away will only reinforce her belief that she isn't valued. You don't want her to grow up believing that, do you?"

Sydney swallowed. "No."

She dropped her head to her hands and massaged her temples. "End of the year. I can postpone her enrollment at the academy until the end of the year, but I won't make any promises beyond that. If it isn't working here, then . . ."

"Okay."

She lifted her head and again her eyes focused on the framed picture at the corner of her desk. I took a small step forward to see past the glare of the glass.

A middle-aged woman with short blond hair and a tired smile slung an arm around a much younger Sydney. I blinked, my heart squeezing tight. On the woman's hip sat the toddler version of Alex.

"A second chance is one of the best gifts we can offer someone in need." Though I spoke the words, I couldn't help but think of a similar phrase Patrick had said to me the day I shook his hand at Cougar Mountain.

Sydney's meditative silence broke as I turned to leave.

"I hope you're right."

Chapter Seventeen

Patrick was seven minutes late. Not that I'd checked the clock or paced the front room or obsessively smoothed the kinks from my freshly flat-ironed hair.

My heels clicked against the tile as I walked from the kitchen to the entry and back. Savannah had dug out my black pumps from her dress-up box, insisting that a woman must wear real dancing shoes to dance. The little fashionista had also chosen a flouncy black-and-white top to pair with my dark wash jeans. Sure, they were a few seasons old, but their fit was snug and still stylish, hugging the curve at my hips and lengthening my legs.

And for the first time in a long time, I felt like a woman.

A car door slammed and my pulse spiked.

I held my breath while he knocked.

The numbing sensation that spread down my arm and into my fingers intensified as I twisted the doorknob and opened the door.

Patrick stood on my porch, his hands slack at his sides, his lips slightly parted as his gaze traveled the length of me. "You are, without a doubt, the prettiest dance partner I've ever had."

Heat inched up my neck and bloomed in my cheeks.

Under the dim porch light, his hair looked slightly damp, like he'd raked his fingers through it only seconds before—a perfect kind of messy. The ends curled under at the base of his neck and behind his ears. His crisp, smooth shirt was a slate gray that made the transparent blue of his eyes shine in contrast.

"Thank you. I like your . . ." *Everything*. "Shirt."

Eyes still locked on my face, he cleared his throat. "You may want to grab a jacket."

I lifted my arm and my red coat swished around my elbow. "Your observation skills must be lacking tonight."

He shook his head, chuckled. "No . . . they're working just fine."

After I'd locked up the house, he offered me his hand so I could maneuver the concrete porch steps without twisting my ankle. Ever the gentleman, Patrick opened the passenger-side door for me before walking around to the driver's side.

Blakely, the town next to Lenox, was a thirty-minute drive, but so far, the first five minutes had been filled with nothing but road noise.

He merged onto the old highway that belted the mountain. Out of the corner of my eye, I glanced at the strangely quiet Patrick. He was usually the one to carry conversation—to set me at ease with his lighthearted laugh and calming smile. But the persistent tapping of his finger on the steering wheel and his concentrated stare on the pavement ahead tugged at my nerves.

"Did something happen at the clinic today?"

The question snapped him out of his driving coma. "No, why?"

"You just . . . you seem distracted, is all."

He shifted in his seat, eyes briefly flickering to my face. "Sorry. I guess I am—distracted."

"And your parents? Their visit with your grandmother is going well?"

Even through the shadows of dusk, I could see his face soften and his lips twitch. "Everything is fine, Willa. I promise." He glanced at me. "What's the latest with your blue-haired friend?"

"That is far from a short conversation," I mused.

"We have the time."

Time—ironic from a man who lived his life out of suitcases.

I filled him in on the events of yesterday, careful not to violate her confidence, but curious as to his insight. Patrick worked with people for a living; his feedback would prove helpful.

"You offered to tutor her?" There was a hint of surprise in his tone. "And your boss agreed to letting her stay in Lenox?"

"Yes." I nodded, smiling as I thought of my new teenage companion. "Alex comes with some complicated baggage, but she's a good kid."

The green sign on the right indicated ten miles to our destination.

"Why did you stop teaching?"

"How did you know . . ." I shook my head, realizing the answer before I finished asking the question. *Weston.* "Wow. My brother must really lack for conversation if he's boring you with the details of my life."

A single tap on the steering wheel and then, "He wasn't. I asked him about you."

My heart skidded up my throat. "Why?"

He tilted his head toward me, laughter dancing in his eyes. "Are you avoiding my question?"

"Are you avoiding mine?"

"Maybe," he said with a sly grin.

I fingered the lock button on the side of my door and tried to figure out how best to explain why I'd left the career my heart had been set on since grade school. "I just . . . I needed to take a break." I cringed internally. Seven years wasn't a break from a career, it was a death sentence.

"So you're planning to go back, then? To teaching?"

"Is this a life lesson test?"

Patrick flipped on his right turn signal and veered onto the Blakely exit.

"No."

An unruly lock of hair curled over his temple, and I tucked my hands under my thighs to keep from reaching out.

I turned my attention to the blue hue of the streetlights. "Have you been here before? To Blakely?"

"First time. Are you offering me a tour?"

I laughed. "Don't blink for the next twenty seconds and you'll pretty much see the whole town."

"Is that small-town sarcasm I hear in your voice?" He pulled into the parking lot of In Motion Dance Studio and put the car in park.

I feigned innocence. "Never. I love my small town."

"Well, it does have its appeal." Patrick winked before popping his door handle and stepping onto the sidewalk.

Weston and Georgia were inside the studio, along with three other couples. They were all speaking to a woman in her mid- to late sixties with an oversized red feather pinned in her hair. She wore a snug-fitting dance leotard and a flowy floral skirt to match.

She swiveled on the balls of her feet and stomped her right heel as the door chimed our entrance. "Oh, good. Our last couple has arrived. You two must be Patrick and Willa?"

A tiny thrill zipped through me at the sound of our names sharing a sentence. *Stupid.*

Patrick and I each shook the woman's hand.

"I'm Louisa Cherry. You can call me Lou. And this," she said, sprawling her arms out wide, "is your ticket to greatness—dancing greatness, that is. Although I've been dancing since I was a young girl, my tips and tricks can help anyone find passion in their dance steps." She sashayed her hips.

No struggle with self-confidence here.

Patrick arched an eyebrow at me and I quickly glanced away, hoping to avoid an outburst of inappropriate laughter. Georgia trotted over to us and gave me a thank-you-for-showing-up smile while Weston offered Patrick a casual salute.

Lou clapped her hands together in a three-count staccato pattern. Patrick bit back another grin, although I was pretty sure I knew what he was thinking: "Welcome back to kindergarten."

"Please stand with your partner. Like this." Lou stole Weston from Georgia and used him as a class demonstration. Weston's cheeks pinked as Lou tugged him closer. "This position is called the closed dance hold." After just a few seconds, she spun away from Weston and encouraged Georgia to take her place.

Lou's heels clicked across the shiny hardwoods. "First things first. You must become an expert in the basics before you can move on. And ladies, *please* . . . let your partner *lead*. That's his one and only job on the dance floor."

Patrick stepped toward me and placed his right hand just above my left hip, his grip strong and secure at my waist. My left hand rose to rest lightly on his shoulder. Our opposite hands clasped into the classic ballroom hold. Either Patrick was annoyingly perfect at everything he tried, or this wasn't his first time on the dance floor.

"You've done this before," I said.

"So have you."

"Yes, but you already knew that."

He glanced down at me, shrugged. "Well, you never asked."

Lou checked each couple's hold, giving Patrick and me a stiff nod. Apparently we'd passed inspection.

There were a few more tedious instructions before a classical medley played through the studio's corner speaker.

Without any prompting, Patrick led and I followed.

While the other couples bumped and groaned and argued about who was stepping on whose feet, we simply swayed to the music. We were both comfortable with the basic steps and comfortable with the standard eighteen inches of space between us. My black heels felt light on my feet, providing confidence in a skill I hadn't used since Savannah was born.

"So . . . what *don't* you do, Patrick?"

He pulled his head back slightly. "I'm not sure I understand."

The shadow along Patrick's jaw matched the russet brown of his hair. The color was so rich, like the blending of cayenne pepper and cocoa powder.

I blinked away. "Let's see . . . you rock climb, you jump off bridges, you forge across alligator-infested waters, you doctor people around the globe, you ballroom dance . . . oh, and let's not forget your little photography *hobby*."

"That sounds like a badly written online dating profile."

I laughed and then quickly bit my bottom lip when Lou glanced my way. "Stop trying to get me in trouble."

He lowered his voice. "Then accept the fact that there are plenty of things I don't know how to do—and an even longer list of things I don't do well."

"Prove it."

He stopped midstep and my feet staggered on either side of his right shoe.

"How exactly do you propose I do that? Would you like me to cook you the worst omelet you've ever eaten? Because I'm horrible with eggs. Or maybe you'd like me to show you my mess of an e-mail account? I'm awful at replying—no matter how vital. Or maybe you'd like to hear about my woodworking skills. That is to say, I have none."

I dipped my head, allowing his arm to block my outburst of giggles. "Those aren't even real flaws."

"No? Then tell me yours."

Perhaps I should have thought this through a bit more. This game wasn't exactly in my favor. Not when I was dealing with a man who thought bad omelet making was a weakness.

"Pass," I said, holding his gaze just long enough to feel the flurries in my belly.

"Pass? You get to pass?"

I rubbed my lips together. "Mm-hm."

"Then I should get a redo question, right?"

Anything to move away from my "issues." We started dancing again and Patrick turned us in a circle. Weston and Georgia were at a standstill as Lou lectured them once again on the roles of leading and following.

"Sure," I said.

"Who is Davis Carter to you?"

Patrick's question killed all sensation below my chest.

"A family friend."

Patrick tipped his head back and scanned the ceiling—for what? I had no idea. "Does *he* know that?"

I studied the button at the base of his collar. "I've known him a long time."

"I've known my grandma a long time."

"He's . . . been very helpful over the last couple of years." Loyal to a fault. "And considerate."

Patrick said nothing, and I racked my brain for a new conversation starter, something to take us far away from the Davis Carter trail.

Several inches evaporated between us. "There's a balance between being considerate of someone's needs and thinking a person is incapable of dealing with their own." His breath swept over my ear. "You're far from incapable, Willa."

A prickle of heat burst in my chest like a sparkler.

Lou clapped and we broke apart. We awaited our next set of instructions, though Patrick's attention wasn't on the front of the room.

Why did he care who Davis was to me? He might have a "family friend" waiting around for him in some war-torn village in Africa. Maybe he had *multiple* "family friends." I would never know, and therefore, couldn't—wouldn't—ask. The same way he shouldn't have asked about Davis.

Patrick was only here for a season.

And just like summer turned to fall and fall turned to winter, Patrick's time in Lenox would come to an end.

Weston caught my eye and ran a finger across his throat, his tongue hanging out of his mouth like roadkill. Unfortunately, Lou saw the gesture, too. She called him to the front of the class once again. He'd just secured himself the role of Lou's designated dance partner.

Georgia nearly buckled with silent laughter.

Lou showed the class two classic spins—both of which I'd learned years ago, and chances were good that Patrick knew them as well.

A new song played through the overhead speakers, and the couples drew together again.

I readied myself for the closed-hold position, only this time when Patrick stepped forward and gripped my waist, he tugged me closer, the space between us melting away. Everything from his gaze to his touch to his breath on my cheek hummed with new awareness. This dance was no longer instructional but intimate. No longer practice but personal.

One step, then two. Three steps, then four. Our feet were quick. He led and I followed.

The air thinned into a universal pause—time measured in beats and blinks and breaths. Heat seared at our every point of connection.

And then he let go—only not entirely.

He spun me out and then back.

My hair was a golden whip, flinging into my face and then curling back over my shoulder again. When he spun me in a third time, my palm thumped flat against his chest. Our breaths a soft pant. Our hearts a steady thrum.

Chins tipped toward each other; a current of recognition crossed our gazes.

"Bravo!" Lou applauded. "Now *that* is how you spin with *passion*."

Patrick slid his arm from my waist and my hand from his grasp. I stepped back, believing that distance alone could break our connection.

I was wrong.

Chapter Eighteen

The vintage fainting couch in my mother's sewing room might have been ornately carved and structurally sophisticated, but what it offered in aesthetics, it lacked in comfort. I didn't have the heart to wake Savannah from her special princess bed at my parents' house, so instead, I tossed and turned all night on a glorified park bench, replaying the memory of a certain dance with a certain doctor. Thankfully, my good-morning/good-bye kiss from Savannah before heading off to Fitness Day had made the long night worth it.

As I pushed through the doors of the fitness center, my phone beeped, and my heart leapt.

False alarm.

ALEX: If I don't come back alive you can keep my black boots.

ME: Funny. Be nice to your sister and I'm sure you'll make it back.

ALEX: Maybe you should try texting her that, too.

ME: Alex.

I'd done my best to encourage Sydney to enjoy her previously scheduled day off by spending some much-needed time with her baby sister, especially since the subject of a certain all-girls boarding school had been placed on hold for the time being. Surprisingly, she had taken my advice.

ALEX: Fine. We just got to some fancy spa place.

ME: You dyeing your hair?

If I squinted I could almost imagine Alex as a blonde.

ALEX: Yup. Gonna go purple.

I laughed out loud and slid my phone back into my pocket. Only Alex.

Squatting, I opened the ice chest and added a few dozen mini water bottles to the mix of energy and protein drinks. Since the assessment began, a steady stream of Lenox residents had passed through the glass doors of the lobby. Sydney's thorough memos and bullet-point instructions had been easy enough to follow, and the personal trainers had kept busy with dozens of potential new members. So far, my only break from the monotony of body fat testing and sit-up counting was the momentary mental invasions of a ruggedly handsome man who wouldn't listen to my halfhearted pleas to exit my mind.

I didn't even have to close my eyes to see the curve of his smile or to remember the pressure of his hand on my waist. It was all right there, floating on the surface of my subconscious. The lure of a daydream I couldn't allow myself to fall into. Not completely.

"You're far from incapable."

I ignored the memory of the feather-soft words spoken against my ear and instead took a long swig of ice-cold water.

The large picture windows in the lobby perfectly framed a vast, cloudless sky. For the fortieth time that day, I calculated the remaining hours left in my workday. One hour and thirty-two minutes. It was too perfect an afternoon to be cooped up indoors. My mind drifted again. What was *he* doing today? No doubt Patrick was taking advantage of this rare fall weather. Oregon only had so many rainless days in autumn. Snow would be here within a month, and with it the commencement of winter hibernation.

I imagined Patrick on an exploratory day hike, or maybe he'd taken the guided rafting trip downriver, or—

"Excuse me—Mrs. Hart?"

Preston Wilkerson—Alex's least-favorite jock—stood at the front desk, baseball cap snugly fit to his head. His arms cradled a large paper sack.

"Hi, Preston. The locker room's open if you need to drop that off. Don't mind the crowd." I pointed to the dwindling line.

He glanced down at the bulky bag. "No. Uh, this isn't mine. It's a delivery."

"A delivery?"

He tipped his head, the bill of his cap shadowing his eyes momentarily. "Yep."

He lowered the bag to the counter and slid it toward me. A colorful tubular package stuck out from the top. I rotated the bag, examining the outside for some kind of instruction or note. Nothing.

I peeked inside, not recognizing any of the contents as my own.

"Um . . . I'm afraid I don't have a clue who this is for—"

"It's for you." The inflection in his tone held more of a question than a statement. "I was told you'd know what to do with it."

"You were told? By who?"

He took an easy step back, one side of his mouth twitching. "Sorry, I'm not supposed to say any more than that. Have a good day, Mrs. Hart."

With a simple wave, Preston jogged out the front doors.

I reached into the bag and my fingers brushed against a crinkly piece of paper. I pulled it out into the light and read the familiar handwriting.

Willa—

Lesson 3.5 (see, I told you dancing would earn you extra credit): "Always reward a hard day of work with an even harder day of play."

Meet me at Lenox Community Park at 3:30. Bring Savannah. And this bag.

Patrick

Pursing my lips, I took inventory of the contents: a peacock-inspired kite, a glow-in-the-dark Frisbee, a rubber foursquare ball, and a yo-yo.

Savannah tore from the car, rushing through the mushy park grass toward the swing set nestled between an old-fashioned merry-go-round and a vintage metal slide. I hollered for her to slow down, to be careful of her knee, but that was the equivalent of telling our dog not to bark when company knocked at the door.

Her feathery blond hair caught the breeze as she ran, sending my already spastic heartbeat into another fit of wild delight.

Vibrant leaves clung to their branches, teetering on the edge of a changing season. The cloudless blue sky was the cherry on top of a forecasted fifty-nine degrees. But it was the sunshine—that gloriously bright orb in the sky—that seemed to warm something inside me I hadn't even registered was cold.

Until today.

Wearing dark jeans and a black lightweight pullover, Patrick jogged toward me from the picnic table, relieving me of the Bag O' Fun.

"You've stooped to using delivery boys now, huh?" I asked, keeping my stride even with his.

"He owed me a favor."

Patrick's reply made me do a double take.

"What?" He laughed. "You don't think I'm capable of making friends outside of you and Weston."

Patrick thought of me as a friend. I gave myself a silent reprimand. *Friend* was the term I *should* be thinking, too.

My efforts to climb up the slippery slope of idealism back to reality seemed to be a solo trek. If Patrick's easy way of conversing was any indication of his inner dialogue, he was just fine reverting to how things had been before the dance class. And despite the pinch in my chest, I had to be fine with that, too. I couldn't remember the last time I'd looked forward to spending time with a friend as much as I did with Patrick.

"How do you know Preston?" It was easy to forget that Patrick likely knew half this town because of his profession. "Of course, if it's patient confidentiality you don't have to—"

He bumped into my shoulder. "It's not. He got a camera for his birthday so I gave him some pointers. His mom is—"

"Marsha, the receptionist at McCade Medical. I should have put that together sooner." The small-town circle connected once again.

"Yeah. Small town." He looked at me. "Think you'll stay here? In Lenox?"

"I can't imagine living anywhere else. Not permanently, anyway." I spotted Savannah near the swing set and waved. "When we stayed near the hospital in Portland last year, I could see the appeal of living in a big city. But at the same time, I realized that city life just isn't for me. There's something really special about knowing your neighbors and the checkers at the grocery store and the grandkids of the pizza parlor owners." We stopped in front of the picnic table. "It's easy to get distracted by the busyness of life, ya know . . . miss the people right in front of you."

His stare left a tingling sensation in my cheeks, and I realized how small-minded my answer probably sounded to a man who had spent years traveling the globe, extending himself to hundreds and thousands of people. "It's not that I never want to travel and see the world, I do. It's just—"

He placed a hand on my shoulder and squeezed. "I get it. The residents of Lenox are as much a home to you as the town itself."

"That's it, exactly."

Savannah hopped off a slowing swing and ran to meet us. "What do you have in that bag, Dr. Patrick?"

Although Patrick had encouraged her to downgrade from Dr. Patrick to Patrick given our ever-mingling professional and personal lives, I hadn't been a fan of that idea.

He dropped to his haunches. "I'll tell you what, if you can guess one of the items in this bag . . . I'll give it to you."

Her dark-brown eyes went round. "For keeps?"

"Yep. For keeps."

"How many guesses do I get?" she asked.

"How about three."

"Okay." A crease indented her forehead. "Is one of them a toy?"

"Um . . ." Patrick glanced to me for confirmation. "Yes. Definitely one could count as a toy. Possibly more."

She tugged at her fingers, and I knew by the look on her face that her brain was hard at work. "Is one a playground toy?"

Patrick grinned. "You're good at this game. Right again."

Savannah tapped her finger on her chin. "Is there a ball in that bag?"

"Do you have X-ray vision?" He ticked his chin at me. "You should have told me I was at an unfair advantage with your little prodigy here."

I laughed. "She is that."

He set the bag down and reached inside to grab the red rubber ball. Savannah *whooped* as he handed it down to her.

"Don't kick that too far into the trees. If you can't see me, then I can't see you."

"I know, Mommy," she said in a voice that was way closer to seventeen than seven.

With a swift kick, the ball went bouncing into a long stretch of dewy grass.

Together, Patrick and I watched her bob and weave through two large oaks bordering the spacious field.

"Her knee seems to be healing up well. Remind me to take a look tonight."

I pulled my attention from Savannah. "We can make an appointment for that. I don't want you to have to—"

"There's no *have to* involved. I offered." He reached into the bag again and pulled out the kite. "Here." He tried to offer it to me, but I shook my head.

"Why don't you go first . . . I don't know the first thing about flying a kite."

"Says the woman who wasn't sure she would remember how to dance." He held my gaze for one, two, three stomach spasms, then pushed the kite into my hands and let go. "And we both know how that turned out."

Actually, I hadn't a clue. I'd give my right dancing foot to hear his thoughts, though. We'd avoided the topic driving home, choosing to discuss upcoming wedding commitments rather than what had passed between us. Part of me—primarily the lonely part—still wondered if I'd only imagined that sexy smolder in his eyes and the racing thump-thump-thump vibration of his chest.

"Fine. I'll try it." I unwrapped the diamond-shaped kite from the plastic.

"A try is to step onto the road that leads to success," Patrick said as if quoting straight out of the book of Proverbs. Only I'd never heard that verse before in my life and I'd grown up in church. Wait—

I whirled around. "Was that a line from Rex's journal?"

Patrick kicked a runaway ball back to Savannah with a laugh. "You're catching on, Willa."

I fiddled with the package in my hand and Savannah skipped over to us, ball tucked under her arm. "Cool kite. Are you gonna fly it?"

"I guess I am." I set the kite on the picnic table and picked up the two loose wooden rods, poking the ends into each of the four corners. And just like that, the kite went from flimsy to taut and ready to fly.

I carried the peacock kite to the center of the field, a tightly wound spool of string in my fist, then glanced back at Patrick. He followed about three paces behind me, wearing the same face as the night of the auction. That now-familiar hands-off expression.

"How does it fly, Mommy?"

"Um . . . well, I guess you just hold it out sort of like this." I held the diamond out, stick side to the ground, in the air. The breeze popped it up immediately and Savannah squealed, but the string was too short and within half a blink, it nose-dived straight into the ground.

I jogged toward it, hoping I hadn't broken the thing on my first try, and waited for Patrick to lend some magical kite-flying words. But he offered only a smile.

"Fine. I'll do it again."

This time, I unwound the spool a little more, held the kite above my head, and waited for the ideal breeze to sail it into the open sky. Or at least keep it from dive-bombing in the first two seconds.

I let it go.

The kite flew free, gliding and snaking and twisting in the air. I trotted ahead, pulling it with me, Savannah on my heels.

And for one euphoric moment, everything was perfect. The sky, the sun, the wind. All of it melding and blending together into a reverent harmony that made my heart sprout wings of its own. I smiled back at Patrick.

Then the line grew slack and the kite took a suicide plunge back toward earth.

In a frenzy I coiled the excess string over and over onto the spool. It was a frantic fight of tugs and pulls to keep the kite from falling. To keep me from failing.

I felt Patrick's chest press against my back and his hand slide down the length of my arm until he reached the spool in mine. With a quick rescue maneuver—a single flick of his wrist—the kite soared free once again.

He handed the reins off to Savannah, but he didn't take a step back.

And I didn't take a step forward.

We simply stood together in the middle of the park and watched my daughter fly my rescued life lesson into the sky.

I tipped my head to the side, his body so close that I could almost feel his chest expand. "I thought you weren't allowed to help me?"

"I never said that."

"But you—"

"*Timing*, Willa. Another one of Rex's proverbs. 'Know when to press in and when to let go.'"

A shiver traveled down my spine. Not from the wind, but from his words.

There was only one thing I knew about life's timing.

It was impossible to predict.

Chapter Nineteen

Alex collapsed into the rolling chair at the front desk, the way she had every afternoon since Sydney enrolled her at Lenox High School two weeks ago. Her hair a shocking shade of eggplant purple, she pulled a leg underneath her and chomped on a piece of gum she'd taken from my purse.

"I saw the calendar on your fridge last night," she announced as I updated member profiles. "And you can't leave."

"I'm only gone for a weekend, Alex. You won't even miss me." Although I knew that probably wasn't true. The drama between Sydney and Alex had taken a much-needed intermission now that Alex was in school, but she'd been at my house almost every night, going over her syllabus and checking her assignments with me before turning them in to the teacher the following day. In a strange twist of irony, Savannah and I had become Alex's social life.

"I thought you were like . . . a homebody or something. Where are you even going for this *vacation*?" Her air quotes around the word *vacation* were not nearly as comical as she thought they were.

I clicked out of payment scheduling. "Your flattery is overwhelming."

Her boots thudded against the cement floor. "Wait a minute . . . is Dr. Hottie involved in this mini vacay? Or is it the other guy—the vet with the nice teeth? Now those two . . . they make your life interesting."

"Alex." The word hummed from my lips with exasperation.

"What?"

What Alex deemed interesting could have given me an ulcer. Or five. This annual family weekend at my parents' cabin was needed. Not only because Davis had dropped by unannounced more times in the last two weeks than in the last two years, but also because Patrick and I hadn't gone a single day without communicating in some form or another. Something was shifting . . . something I could neither explain nor deny. Yet it lingered between us. In every text, in every conversation, in every bravery lesson I conquered.

This weekend was a pause. A breather. A detox for my heart and my head. "It's a family trip. My parents have a rental cabin a couple hours from here. We've gone there the first weekend of November every year since I was twelve—well, with the exception of last year."

Last year we were well into the second phase of Savannah's treatments.

Alex scooted closer to me, smashing herself against my side to peek over my shoulder at the membership profile screen. Some days working with Alex was like trying to fold a pile of clean laundry next to a toddler. "So do you ski?"

"No."

"Snowboard?"

"No."

"Inner-tube, sled, toboggan?"

"No."

She grunted in satisfaction. "I didn't think so."

I swiveled the chair around and gave her my undivided attention. "What's that supposed to mean?"

"Nothing. Just proving myself right. I have a gift for typing people."

"You *typed* me?"

Cold air rushed in from the front doors.

"Do you two even work?"

Alex jumped to her feet and rushed to fist-bump my brother—her new favorite teacher. "What's up, Mr. Wes?"

"What's up with you, Barney?"

Weston was likely the only person alive who could get away with comparing Alex's new hair color to an overweight purple dinosaur. But then again, Weston could charm a cobra into being a house pet if he wanted to.

"I'm just schooling your sister on her personality type."

"Oh?" Fully baited, he leaned his elbows on the counter. "Now this I have to hear."

Oh no. "Alex—"

"I say she borders between Classic Bore and Wound Too Tight."

At least my brother had the dignity to refrain from howling. "I'll take Wound Too Tight for two hundred please."

"Ding, ding, ding!"

It was hard to tell who was more annoying at the moment: the seventeen-year-old or the man who shared my DNA. It was a toss-up.

"Okay, okay." I said, shutting the obnoxious duo down before another round could begin. "Don't teachers have meetings today— hence the early dismissal for high school students." I gestured to Alex. Case in point.

"Not me." His smile notched wider. "So I thought I'd pay a visit to my big sis."

I didn't buy it. Not for a second. Not with that look in his eye. "Okay, so what's the real reason you're here?"

He snatched a pen from my desk and drummed on every nearby surface. "You'll never guess what we're taking up to the cabin this year."

He was right, I couldn't guess. The list of options was never-ending where Weston was concerned.

"Snowmobiles," he supplied.

"Really? How did you get—"

"Not me." His pen stopped midtap but didn't wait for me to fill in the blank. He never had the patience for guessing games. "Good ol' Ricky."

"Patrick," I corrected without thought, his name echoing through me as though I'd shouted it from a mountaintop.

Had Weston really invited Patrick on our family vacation? The idea shouldn't have surprised me, but another weekend spent with Patrick . . . I bit my lip.

"What's that look for?" Weston asked me.

I eyed Alex, hoping she'd catch the hint to give us some privacy, but she was too busy emptying the stapler into her palm.

Plan B. "Alex, can you manage the desk for a minute? I'm gonna grab a drink from the break room."

"No prob," she said, stacking the metal pieces into a miniature skyscraper.

I led Weston to the staff lounge. The mini kitchen held a small dining set, fridge, sink, and pantry. The deodorizer plug-in to the left of the sink wafted a continuous aroma of coconut and lemongrass.

Weston let the door swing closed behind him.

"Whoa . . . why does it smell like I'm caught on an island surrounded by a sea of bathroom cleaner?"

Ignoring him, I pressed my cold palms to my warm cheeks in hopes of coaxing them back to a preflushed state. "You really invited him on our family vacation?" My voice was thin, my words strung out on a fragile thread.

He gripped the edge of the steel countertop and pulled himself up, heels banging against the bottom cabinets. "I thought you'd be happy. You spend more time with him than anyone else . . ." His eyebrows wrinkled. "Wait, did something happen that I should know about?"

Stunned, I blinked. "What? No . . . of course nothing happened."

"Because if there's anything I need to discuss with him—"

"Weston. Stop." I shook my head, my insides a tangle of anxiety. How could I even begin to explain what I didn't understand myself. "He's done nothing wrong. It's just . . . *he's leaving*."

"Not for a couple months."

Actually, seven and a half weeks. Not that I was counting. But it was that inevitable ticking of the clock that unclouded the fogginess in my mind.

We were all investing too much in a man who *lived* to *leave*.

"Have you actually thought about that—him leaving, I mean? Because it doesn't seem like you have." I held out my hand, ticked off my fingers one by one. "First he's your new gym buddy, then your rock-climbing pal, then he's a groomsman in your wedding, and now he's invited on our family vacations? Your expectations aren't realistic. Lenox is just one quick stop on his life map."

Wes studied me for several seconds. "You've thought a lot about this."

I wanted to deny it, but even if I tried, my finger ticking had already done me in.

He slid off the counter. "You *like* him."

"As a friend." I spaced the words out evenly, made each syllable count.

"Hmm."

"I'm not one of your students. I don't get crushes . . . so you can stop with that gloating smirk. This isn't about me."

"Right." His bright eyes reminded me of when he was hard at work in his shop, inspired by a new concept or design. "It's about *him*."

This wasn't going well. "Stop thinking whatever it is you're thinking right now. There is only friendship between he and I—not that there even is a he and I." I shook my head. "Or a him and me. Whichever. Whatever. This entire conversation is pointless . . ."

"You do hear yourself rambling, right?"

Time for a conversation U-turn. "I don't think it's a good idea for him to come out this weekend."

As if with an invisible paintbrush, Weston drew a circle around my head with his pointer finger. "Well, then I suggest you figure out how to deal with whatever girl drama is happening in that head of yours. Because he's coming on Saturday. And he's bringing snowmobiles."

Weston regained his full smile and pulled open the door to the lobby. "Hope you can handle him for one night."

Hot on his heels, I wasn't about to let my baby brother have the last word. "There will be no handling of him at all."

Alex's head shot up at the front desk. "Wait—who's she handling?"

Weston strode toward the exit and lifted his hand in a two-second wave. The Thursday step class poured out from the upstairs studio, washing him out to sea with the crowd.

I stood frozen, my lungs failing to expand.

"Hmm. Maybe I *typed* you too soon," said the familiar female voice at my back. "I think your excitement meter's about to kick up a few notches."

Alex's observation skills were hit-the-nail-on-the-head accurate.

Chapter Twenty

My mother's infamous traveling mantra, "It's always better to be over-prepared than underpacked," was a mentality I'd adopted long ago.

"You're kidding with this, right?" Weston asked, popping my trunk and scanning my luggage.

"Weston, leave your sister alone," my mom called from the porch of our three-bedroom log cabin. "She's just prepared."

"For what? A winter apocalypse?" He shook his head and grabbed my duffle bag and Savannah's suitcase. "You do realize we're only here for three days."

"Weston," my mom scolded again. "Knock it off."

Smashing his lips together, he rolled his eyes in my direction and then hiked up the snowy front porch steps with my bags. Georgia was already inside, dusting off the vintage board games from the hall closet. She was dead set on starting up a family game tournament this week-end. As if she and Weston needed more competition. Whatever new rivalry had begun on their drive up the mountain, I was thankful that Savannah and I had missed it. Two hours of listening to those two try to one-up each other was two hours too long.

My dad rose from his well-worn spot on the elk-printed couch and hugged me. "We could have brought you up with us—I wasn't thrilled when Mom told me you and Savannah were driving alone."

Even though I'd driven in the snow and ice my entire adult life, my father still worried over me like a teenager with a shiny new license. "No, Daddy. I wanted you and Mom to be able to stay an extra night or two. Besides, I followed behind Wes and Georgia the whole way up." I kissed his cheek, his graying mustache tickling my chin.

My father's expressive eyes always said more than his words. "I just worry about you." But those words could have gone without saying. I knew them well—had heard them countless times.

I rubbed the shoulder of my dad's fuzzy flannel shirt and told him I was just fine and that he could relax. Even after he sat down, I could still feel the concern of his gaze trailing after me.

Savannah sat at the large oak kitchen table with my mom, eating a slice of banana bread that Nan had sent over with Georgia. "Mommy, this is almost like yours. Except squishier."

Her remark surprised me. "You remember my banana bread?" Gosh, how long had it been since I'd baked a loaf for her?

"Your mommy makes very good treats, doesn't she?" my mom said.

Mouth stuffed full, Savannah talked around her massive bite. "Yep." She swallowed. "Dr. Patrick asked her to make brownies, but she still hasn't yet."

My mom's gaze flitted up to mine. "Dr. Patrick? Weston's friend who's joining us tomorrow?" There was a hint of strain to the way she asked it. "I didn't know you two knew each other all that well."

"Oh, well—"

"We do lots with him." Savannah nodded. "He fixed up my bloody knee and showed Mommy how to fly a kite. Oh, and he taught her a cool trick with a yo-yo, too."

My mother's curious expression was downplayed in Savannah's presence, yet there was only so much she could hide on her open face.

Unlike me, she hadn't mastered the onion layers of protection and pretenses. She hadn't needed to.

I backed away from the table, thankful Savannah had moved onto a new story about school, and pointed down the hall. "I'm gonna help Georgia sort out the games."

"Hey," Georgia said, sitting cross-legged at the end of the hallway, closet door propped open. She held up a 1960s edition of Monopoly. "Can you believe this one has all the pieces to it?"

I stifled a groan not because I disliked the board game, but because I doubted Weston and Georgia could survive a round of Monopoly this weekend—the way they played it anyway. Their brand of cutthroat competitiveness didn't work so well in a tight space with several houseguests. "Oh, wow, yeah. What other options have you found?" I sat, leaning against the door that led to the pink room—which for the weekend would house Georgia, Savannah, and me.

"Um, all of these ones here." She pointed to the pile to the right of her: Candy Land, Sorry!, Twister, Clue. "Your mom has some awesome games. Look at this one!" She picked up a washed-out box and handed it to me.

"Mystery Date." I rubbed my hand over the old dusty rectangular box with a woman in a pink dress pictured on the front. "My mom's told me about this game."

I lifted the lid and Georgia peered over my shoulder.

"Look at that giant door."

In the center of the pastel-colored game board was a large white door, plastic hinges, and blue doorknob. "Meet your secret admirer?" I read off the side of the box lid.

She picked up the pile of cards and the game pieces—cutouts of women in 1960s attire. "I guess they have to open the door to see who they'll date." She thumbed through them. "There's a formal dance date, a beach date, a bowling date, a skiing date, oh . . . and the dud."

We laughed.

The door to Weston's room pulled open to reveal my brother clad in snow pants, ski boots, and a thick padded jacket. Apparently he was ready to go up to the mountain. "Are you still sitting there looking at games?" He reached his hand down for Georgia and, when she was standing next to him, kissed her square on the mouth.

She peered down at me. "I guess I know who my mystery date is." She patted him on the chest. "Give me five minutes to dig out my gear and then we'll go."

She practically danced into our room and closed the door.

Weston spied the game next to me. "Mystery Date?"

I shrugged and sorted the pieces. "It's just a silly old game."

He snatched the cards from my hand and held them out of my reach. "These are your choices?" He laughed. "I think this game should have an edition where the brother chooses the contestants."

"That would never sell." I collected the other pieces and put them back into the box and then reached out my hand to retrieve the cards.

He pulled them back. "But don't you want to know who I'd choose for you?"

"I already know who you'd choose for me. The dud. Hardy har har," I deadpanned.

"Nope. But it's nice to know what you think of me." He flicked the cards down on top of my head, one by one, keeping the last card in his palm. "It's this guy." He turned it toward me. "Because I've never seen you smile the way you did the night you came dancing with us."

The ballroom dance guy. Weston handed me the card.

Georgia opened her door. "I'm ready, Mr. Ski Date."

Weston took her in, his gaze sticking on her bottom half. "Mm-hmm . . . snow pants never looked hotter."

"Okay, you two." I shooed them. "Go cool off in the snow."

Hand in hand, they walked to the end of the hall. Weston peeked over his shoulder at me. "You sure you don't want to come out? We can take you up on the starter hill."

"No, thanks. I'm good here," I said without even considering the alternative.

The front door closed a minute later.

I stared at the vintage card in my hand. The charming figure drawn on the front had a smile that belonged on a toothpaste commercial and arms held in the traditional closed-hold ballroom dance position. My stomach swooped.

Patrick would be here tomorrow. Along with all the butterflies that went along with his name and face and smile.

With one last lingering look at Mr. Ballroom Dancer, I opened the lid to the old dusty board game and slid the card back inside.

If my parents hadn't taken off after breakfast to run up to the lodge and visit with old friends, my mom would be scrunching her nose at me, shaking her head in disapproval when I poured my third cup of coffee.

Patrick would be here within minutes. He'd texted me on his way up, and though my fingers itched to respond and reply with a big smiley face, I stared at the screen for a full ten seconds before it darkened.

And then I pushed the phone out of reach.

I inhaled the cloud of coffee steam, hoping caffeine would lift the confusion circulating inside me, provide me the strength I needed to let go—of the bravery challenges and of Patrick.

I'd passed all his tests, memorized his favorite one-liners, and cut my peppermint addiction by half. The only thing left to be gained from more time spent together . . . was heartache.

Tires crunched over the snowy driveway and a blur of gray pulled my gaze to the window above the sink.

"Mom! Look what Dr. Patrick brought!" Savannah tugged open the front door and padded down the porch steps in her purple snow boots.

"Wait—"

Weston was slapping Patrick on the back when I rounded the corner to stop my little blond pixie. Too late. My brother scooped her up in his arms and plopped her down on the black snowmobile seat.

"Morning, Willa." Patrick's tone was easy, expectant in a way that made me reevaluate my earlier resolve.

I spared the briefest of glances and nodded his way. "Morning."

"I want to ride this! Please, Mommy!"

"No, baby. That's not for you."

Savannah stretched her arms wide and gripped the handles. She leaned from left to right. The girl's love for speed was bound to give me a heart attack before my thirtieth birthday.

"Hop off, sweetie. Let the big boys have a turn."

"But, Mooommmy," she said, stretching the word into a classic Savannah-whine. "I want to play in the snow, too."

"Then I'll play out back with you in a little bit."

"But that's not fun. Not like Uncle Wes's kind of fun."

Weston's flippant chuckle caused my chest to heat. No matter how many bravery tests I passed or how many times I stepped out of my comfort zone . . . it would never be enough. My family would never see the me I wanted them to see.

"She borders between Classic Bore and Wound Too Tight." Alex's statement from the other day echoed in my head like the ringing of a gong.

Weston plucked Savannah off the seat. "Go on, kiddo. I'll build a snow den with you this afternoon."

Sulking, she rounded her shoulders and kicked the top layer of snow with the tip of her boot.

I heard the front door latch and turned to follow her, offering Weston and Patrick a small wave without eye contact. "See you guys later."

Tucking my frozen fingertips back inside the pockets of my jeans, I stepped in Savannah's shallow footprints.

"You want the first ride? I'll take you up."

I stopped midstride. A tangled feeling of hope and dread wove through my rib cage as I glanced back at Patrick. The answer was already forming on my lips when Weston interrupted.

"Ha! I'd give you a hundred bucks if you got her on that thing." There was no backbone in Weston's words. He knew the risk to his pocketbook was minimal, if not obsolete. He unlatched the trailer to remove his new toy.

My gaze locked with Patrick's and in that moment, my fear hardened into something firm and fierce and fiery. Something that whooshed in my eardrums and marched in my chest. Something that wouldn't allow me to walk away.

"Pay him."

Weston whipped his head around. "What?"

Patrick's patient facade broke into a heart-shattering grin.

"I said, 'Pay him.' Just give me a minute to suit up."

Chapter Twenty-One

One might think that accepting a sibling bet would provide the kind of adrenaline boost that could trump even the strongest wave of nausea. Not so. I clung to the handlebars below my section of seat. While trapped inside a giant helmet, I focused on my Darth Vader breathing.

We idled in the driveway for what felt like a month. *What on earth is he waiting for?* My pride and common sense were engaged in a battle, and in approximately one minute a white flag would be waved if Patrick didn't squeeze that throttle.

Ducking his head as if to obscure my brother's view, Patrick's muffled words rang clear through the vent near his mouth. "Wrap your arms around my waist."

"But I'm holding on to the bars." He couldn't see the ghostly shade surrounding my knuckles through my thick gloves, but I was sure my grip could rival Samson's.

"It will make our turns easier. And you'll feel safer."

If I hadn't been straddled to the back of this death machine, I would have laughed. Touching Patrick was anything but safe. Yet, ever the abiding rule follower, I obeyed.

The white-flocked pine trees in the distance held my focus—at least for the moment—but the millisecond Wes and the cabin were out of sight my plan was to close my eyes and keep them closed until we slid to a stop. I could only hope that Patrick's idea of a "ride" was something comparable to the kiddie coasters at the fairground.

The motor engaged and the muscles of Patrick's stomach flexed under the strain of acceleration. My boa-constrictor hold tightened. I guessed it would be weeks before the imprint of the helmet faded from my left cheek—and weeks before the imprint of my helmet faded from Patrick's upper back, too. Eyes squeezed closed, hair a tangled whip behind me, I swallowed against the reflux creeping up my throat.

I leaned through every turn with him, doing my best not to resist or react when my backside left the seat because of a bump in the trail. Blind as I was, the two of us worked as a unit.

A hand gripped my knee, squeezed three times, and then disappeared. And for the briefest of seconds, disappointment overshadowed every other sensation that coursed through me.

Our speed downshifted into a sluggish crawl. And then we stopped.

Vertigo swirled my vision as I blinked and lifted my head. Even so, I could see we weren't back at the cabin. Instead, we'd reached a clearing. A flatland of sparkling white with patches of dense forest on either side. Pulling the key from the ignition, Patrick swung a leg over the front of the snowmobile and tugged off his helmet.

"W . . . what are we doing?"

Nose pink, breath white, he reached for my helmet and lifted it from my head. "I figured you could use a break."

Static tingled though my scalp as I finger-combed my hair. "Oh, uh . . . nope. I'm doing fine—having a great time." Stupidest lie ever.

"Oh, really? Burying your face in the center of my back is you having a great time? Come on, Willa. I know you better than that."

I scrunched my shoulders. "Well . . . at least you made a hundred bucks, right?"

He stared, unblinking. "I'd take a genuine smile from you over a hundred bucks any day of the week."

His words punched straight into my chest.

With a strong tug, he guided me off the seat and onto the snowy ground. He gripped my arm above my elbow, strong and steady, as if to stabilize me from the outside in.

One shallow breath led into the next, and I knew this was my chance—that I should tell him now that our lessons needed to end. That our time together needed to end, too.

But something about the way he stood, something about the dip in his smile, something about the intensity of his gaze made my knees buckle. He pulled off his glove and reached his hand out toward my face, his fingertips skimming the side of my knit hat before pushing into the curtain of my hair.

The pulse point in my throat was hammering the Morse code of my most secret desire. Could he hear it?

He tugged gently on my shortest lock of hair, the one that incessantly curled under my chin no matter how many times I tucked it behind my ear. It became our tether. His fingers slipped down the strand, freeing a pine needle that spiraled in the wind like a pinwheel.

Neither of us watched it land. Neither of us willing to be the first to look away.

He didn't drop his hand or take a step back. Instead, he cork-screwed the ornery piece of blond around his finger like golden thread, and the space between us shrank to nothing.

His breath swept across my face in cloudy patches. "You trust me, Willa?"

I nodded without hesitation.

He uncoiled my hair. "Then take the keys."

"What?"

"I want you to drive."

Two beats, and then three. "The snowmobile?"

"Yes. The snowmobile." His smile felt like a sedative for the over-worked neurons in my brain. He pressed his thumb against my bottom lip to prevent the most commonly used word in my vocabulary from slipping out—*no*.

"What would happen if you said yes before you thought of all the reasons to say no?"

The lump in my throat swelled. *What would happen?*

He dropped his hand and reached into his jacket pocket for the key. "I'll teach you—this is the ideal place to learn. Mostly flat with a wide, clear path."

A thousand *what ifs* entered my mind, yet amazingly I shut each of them down and took the key from his palm.

"I'll be right behind you, okay?"

"Okay."

The triumph in his smile spread through me like a virus, and soon I was smiling, too.

Stiff-legged, I climbed back onto the snowmobile. Patrick clipped the safety pull to the front of my jacket and pointed out the hand brake, the throttle, and the kill switch. He scooted on behind me and patted my thigh, my cue to start the engine.

His arms wrapped around my sides at the first squeeze of the throt-tle. And for a moment I wanted nothing more than to close my eyes and relax against him, to relish this rare feeling of security for as long as possible.

I accelerated cautiously.

The twin skis at the front of the snowmobile pointed in the direc-tion of the flat, snowy plane before us, and a billow of smoky exhaust tinged my nostrils.

How quickly perspective could change.

The difference between the passenger seat and the driver's seat was like the difference between reading about the taste of chocolate and eating it.

I scanned the scenery the same way I had scanned every minor detail of the panoramic photograph that hung on my dining room wall, courtesy of Patrick McCade. Only the landscape in front of me wasn't a piece of art.

It was real life.

And I was living it.

The sun, the sky, the trees, each and every dip and bend and peak in the mountain range—all of it was another layer of freedom exposed.

I pressed the throttle harder.

My body vibrated from the powerful pull of the engine. I inclined into another turn and Patrick followed my lead.

"You're doing great!" he called over my shoulder.

My smile felt wider, bolder, freer than it had in years. Patrick had given me a gift today.

After I made one last pass, I released the throttle and rounded back toward the cabin.

He patted the outside of my right thigh and leaned closer. "You sure you don't want to go any farther?"

I wasn't sure of anything anymore, but I nodded anyway. I'd promised Savannah some fun in the snow today, and I needed to relieve Georgia and Weston of their babysitting duties so they could have some fun of their own.

I eased the hand brake back and glided us to the side of the house where Patrick had parked the borrowed truck and trailer.

Only something was different.

Our helmets off, Patrick's upbeat words and positive affirmations pinged against deaf ears as I scanned the property.

A cold hard panic scratched at the base of my throat, my heart punching bruises into my rib cage.

I pushed off the snowmobile, my legs stumbling into motion.

I broke for the cabin.

"Willa?"

He ran after me, yanked me to a stop. "Why are you—"

"The other one," I panted out, pointing to the blank space near the truck. "It's gone."

He craned his neck, registering the missing snowmobile for the first time. I ripped away from his grasp, and with each harried stride I muttered a chant I wished I could believe.

He wouldn't. He wouldn't. He wouldn't.

I threw open the front door to the cabin. Georgia sat at the dining room table, flipping through her wedding planner. Alone.

"Where's Savannah?" I demanded, breathless.

Confusion crossed her face. "Weston took her on a ride. Up the mountain. What's wrong?"

Bile lurched up my esophagus.

I let the door swing shut without offering a reply and flew down the porch steps, my boots sinking into the snow like anchors.

Georgia called after us and Patrick answered. "It's okay. I got her."

Only he was wrong; it wasn't okay.

Stride for stride, Patrick matched my frantic pace. "Your brother isn't reckless. They'll be fine, Willa. Slow down."

I halted at our snowmobile.

"Take me up there—I need to get her." I pointed up at the mountain, and a dizzying pulse pounded behind my eyes and in my temples.

"No."

My attention snapped back to his face.

"What?" *What didn't he understand?* "I have to get to her."

"No, Willa. You don't. You need to stay here and wait for them to come back."

Tears blurred my vision but I pushed past him anyway. Curling my numb fingers around the handlebars, I planted my left foot onto the running board and prepared to swing my right over the seat.

Patrick gripped my waist and pulled me back.

I squirmed free, pushed him away again. "This. *This* is the reason I can't say yes, Patrick."

"What is?"

I sidestepped him, no time to explain, and dove again for the snowmobile.

Only it wasn't Patrick that stopped me this time, it was a cramp in my stomach.

As I crumpled to my knees, an all-too-familiar pain spread through my abdomen and radiated north. Restricting my lungs. Tightening my airway.

I can't breathe. I can't breathe. I can't breathe.

Patrick dropped in front of me and ripped off his gloves. Rough, warm fingers lifted my face and forced my gaze to his. My eyes widened and a desperate wheeze sliced from my throat.

I can't breathe. I can't breathe. I can't breathe.

"Listen to me, Willa. Take a slow, deep breath—"

But not even the smooth tenor of Patrick's voice could make my panic obey. I tore from his hold and dry-heaved in the snow.

A steady pressure remained on my back until the last spasm subsided, and then he cradled the back of my head into his chest, his mouth against the tip of my ear.

"Breathe with me, Willa." There was a new sternness in his tone. "Inhale through your nose." He lifted my hand and pressed it to my abdomen. "You should feel your breath expand *here*. Not in your chest. Now hold it."

I nodded, the technique a forgotten kind of familiar.

"Good. Now exhale through your mouth. *Slowly.*"

I did as he said, fighting against the burning sensation inside my lungs and the hysterical voice in my head screaming for *more air*.

"Again." He coached me through my next few breaths, a continuous rhythm of holds and releases. "Now, picture that sunset. Focus on the colors, the tips of the trees, the way it makes you feel. Good."

The back of my head rubbed against the front of his jacket, the sound like the peeling of Velcro. But breath by purposed breath, the buzzing in my head and my body quieted.

The sunset canvas had been my go-to place for peace and calm since the attacks had come back, the only image that seemed to stop my spiral of worry and—

The whistling hum of a motor catapulted me forward.

"Willa—stop," Patrick called after me, getting to his feet. "You don't want to do this. Not here. Not now."

Adrenaline fueled each wobbly stride.

Weston parked and dismounted and then removed their helmets. Savannah's giddy laugh echoed throughout the carved-out space between the cabin and the forest line beyond.

"Hi, Mommy! Uncle Wes took me almost all the way to the tippy-top."

A metallic taste filled my mouth.

Patrick flung his arm out like a barrier, stopping me only a few feet away from the duo. *"Wait."*

The word stretched like a taut rubber band inside my head as Patrick called for Georgia. Immediately, she was there. Had she been watching us, waiting for an opportunity to help—to make up for my brother's stupidity?

She grabbed Savannah's hand and took her inside.

Patrick lowered his arm and Weston scanned my face, a crease formed above his brow line.

He'd always thought of me as the weaker one. The quiet one. The delicate one. The fragile one. But not today.

"How could you?" I lunged at him, ramming the center of his chest with my open palms.

His eyes rounded and I wanted to shove him again, but Patrick's hand, the one clamped to my right shoulder, assured me he wouldn't allow me a second chance.

"It was one ride. Calm down. An inchworm could have traveled faster than the speed I took her." Weston had the audacity to throw his arms up in the air, as if my words, my worry, my role as Savannah's mother meant nothing to him at all.

"I don't care! It wasn't your call to make." My finger slashed through the air. "It was mine. You *knew* I'd never give my permission. And yet you did it anyway." The words tipped the scale away from a panic relapse into a powerful rage.

His eyes narrowed. "You're right. I knew you'd never give it. Just like I knew you wouldn't say yes to soccer. Just like I knew you wouldn't keep your promise."

Tears climbed my throat. "Don't make this about me."

"Fine. I'll make it about me." He pushed closer, his eyebrows pinched into a stony expression. "Because if I don't teach her to enjoy life, who will?"

Patrick planted a firm hand on Weston's chest. "Weston," he warned. "I think you should take a break."

My brother's steely eyes didn't blink; his hardened mouth didn't twitch. "When will you get it through your head that you can't prevent tragedy from happening—*you're not God, Willa.*"

I clenched my fists. "You don't know the first thing about loss!"

The flash of pain in his eyes made me shrink back. "I almost lost *you*! And sometimes I still wonder if I didn't."

"That's not the same."

Patrick's gaze burned into the side of my face.

"Isn't it?" Weston ripped his hat off his head and fisted his hair with both hands. "You think it's been easy for me—watching you in pain? Watching you hide? Watching you wait for the next disaster to strike? It's not. It's the hardest thing I've ever had to do." His eyes turned glassy. "But I refuse, I *refuse*, to sit back and watch your fear rob your daughter the way it's robbed you."

My heart slammed into my throat. "That's not fair. I've tried . . ."

"Then tell me, Willa. Tell me how your life looks different now than it did last year? Or the year before that? Or the year before that. Tell me that your fear doesn't control every little thing you do—or I should say, every little thing you don't do."

I didn't respond, and he shook his head. "I don't know who I'm more disappointed in—you for giving up, or me for believing that you would try."

"That's enough." Patrick pulled me back a step. "You both need to take a walk."

I swiped at my damp cheeks. I could do better than that. "I'm going home."

Chapter Twenty-Two

Georgia closed the door to our bedroom while I tried in vain to fit Savannah's nightgown and teddy bear into her suitcase. My window to escape without the interference of my parents was growing narrower by the minute.

"You don't have to leave." The tears I heard in her voice tore at my heart.

Georgia's gaze remained fixed on the old hardwoods. "I should have stopped him from taking her up—"

I closed the suitcase with a snap and turned to hug her. "This has nothing to do with you."

She held on to me. "I know you're hurt, but your brother loves you so much."

But that truth didn't change anything.

I pulled back just enough to see her eyes. "I promise you, I won't let any of this interfere with your wedding plans."

"The wedding is the least of my concerns." The inflection in her tone indicated what her words had not. "How long . . . how long have the panic attacks been back?"

My bones suddenly chilled, I dropped my arms to my sides. She wasn't here to discuss Weston; she was here to discuss me.

"You saw?" Although I knew the answer before the question even registered on her face.

"Are you okay?"

I reached for the strap of my duffle bag. "They don't happen often." True. But they had come back, a fact I'd failed to reveal to any person in my family.

With a resigned sigh, she grabbed Savannah's blanket, suitcase, and pillow. "What should we tell your parents when they get back?"

She might not be an official member of our family, but even Georgia knew that nothing beneficial would come from my parents knowing—either about my attack or about my argument with Weston.

"Tell them I wasn't feeling well and I wanted to sleep in my own bed. I'll call them once I'm through the pass."

She opened the bedroom door and together we carried my luggage down the hall.

Savannah sat on the sofa, her arms crossed over her chest and a pout on her mouth. "I don't want to go home."

"I know, baby. But we are."

Georgia held out her hand, and begrudgingly Savannah accepted it.

I'd prepared myself to see Weston waiting beside my car, braced myself for his quick apology and refusal to let me leave.

But it wasn't Weston standing at my car. It was Patrick.

He met me as I stepped off the front porch and took the bags from my hands. "You're sure about this?"

"Yes."

"Okay, then. I'm going to drive you back. I gave Weston the keys to my dad's truck. He'll take care of getting it back to Lenox."

"Oh, no. No, Patrick, please . . . don't let what happened today ruin your stay—"

But by the look on his face, he was as set on driving me as I was on leaving the cabin. He popped the trunk, loaded my bags, and helped Savannah get situated in the backseat.

With one last glance over our property and cabin, I slipped inside the car, refusing to acknowledge Weston's final blow.

His absence.

At Savannah's seventeenth Kid Travel Trivia card, I was starting to wish I'd never purchased the car game. Ever the gracious companion, Patrick answered her riddles, laughed at her made-up jokes, and even pretended to be stumped on the bonus multiple-choice questions. I kneaded my temples in a circular motion, hoping the effort might stop the throb of this post-panic-attack migraine. So far, my efforts had been in vain. The pressure behind my eyes was enough to wish for voluntary blindness.

As she read a new question from the backseat, Patrick snaked his hand behind my neck. With expert precision, he managed to pinpoint each of the tension spots.

He answered Savannah and then quieted his voice. "You get these every time?"

Every time. Amazingly, what I'd managed to keep hidden from my family for years, Patrick had picked up on in one afternoon.

Maybe he wasn't a doctor after all, but a detective.

"Yes."

The massage down the column of my neck continued until we pulled off the highway and passed the WELCOME TO LENOX sign.

Tilting my head in his direction, I peeked through the narrowed slits of my eyes. "I can drop you off at your house. It's just a few blocks away."

"I don't think so."

He turned onto my street.

"But—"

"Let's get you and Savannah taken care of for the night, okay? Don't worry about me."

Even through a raging headache, Patrick's profile was shockingly handsome. The messy tufts of hair sticking out at various angles begged to be touched, as did the light stubble along his jaw. I closed my eyes to keep the temptation at bay.

My phone buzzed from the middle console.

He picked it up. "It's your mom again."

I held out my hand and silenced the call as he parked. If I hadn't had a headache before, there wasn't a chance I'd escape one after that conversation.

Patrick came around to open my door. "How about you settle on the couch while I get you some ibuprofen and figure something out for dinner." His hand, firm on my lower back, guided me up the driveway. "Then you can call your mom back."

Holding the front of my head, I stepped lightly. "Can we trade places? I think you secretly want to talk to my mom instead."

He laughed. "Not on your life, sweetheart."

Savannah jogged ahead. "Can I unlock the door? I know which key is for the house. It's the green one."

"Sure. Here you go." Patrick handed her the keys. She turned it with ease and opened the door.

Two steps past the entryway, Savannah spun back around, hands on her hips.

"I think you're like . . . the bestest, Dr. Patrick."

He placed a hand on her head. "Feeling's mutual."

Maybe I didn't need medicine for my head as much as I needed it for my heart.

Though it was only half past eight, exhaustion radiated from my bones.

The remnants of Patrick's take-out order from the Golden Dragon were still scattered between the coffee table and the breakfast bar, and as much as I wanted to clean up, I'd been doctor-ordered to stay put. To rest.

He handed me a hot cup of tea. I took it, grateful for the quiet, and even more grateful that I'd managed to convince my mom to stay at the cabin.

"How's the headache?"

The soft scent of chamomile soothed the remaining tension in my skull. "Better, thank you."

I pulled my knees up to my chest. "Please, feel free to take my car for the night, I'm sure you're ready to be home." *And away from my crazy.*

Patrick shifted on the couch opposite me and leaned forward, the vivid blue of his eyes glinting in the low evening light. "If you don't mind, I'd feel better if I stayed."

Something grabbed in the pit of my stomach.

"Really, I'm okay now."

"Even still, today was . . . eventful."

As my hands pressed against the warm mug, I toyed with the hang-nail at the edge of my thumb. "Yes, too eventful, I'm afraid." I tried to smile but knew it fell short. Much like my attempt at small talk. "I owe you an explanation and probably the world's biggest apology."

"No, you don't."

"If you hadn't been there today . . ."

"I don't play the what-if game, Willa. It's a lose-lose. For everyone involved."

I considered him, took a deep breath, and then started again. No games or pretenses. No sugarcoated words. No therapeutic mantras.

Just truth, raw and ugly.

"I was never the kind of kid to chase a ball into the street or climb a tree in the neighborhood park or jump off the diving board at the city pool. My mom called it being 'extra careful,' which was exactly how my parents wanted Wes and me to be, only . . . one of us didn't mind them so well."

Patrick gave me a meditative smile.

"But as I grew older, I knew this feeling—this nagging static—wasn't just caution. It was fear. And it didn't matter how rational or irrational the worry, the fear—the anxiety—felt the same on the inside. Chad was always so good at reminding me to focus on the here and now while still encouraging me to chase after my dreams. And for a while, life felt almost perfect. I got hired on at Lenox Elementary as a second-grade teacher, and we found out we were expecting six months later. We were so happy."

I sighed into my mug, watching as the hot liquid swirled with my breath, the way I wished I could avoid the truth of my next words.

"I had my first panic attack the week Chad died. I was in my second trimester. And it was . . . much worse than today's." I searched the darkness outside the window that faced my backyard. "I was hospitalized several times during my pregnancy because of them, saw a grief counselor weekly, and ingested all the right herbal supplement combinations I could find. Savannah felt like my only reason for hope—my only reason to be alive, really. The second she was born, all my energy shifted to her. To being the best mom I could be despite . . . despite my issues." I reached into my pocket and pulled out three peppermints. "I know there's nothing scientific about these . . . but for whatever reason, they became a comfort, and the attacks stopped."

Patrick stared at the candy and then lifted his eyes to me again. "And then Savannah was diagnosed with cancer."

My grip tightened on the warm mug. "The doctors assured us time and time again of her optimistic prognosis, but I felt so helpless, so powerless, so distant from the God I'd always believed in. I had so many questions and so few answers. I struggled to pray, couldn't even form the words most days." I glanced up at the art on the wall above the dining room table. "When your father gave me the sunset pictures before her first big treatment . . . something, something shifted inside me. It's hard to explain." A wave of self-consciousness rolled through me. I'd never been so honest, so vulnerable.

"Will you try?"

"It felt like your father handed me a picture of hope, not the kind that comes in the form of a good prognosis, but the kind of hope that can transform the horizon. If I could believe God was responsible for every sunset, then I had to believe He was with us, too."

Patrick's expression was so thoughtful, so peaceful, that I wished I could end this story right there. But that wasn't the end.

"The day we heard the words *cancer free*, I truly believed that Savannah's cure would be my cure, too. That all my fears would vanish and that all my doubts would lift."

"And that's not what happened."

"No. It's not." I tapped my fingernail on the ceramic, the soft ting, ting, ting pushing me to continue. "It's back—all of it. The anxiety, the restless nights, the constant fear that someone I love will be hurt. Sometimes it feels impossible to turn the worry off." I lifted my gaze to Patrick. "But I promised her that things would be different when she was well again. I promised her that I would be different . . . and I just keep failing."

"You haven't failed." His voice pierced the space between my chest and throat.

I sucked in a sob. *Hadn't I? Hadn't I failed over and over and over again? Too afraid to say yes, too afraid to let go, too afraid to—*

Patrick was on his feet, lifting the mug from my grasp and setting it on the coffee table. He positioned himself on the sofa beside me and captured my hand, folding it into his as silent tears streamed down my face.

"Willa, you haven't failed," he repeated. "That little girl has more love in her life than she knows what to do with. And if she were given a choice, she would choose you as her mom. Over and over again. This battle you're fighting is much bigger than keeping a promise you made to Savannah. It's about dealing with what's going on inside you." He looked down at our joined hands, and a surge of hope filled me. "The only way you fail is by giving up."

"I'm not giving up." I meant it. I was tired of running in circles, tired of living in a maze with no way out. I needed to keep trying—for me as much as for Savannah.

"Good. Because we have work to do."

"*We?*"

"What—you thought I was going to quit on you?"

Laughable, really, the idea of Patrick quitting anything. "No." *But I might have thought about quitting you. Only about a million times in the last few weeks.*

"What aren't you saying?" he asked.

"It's just that . . ." *How do I even . . . ?* "Your time here is just so limited and sometimes I worry about . . . complications."

I slipped my hand from his and gripped my kneecaps. *Safer. Much safer.*

"My time here is limited, yes." Patrick's voice was strong and steady. "But I'd say *complication* started the minute a beautiful blonde challenged my credentials."

The cadence of my pulse shifted into a rhythm of stutters and stops. "We've switched roles since then."

"A lot of things have changed since then." A whisper of fingertips skimmed the base of my chin and forced my gaze upward. "I'm not sorry about the days we've spent together, Willa. I value your friendship." He exhaled. "That said, if you think it's best we don't—"

"No." I wouldn't quit. He'd helped me far more than I'd ever believed possible. "I meant what I said. I want to keep going. I want to kill this fear."

"Then we're gonna have to raise the stakes."

Chapter Twenty-Three

I dreamed of coffee: dark and rich and boldly brewed. The aroma was so strong that it lingered even after my eyes searched the spaces between my dusty blinds. But there was no wink of dawn to be found. No golds or reds or pinks illuminating my bedroom ceiling. The sky was still asleep.

I tapped the screen on my phone. *5:13 a.m.*

Patrick is on my couch!

A trail of goose bumps sped up my spine.

In record-breaking speed, I swung my feet to the floor, tied my robe around my waist, and smoothed the bed-head out of my hair. After a quick traffic check outside my bedroom door, I tiptoed across the hall and into the bathroom. Crazy hair was one thing, but there was no excuse for morning breath.

Mouth minty fresh, I padded down the dark hallway and into the living room.

The couch was empty. *Has he already gone home?*

"Morning." Elbows on the breakfast bar, pen between his fingers, he lifted his head. "I hope I didn't wake you."

For the third time since leaving the bathroom, I checked the knot at my hip. *Secure.* "Coffee is always the best way to wake up." By the sound of my raspy morning voice, I could use a cup. Or maybe ten.

"I'll pour you a cup before I go, unless you think you can get back to sleep? It was a pretty short night." Yet he looked ready to take the day by force. His clothes from yesterday had been replaced with workout attire. And running shoes. I scanned the room. The fire was roaring hot in the fireplace, the blankets and pillow were folded near the couch, and his overnight bag sat next to the front door.

Wait. The kitchen. Spotless. No sign of Chinese take-out to be found. Not a noodle or even a fortune cookie.

"Um . . . looks like you had an even shorter night. How long have you been awake? I can't believe you cleaned up like this—"

"Is this a scolding?"

My laugh sounded rusty. "No, it's a thank-you. Thank you, Patrick. For . . . everything." That pretty much summed it up. Everything. For every day. For every conversation. For every moment of friendship he'd given me.

His grin said so much about him—especially considering he couldn't have slept more than a few hours. "I was just leaving you a note."

"Oh, you're leaving . . . now?" Again, I glanced at the presunrise time on the clock.

He handed me a steaming mug of my favorite drink on earth and gave me a half grin. "Thought I should probably be gone before Twenty Questions wakes up."

My heart double-tapped. "Right." I hadn't thought about my daughter's curiosity. "Thank you."

He dipped his chin. "I think your *everything* clause has you covered on the thank-yous. You don't have to keep saying it." He reached for a leathery object on the countertop. A book. "Here's some required reading material for you. And yes, there'll be a quiz."

I set the mug to the side and took the worn book from his hands. The cracked leather was rough to the touch. Opening it, I gasped as I read the name on the inside cover.

"This is Rex Porter's journal?"

He eyed the book appreciatively. "Yes."

"You had it with you?"

A lazy shrug, as if this weren't one of his most valued possessions. "I was planning on giving it to you at the cabin."

The word hit like a boulder in my gut. The cabin. "Oh, right."

I slumped against the doorjamb, and like a remembered nightmare, the events of yesterday replayed in my mind.

"Your brother texted me last night after you went to bed."

I stared at the journal, unblinking, hoping my internal wince hadn't been audible.

Patrick touched my shoulder, squeezed it lightly. "I let him know you were home safe."

"Is that all you said?" I hadn't wanted to ask, but I needed to. Patrick was Weston's friend before he was mine, and it wouldn't be the first time they'd shared information about me.

"Willa."

I bit the inside of my cheek.

"I may be a family doctor, but I'm no family therapist. And I won't pretend to be."

My forefinger inched along the binding of the old travel journal once more. "Okay."

"Okay." His tone was hesitant. "I'm gonna run back to my place and shower. I'll come by later this afternoon with my car and grab my bag."

He leaned forward and then quickly pulled himself back.

Maybe it was my foggy morning brain, or the short night's sleep, or the emotional storm of the last twenty-four hours, but I could have sworn Patrick was about to . . . *to what?*

Nothing. He wasn't about to do anything.

I spun toward the entryway and opened the door for him. "So, about this quiz . . . will it be multiple choice?"

"Essay," he teased.

"Ah. Well, I better get busy, then."

He jogged down the front porch steps, and a blast of frigid November air swept into my house. "Oh my gosh! You're gonna freeze. Please, just take my car."

His breathy laugh was a billowy white as he jogged in place. "I love to run at sunrise. Plus, we're supposed to get snow later."

"Then you better watch for ice."

"And you better keep that fire going."

He raised his arm in a wave, and I closed the door and latched the chain. I let out a tension-filled sigh and then grabbed my coffee, a stack of pink Post-it Notes, and today's special reading assignment off the counter. I snuggled into the sofa.

If Savannah followed her normal sleep routine, I'd have an hour of kid-free reading time. Better get started now.

For being fifty-odd years old, the travel journal, stuffed with trinkets, scribbles, and photographs, was in remarkable shape. It was the kind of treasure my mom would showcase in her antique store, the kind of artifact that should be on display in a museum.

By noon, I'd been transported to three different continents, read about a dozen cultures, and touched coins and bus tickets, brittle leaves, and sketches of wildlife. Patrick was right. Rex Porter had lived an incredible life, and his faith was at the forefront.

Savannah snuggled into my side, a bowl of trail mix in her lap. "Be strong and courageous," she read.

I kissed the top of her head and followed her finger to the messy cursive at the top of the page. "That's right. Be strong and courageous." Those same words had been scrawled at the top of nearly every page, written with narrowly connected strokes.

She chomped on several peanuts. "Hmm."

"It's from the Bible," I said.

"Oh! Like a scripture verse?"

"Yes, like a scripture verse. It's from Joshua."

"My favorite story is David and Goliath," she said proudly.

Naturally. "That doesn't surprise me."

"Uncle Wes says I'm brave, just like David was."

It hurt to swallow. "You *are* brave."

She slid off the couch. "I'm gonna get my tea set ready. You can be the hostess this time."

Just as predicted, the first snow flurry started around three in the afternoon. Savannah's tea party guests—Barbies, stuffed bears, and several princess figurines—had been pushed closer to the sliding glass doors so they might better enjoy the wintry view. We'd already "served" them crackers and juice, but Savannah was convinced they needed a tiny helping of chocolate chips, too.

I felt the familiar vibration of a text in my back pocket as I reached into the pantry.

Was this my first pop quiz on Rex's journal? I slipped the phone out. Not Patrick or a pop quiz.

DAVIS: Don't know when you get back into town, we left church a while ago. Headed to the clinic now. Have a new litter of puppies if you want to join us. Tell Savannah Prince Pickles says hi.

I sighed and leaned against the counter, biting the inside of my cheek. He'd boarded Prince Pickles during our weekend at the mountain— just one of the many ways he continued to show kindness to us.

I glanced out the window again. The accumulation of snow was minimal, and it would be better to pick up Savannah's fur ball sooner rather than later. Plus, she would absolutely flip over a litter of puppies. Her animal obsession was almost as intense as her obsession for all things glitter.

I texted him back.

ME: We can be there in twenty minutes?

DAVIS: Look forward to seeing you.

Valley View Veterinary Clinic was an A-frame building with cedar siding and hunter-green trim. The prime location had cost Davis a small fortune, sitting just two blocks from downtown Lenox, but it had also made him the most visible vet clinic in the area, and therefore the most popular. Everyone knew Dr. Davis Carter. And there wasn't a person around who didn't sing his praises.

Ignoring the CLOSED ON SUNDAY sign out front, Savannah pushed open the glass door as bells chimed our entrance.

The waiting room was dim and empty except for Brandon, and Savannah spotted her friend immediately. "Hey, Brandon! You got puppies here?"

"Yep, sure do!" Minus the freckles, Brandon was a mirror image of his father—cropped dark hair, happy eyes, and a generous smile. "Hi, Ms. Hart."

"Hi, Brandon." I gave him a quick hug.

"I'm supposed to take you to the back. Dad had to clean up a mess."

It was likely Davis had to clean up many messes on the weekends. He was here more than he was anywhere else. That was the price of having your name on the front door.

The high-gloss linoleum floors were a smart choice, considering the paws that walked them daily. Everything we passed—whether it be equipment or exam rooms—was pristine and polished. Although cleanliness was a top priority, they hadn't been quite as effective at eliminating the odors that went along with pet management. My nose crinkled as we neared the boarding area and a waft of "wet dog" stung my nostrils.

Brandon pulled open the painted green door to reveal a large rectangular room, one I'd been inside several times—usually to pick up and drop off Prince Pickles for a trip to Portland. Eventually, when the back-and-forth of it all had become too much, we'd decided to stay in the family apartment connected to the hospital and Prince Pickles had made a short-term home here. I couldn't thank Davis enough for that.

The room was bordered with doggie kennels, some larger than others, painted like boxes of crayons; the door to each was trimmed in primary colors. A few dozen whimsical paw prints had been stamped onto the concrete floor. The whole area resembled a child's play land rather than a pet's paradise, but perhaps it was that extra attention to detail that kept it full.

Davis dried his hands near a deep stainless steel sink and craned his neck to smile at me. And when he did, I couldn't help but notice his perfect teeth—the one feature that Alex knew him by, not quite caring enough to learn his name. *The vet with the nice teeth.*

I stifled a giggle at the memory.

Davis pulled me in for a hug and then held me out at arm's length to scan my face. "You doing okay?"

"Yes, I'm fine." Maybe not exactly the truth, but close enough.

I turned my attention to our kids, who were squealing over puppy licks. "They're really cute."

His gaze trailed my face. "You look tired."

Apparently, he wasn't quite ready to discuss the puppies. Despite his manners and good intentions, Davis was difficult to divert once his mind had been set. "Doesn't your family usually stay on the mountain for the whole weekend? Doesn't seem worth the trip for less than that."

"They stayed. I just decided to come back early. Had some things to do." I tried to hide the tensing of my shoulders with a simple shrug, yet with Davis's palm still pressed to my upper back, there was no way he hadn't noticed.

"You came back on your own?"

"Oh, uh . . . yes." *Sort of, if you don't count the charming man driving my car.* That was the thing about lies. Like mice, they multiplied quickly.

Savannah held up a golden retriever puppy and called me over. Facing the panting puppy was far easier than facing the crinkle of a disapproving brow. I'd seen that look too many times this weekend.

"He's adorable." I scooped the puppy into my arms and it licked my hand over and over. "Aww."

"Can we take it home, Mommy?"

I laughed at the optimism in her voice. Prince Pickles would never stand for another dog in our house, not even one as cute as this. "Have you even said hello to *your* dog?"

"Oopsie." She padded to the end of the room, knelt, and stuck her hand through the slats of Prince Pickles's gated door. Her little off-white dog with fur like the soiled end of a mop nuzzled her fingers. "Hi, boy. Don't worry . . . I could never forget you."

I watched as my healthy daughter murmured soft words to her devoted canine.

Davis slung an arm around my shoulders. "I ordered pizza—your favorite, with extra pineapple. Thought we could all eat together in the lounge." The one place that was pet—and pet odor—free.

The tiny puppy in my arms whimpered and I nuzzled him against my face, let him swipe his wet nose across my cheek. "Oh, that sounds yummy. Thank you."

He rubbed the side of my arm and nodded toward our children. "It's good to see them playing together again."

"Brandon's a great kid," I said.

"So is Savannah. She takes after her mom."

Davis wasn't a flirt—not in the classic sense of the word. He'd always stayed true to his faith and to his heart. Maybe that was why spending time with him didn't come as easily for me anymore. Because when I was with him, I didn't feel I was being true to mine.

He dropped his arm suddenly and slapped his thigh. "Hey, did you get my text last week—about the bazaar?"

The bazaar. "Oh! The Christmas bazaar? Sorry, I totally forgot to respond, it must have been a crazy day at work. What was it you needed help with?"

As the main sponsor of the annual Lenox Christmas Bazaar, Davis was in charge of organizing the volunteer staff for Santa's Village.

"I need you to be my wife."

The puppy nearly slipped out of my hold. *What?*

He laughed freely. "Sorry, but I've been waiting to use that line all week." He bumped my shoulder with his. "Actually, I just need you to play my Mrs. Claus for the day."

"Uh . . ." I'd imagined helping kids with crafts or handing out cookies at the entrance. Not playing his make-believe spouse.

"Willa, come on. I'll take care of everything. All you need to do is wear the costume and show up."

I thought of my new anti-fear motto, the one Patrick had inspired: *Say yes before thinking of all the reasons to say no.* "Okay, fine. I'll do it."

"Great." His near-perfect smile brightened his entire countenance— a man as attractive on the outside as he was on the inside. "I knew I could count on you." He checked his cell phone for the time. "I should probably go check for the pizza guy. Wanna help the kids wash up?"

"Sure thing."

He started for the door and then turned back. "Hey, Willa?"

"Yeah?"

"I think you'll be the prettiest Mrs. Claus this town has ever had."

He winked before pushing out the door, and I waited for a flip or a flutter or a spark . . . But instead, I felt a not-so-gentle nudge. From my head to my heart.

Davis could offer me a future. Love. Commitment. Family. While the man who invaded my thoughts, the man on his way back to my house this afternoon, the man who gave me all the feels . . . could promise me nothing more than today.

Chapter Twenty-Four

A black sedan sat in my driveway, no driver in sight.

When I parked to the side of it, Savannah, in the backseat with Prince Pickles, perked up. "Isn't that Dr. Patrick's car?"

An electric current traveled up my spine. "Yes."

I opened her door and Prince Pickles jumped from her lap and hopped through the freshly fallen snow like a jackrabbit. I waved them onto the front porch, glancing around the property for Patrick.

As Savannah turned the knob to go inside, Patrick rounded the corner between my parents' house and mine, an armful of dry firewood from the woodshed cradled to his chest.

He halted. "You're home." Shimmering flecks of ice clung to the thicket of his hair.

"So are you, it seems—" A laugh slipped through my lips. "I mean, at my home. You're at my home." My cheeks flushed. *Stop talking. Stop talking now.*

Patrick's face broke into an ethereal grin.

When he shifted the load in his arms, I raced up the five porch steps and held the door open for him to enter.

"Thanks," he said.

"I'm pretty sure I should be the one thanking you." *Again.* "You didn't have to do that."

He set the firewood in the steel bucket near the hearth, splinters and wood chips frozen to the sleeves of his dark jacket. "And *you* didn't have to make me brownies."

I crinkled my forehead. "Brownies? But I didn't make you . . ."

He cocked his head in my direction, mischievousness dancing in his eyes.

Laughter bubbled up my throat. "Ah . . . I see. Firewood for brownies? And is this payment expected tonight?"

"I don't mind sticking around."

I didn't mind having him stick around either. "Okay, I'll go rummage through my mom's pantry in a minute."

Savannah plopped on the couch nearby, Prince Pickles glued to her hip. "Guess what we did today?" She ruffled the fur between her dog's ears.

Patrick swiveled and dropped to his haunches. "Um . . . let's see. You met a mermaid?"

"What? No." She was lost to a fit of giggles. "Mermaids don't come out in the winter. Everybody knows that."

I bit my bottom lip as Patrick tried his best to keep the chuckle from his voice. "Hmm . . . yes, I forgot about that. So, did you run to the store? Stock up on winter hibernation snacks?"

"Nope. We saw puppies." Eyes rounded and full of wonder, she held out her arms. "A whole basket full of them. And they were the cutest things ever. Mr. Davis said we could come back anytime and play with them."

Patrick stiffened, his gaze a slow-moving bullet, its accuracy rate 100 percent. My chest thudded upon impact.

"Did he? How nice." His level of enthusiasm hovered at zero.

Despite my mental pleas for her to stop sharing, Savannah continued on with her puppy-dog story time. "Yep. And he bought us pizza, too. Brandon and I love pepperoni and pineapple. It's what we get every time."

Patrick's hand roved along the back of the sofa, stopping at Rex's journal. He tapped the cover with his fingernail. "Sounds like a winning combination."

The hard edge I detected in his voice made me doubt he was still speaking about pizza toppings.

"So." I clasped my damp palms together. "About those brownies—"

"Brownies?" Savannah bounced on the cushion. Prince Pickles barked at the abrupt change in atmosphere. She patted his head. "Sorry, buddy, too bad you can't have those. They're so yummy."

I pointed toward my parents' house. "I'll just be a second next door if you don't mind hanging out?"

The faintest of smiles tugged at his mouth. "I don't plan on leaving"—he paused, and my heart paused, too—"without one."

Per the thermometer nailed to the banister on the back porch, the temperature had dropped eight degrees since Patrick sauntered into my house with an armful of wood. Yet I was about one minute away from combustion.

A bead of sweat rolled down the planes of my stomach. Maybe it was the blazing fire in the hearth, or maybe it was the preheated oven two steps to my right, or maybe it was the fact that Patrick had said so little during the cracking and the whisking and the pouring of brownie batter. Instead, he'd just watched me, studied me, contemplated me as if an entire conversation were going on inside his head. Chin resting on his fist, he sat at the breakfast bar across from the sink. His gaze seared through my back.

I silenced the buzzer on the oven, slid the soupy concoction onto the middle rack, and let the door snap shut.

"I'll be right back." And then I tore down the hall to my room and stripped my sweater over my head. Relief was instantaneous, like a plunge in the river on a hot summer day.

I flapped my arms to circulate airflow and then flipped my head, twisting my hair into a topknot. After taking a quick inventory of the shirts in my closet, I sagged against the door. Sweatshirts, thermals, fleeces, jackets . . . The thought of pulling on another long-sleeve top made me queasy.

I yanked open the second drawer of my dresser and rummaged through panties, bras, and wool socks until . . . a black tank top. How it had survived the Great Winterization of my wardrobe two months ago, I had no idea—but I certainly wasn't about to complain about the oversight. It was either wearing this tank top or serving hot brownies in the snow.

As I tugged it over my head, the thin, ribbed fabric was a cool kiss against my smoldering skin. Not that I was thinking about kisses. Because I wasn't. I was thinking about brownies. *Only* brownies.

Hair off my neck, arms exposed, I stepped back into the hall. I quieted my steps when I heard my daughter discussing the finer points of art with Patrick.

She'd claimed the stool next to him, a coloring book spread wide on the bar and a pink crayon in her hand. Apparently she was teaching him her award-winning technique.

"You need the orange now," she bossed.

"Ah, got it." He selected a crayon from the box. "Now what?"

"Now trace the outside lines, like this. You try." She slid the book to him and he obeyed.

I tiptoed behind them, peering over his right shoulder, watching him color the way she'd instructed.

"I'd give you an A."

Patrick swung his head around and then blinked. His orange crayon snapped in two. "You changed." A statement. Not a question.

I tried to shrug off the observation, as if it were perfectly normal to wear summer attire during a snowstorm. I couldn't exactly tell him the truth, that his presence made global warming feel trite.

"My mommy's a teacher again, but she only has one student. Alex." Savannah practically sang the announcement.

"Not a teacher, a tutor—"

"Yeah? I may have heard about that." Patrick steamrolled my comment, his eyes pinning me against the back counter. "I bet she's a great teacher."

"Tutor," I corrected again.

"Yep. She is. Alex told me so." Savannah outlined the hair of her favorite Disney princess in bright purple. Channeling her inner Alex, it would seem.

Patrick's confident smile could melt through bone. "The best teachers are kind, patient, understanding—oh, and they're usually really great at baking brownies, too."

A blush crept up my neck and filled in my cheeks like the shading of a crayon on a blank page. "You don't even know if they're good yet."

"They will be."

Savannah closed her coloring book and picked up the crayons scattered on the countertop. Patrick reached for the box, but before he could shove the bottom half of the orange into the sleeve, she snatched it away.

"Mommy says you can't put broken crayons back into the box."

"Well . . . it's a good thing I like orange, then."

"Yep." Savannah collected the rest of her art supplies and then twisted off the stool to strut down the hallway toward her room.

Patrick held up his sad-looking piece of pumpkin-colored wax. "So, what should I do with this, O Great Rule Maker?"

I shook my head. "Stop."

He pushed back from the breakfast bar and came into the kitchen. "Perhaps Miss Organization has a special banishing place for these unfortunate misfit crayons?" He pulled open a drawer at the farthest end of the cabinet. "Nope. Not in there."

I laughed in earnest as he reached for the next one. "Not here, either. Although your arrangement of Tupperware lids is the neatest I've seen."

He worked his way down the row of cabinetry, getting closer and closer to the corner near the sink—where I happened to be standing. I threw a yellow dishrag at his head.

Too bad his reflexes were superhuman.

He tossed it back onto the counter with a smirk. "A teacher with some spunk. My favorite kind."

Arching an eyebrow, I scraped the inside of the batter bowl with a red rubber spatula and cocked it back. "Don't take another step closer or—"

"I wouldn't make threats you don't intend to keep."

"Good thing spunk and follow-through are a team." But before I could catapult the batter, Patrick's fingers hooked around my wrist.

He squeezed just enough to loosen my grip, just enough to secure his hold, just enough to prove that I was no longer the one in control.

The pressure of his hip against the curve of my waist restricted my next breath. The earthy scent of firewood that clung to his sweater mingled with the sugary sweetness of the batter that dripped onto my knuckles.

A rogue curl draped over his right temple, threatened to block my view of the half-moon scar shadowed by his hairline. In the dim light, it looked nearly silver, a shimmery sort of iridescence that should be saved for ethereal beings . . . but then again.

The pulse point at my wrist ticked harder beneath the pressure of his grip. The warning look in his eyes was like a lit fuse at the end of a firework. He wouldn't be the one to pull back. And neither would I.

With the slightest tilt of his chin, he leaned forward and licked the end of the spatula.

My knees liquefied.

Strong and solid, his free hand snaked around to the small of my back and kept me from sliding down the cabinets.

His chocolaty exhale sucked the air from my lungs, but I no longer cared about oxygen. I cared only about his lips—how they'd taste. How they'd feel. How they'd move against mine.

A silent plea and then his mouth dipped—

The splat of the spatula smacking against the tile floor was the gunshot that broke our trance.

Patrick jerked back and my arm fell to my side, weightless and numb.

The thump in my chest, the heat in my face, the boom, boom, boom in my ears . . . it was all too much.

I spun around and braced myself against the hard edge of the sink. I flipped on the water and began to pump soap into the batter bowl like I was fueling a gasoline tank.

"Hey, Mommy—" The pattering of little feet halted. "Whoa . . . there's a big mess on the floor." She continued without missing a beat, "When are the brownies gonna be done?"

Out of the corner of my eye, I watched as Patrick picked up the forgotten spatula from the floor.

"In a minute." The voice that came out could have been from an animated film—mousy, strained, not fit for real life.

Patrick slid the wicked utensil into the sudsy water as I submerged my hands, wishing I could submerge my head.

He's leaving. He's leaving. He's leaving.

I needed to brand those words on my forehead. Sear them onto my heart. Patrick was only real for a few more weeks. And then he would be gone. No more snowmobiling, or ballroom dancing, or kite flying in the park. And there would certainly be no more batter licking.

"I can't reach the puzzles in my closet."

As I grabbed for the towel on the counter, Patrick touched my arm.

"I'll get them down for her."

I nodded, too afraid to leave my post. Too afraid to face him. Too afraid to think about what tomorrow or the day after or the day after that might bring. *I'd* asked for his help. *I'd* invited him into the most vulnerable pockets of my life.

And yet I couldn't even control the most basic of instincts. I couldn't control the wandering of my heart.

Patrick walked back into the kitchen just as the buzzer for the brownies went off.

I set the hot pan atop the stove. "Cooling just takes a few minutes."

The brownies, that is. Not my heart. That would take much, much longer.

"You know, maybe I should take one for the road. We can discuss the journal tomorrow." He was yards away from me now, standing on the opposite side of the kitchen. Still he felt too close. I wondered if he felt the same? "Can you find someone to watch Savannah for you tomorrow, after work?"

I thought for a moment—*Monday*. My parents would be home in the morning, our routine back to normal. At least for the most part. "I think so."

"Okay. I cleared my schedule to be off by four. I'll pick you up."

"Where are we—"

"Part of the lesson is the surprise."

"I hate surprises."

"I know."

Despite myself, the corner of my mouth twitched. "Fine."

I cut his brownie and handed it to him on a folded paper towel.

He glanced toward the fireplace as I followed him to the entryway, as if checking to make sure it was stoked enough for the night. It was.

I opened the door for him and shuddered at the cold blast of air. "'Night."

He hesitated, a shadow draping his face as he looked back at me. No, not a shadow. A frown. The first one I'd ever seen him wear.

I hoped it would be the last.

"Dress warmly tomorrow," he said. "We'll be outside."

Without another word I shut the door and pressed my forehead to the frame.

Chapter Twenty-Five

Considering that the sky had dumped three inches of snow the night before, today seemed uncharacteristically temperate. Birds chirped from nearby treetops and clouds stretched like thinning wisps of cotton. Squinting, I shielded my eyes from the reflection of sun on the slush.

I lagged several paces behind Patrick.

I didn't know what bothered me more, that what happened last night hadn't been acknowledged, or that his idea of a "surprise adventure" was my idea of a nightmare.

"You coming?" Arms out wide, he pivoted and tromped backward through the melting snow.

I stopped to tuck my pants further into my boots. "Haven't decided yet."

"Will this delightful mood of yours be with us for the rest of the evening?"

I snapped my eyes to his. "Were you really expecting me to be overcome with joy when you pulled up to Cougar Mountain?"

He seemed unfazed by my sarcasm. "You told me you were ready."

I planted my feet. "I also told you I despised heights." I took a breath and tried to contain my irritation. "Can't we just pass this lesson and move on to the next one?"

He inched toward me and then halted in his steps. "There is no next one." He gestured to the brown sign at the start of the trailhead. "This is it, sweetheart."

A rush of icy awareness prickled the skin at the base of my neck. This couldn't be it. Climbing a mountain wasn't the way to kill my fear. It was the way to kill *me*. "Wait—" I held out my hand and stared at the incline ahead. "What about the journal? What about Rex's—"

"There's no point in filling the time we have left by hopping from place to place, not when this one location represents everything you need to face."

The time we have left. The sting of those words distracted me from the sickness in my gut. My gaze flicked again to the switchback. "How far do we have to climb?"

"Wrong question."

I gritted my teeth. *Savannah. Savannah. Savannah.* Her name was a pulse beat, a thunderous boom inside my head. Sure, I needed to be brave for myself, too, but if it were just about me, I would turn tail and head home right now.

"We'll take it one step at a time. Stop looking at the peak and focus on the trail."

Now *that* sounded like Rex. I'd spent most of last night flipping through the yellowed pages, reading his scribbles, notes, and scriptures. And the more I read, the more I thought the man a saint. He truly was fearless—courage for blood.

I swallowed the tight knot in my throat and willed my knees to unlock and bend. Patrick forged ahead, not waiting for my first step. I contemplated chucking a snowball at his back—or better yet, at the bare skin near the bottom of his hairline. But with the extra distance he'd put between us today, playing in the snow felt as lethal as asking for a piggyback ride.

Three steps past the park sign he slowed, which likely had more to do with my snail's pace than his need for my company.

"Tell me about teaching," he said.

"What?" I glanced to my left, to the incline shrouded by trees. No open spaces. No dizzying view. *I'm fine. I'm fine. I'm fine.*

"Teaching. Tell me about it."

"Um." I kept my eyes down, one step and then another. The ground beneath me was soft and wet, squishing like mud through open fingers. "I only taught for a year."

"Do you miss it?"

The question seemed to echo through the wooded path, filling my mind with images I'd tried to replace a thousand times: the smell of pencil shavings and paper and the sounds of happy voices and whispers in the hall. "Some days." A half-truth. "Do you think you'll miss working at your dad's clinic?"

Out of the corner of my eye, I watched him breathe a steady stream of white. It curled around us both. "Some days."

There was a slight incline ahead and my boots were already sodden and heavy. Maybe if I stayed tucked in the shadows, hugged against the mountain on my right, I wouldn't feel the elevation. If I couldn't see the drop-off, I'd never have to look down. My stomach swooped low at the thought, and then my next step snagged on a branch.

Patrick reached out and gripped my elbow. He let go the instant I had my footing again.

"Thanks," I said shakily. "How . . . how are your folks doing in Scotland?"

If I was going to survive the next ten feet, he needed to keep talking.

"I talked to my dad this morning, actually. They've just secured a nice home for my grandmother. Thinking they'll be back sometime mid-December." He glanced at me. "A change of pace and scenery is always good for the soul."

"Okay, Rex." I'd read those very words last night.

He laughed. "That was your first pop quiz."

"So, I decide which words are from you and which are from the journal?"

His smile was answer enough.

"Good thing for you I have a photographic memory." A lie.

"Good thing for me I do, too."

Of course he did.

I rolled my eyes, careful to keep my balance on the uneven terrain. "Your professors probably loved you."

"Winning the affection of my professors was fairly low on my list of priorities back then. My focus was wholly on not killing my patients."

"That's encouraging."

A giant boulder blocked the path, and for the briefest of moments I was certain I'd just passed the test. My face must have shone with delight as I whirled my attention from the rock to Patrick.

"This is it? I finished?"

For some reason he didn't seem dazzled by this show of bravery. "You finished the prehike, yes. But *that*"—he stepped to the side to reveal my erroneous conclusion—"is the trail to the top."

My legs, my head, my stomach. Everything felt woozy.

The passage on the other side of the boulder was open and rocky and utterly exposed. Even with layers of dripping snow, the contrast in terrain was stark: steep and narrow and curved. The tightening in my chest and the tingling in the tips of my fingers were nothing compared to the trembling of my legs. I could no sooner walk a tightrope than step foot on that trail.

"I can't—"

"We're not going farther today."

Relief covered me like heat from a flame, yet Patrick made no attempt to turn around. If anything, his stance looked more solid than it had seconds ago.

My breath came out in quick white puffs. "Is this a trick? Some kind of reverse psychology technique? Like by you *not* encouraging me to go farther, I'll magically realize that I've held the power inside me to conquer my fear of heights all along?"

The corner of his mouth twitched and then he said, "Yep. That's it exactly. You just blew my whole plan. Guess I should stop taking those Disney movies so literally."

I looked beyond him again and focused on the ledge. I could see myself there, grappling for the loose rocks, slipping off the pathway, dangling from the cliffside.

My world tilted on itself.

The boulder in front of us was twice my height and ten times my width. A safe haven. I reached for it, pressed my back to the uneven surface, closed my eyes. *Count with me.* I could hear Patrick's words in my head, yet I couldn't tell if they were real or remembered. I pulled in breath to fill my belly and then exhaled through my nose.

"I went to the Philippines after a typhoon hit."

I lolled my head to the side, and he was there next to me, staring out at the pine trees, his face irritatingly peaceful.

"It was my first time on a disaster relief team. And when we got there, our supplies and inflatable hospital seemed vastly insignificant compared to the need. We'd work until we couldn't see straight, over-whelmed and exhausted by the lines of people that never seemed to decrease."

I studied the slow rise and fall of his chest.

"I would go to bed each night with a pounding headache, doubting my abilities as well as my calling."

"To aid in disaster relief?" I couldn't picture Patrick ever second-guessing himself.

He held my gaze for less than a second before focusing again on the branches overhead. "To work in health care. To go abroad." He blew out a long breath. "All of it."

Cold seeped through my skin and into my bones, but I craved Patrick's voice more than warmth.

"I was there for over a month before I realized the source of my doubt." He rolled onto his shoulder, his breath like a feather against my cheek. "Everything in my life up until that point had a tangible end. A goal. Passing a test, graduating from med school, getting a fellowship. But it wasn't until I was dropped into the middle of a crisis that I was forced to deal with the chaos in here." He touched his temple. "I couldn't just push past the hardship or clock out at the end of a workday. I woke up in the chaos and I went to bed in it, too. My only choice was to pray for a way to make peace with it. And for me, that meant redefining what it meant to succeed. And what it meant to fail."

"Fail?" The word squeezed from my chest. It was hard to believe that word existed anywhere in his mind. "You risked your life going there, working for people you didn't even know. That's nothing short of heroic."

"Heroes aren't made on the field. They're made in the mind."

"Rex again."

"Good." He winked. "It's easy to get overwhelmed when we can't see the end . . . but this mountain is far more mental than it is physical. I don't care if you ever take a step past this boulder." He pressed a palm to the rock at the side of my head, his gloved fingers digging in like claws. "This chaos inside you—what you *feel* when you look out at that ledge, what you felt when Savannah was on the snowmobile with your brother . . . and maybe even the reason behind why you won't teach full-time again. Figure out what the chaos is, Willa. You won't be able to find peace until you do."

His words sunk to a place within me I couldn't even name.

"Make peace." My lips trembled but I realized my heart rate was as calm as Patrick's face.

I'd grown so accustomed to the static in my ears, the choke hold around my throat, the barbed wire that cut through the lining of my stomach at the onset of an attack—so used to the chaos—that I'd stopped searching for peace long ago.

I shivered and hugged my arms to my chest. "Your photographs . . ."

"Yeah?"

"They capture that—peace, I mean. It's why I love them so much."

His chest hitched in a breath two full seconds before he pushed away from the rock. "We should head back down. Your lips have turned purple."

For the briefest moment, his hand pressed to my lower back, ushering me toward the trail. And then, like a whisper lost on a winter breeze, it was gone.

We walked in silence for several minutes.

"You willing to try this again?" he asked.

Three steps.

That was all it took for me to answer.

"I'm willing."

Chapter Twenty-Six

I saw my brother—or at least, I saw his name on the open gym sign-in sheet. The same way I'd seen it every day for the past two weeks.

Arrived at 6:03 a.m. Gone by 7:37 a.m.

His signature was scrawled right under Patrick's—messy and nearly illegible. He probably wrote it half asleep, his hooded sweatshirt tugged over his eyes, his fingers drumming against the counter.

But I wouldn't know for sure. Because our passing on the street, in the checkout line at Gigi's Grocery, or in my parents' driveway without either of us stopping to say hello didn't lend well to patching up the holes between us.

Nor did my inability to pick up the phone and call him.

"Gross. Why are you drinking that? It smells like lawn clippings."

I tossed the Dixie cup into the trash can under my desk and shuddered. Alex was absolutely right. It didn't just smell like lawn clippings, it tasted like them, too.

"Sydney thinks these free samples might increase sales."

Alex scanned the green smoothie display table and scrunched up her nose. "Yeah, well, she also thinks it's a good idea to order microwavable Tofurky off the Internet and call it a *Thanksgiving meal*, too." She added air quotes and rolled her eyes. "Looks like I'll be eating frozen pizza again this year."

It took me all of two seconds to realize she was serious. "No." I shook my head. "You won't. You can eat with us. Sydney's invited, too." Though her presence would make for a very interesting dynamic, I couldn't bear the thought of anyone spending the holidays alone.

"She won't come." She cranked her finger near her temple. "She invited her hoity-toity vegan book club over, which is like sitting in the middle of crazy town—"

I pulled her arm down, hoping the folks wandering through the lobby hadn't overheard. Naturally, this only made her volume increase.

"It's true." She stood her ground as if I were questioning her accuracy and not her antics. Usually I was questioning both. "If I have to hear about how eating a spoonful of hemp a day can cure constipation, then—"

"Okay, I get it. We usually eat around one. Come over to my parents' house whenever you want—just make sure it's alright with Sydney, okay?"

Despite her new fondness for black-winged eyeliner, I could still see her eyes brighten. "Really? Okay. Thanks. I'll bring . . . something."

"Just bring yourself. That will be plenty." I could easily picture Alex sitting at my parents' table—the energy she would bring to the family gathering and . . .

And then I thought of someone else.

What if things with Weston aren't fixed by Thanksgiving?

Alex snapped her fingers in front of my face. "Uh, hello? Where'd you go?"

"Nowhere. Have you done a locker room check yet?" It was supposed to be Alex's first task when she arrived at the fitness center in the afternoons. Given that the school had agreed to community credit for her time here, my extra prodding was completely justified. "And don't let me forget to look over your history quiz when you come over tonight."

"Sure thing, boss lady." She turned away and moseyed down the hall, her boots squeaking against the polished lobby floors.

The phone rang, followed by the flashing of its red light.

I picked up the receiver and watched as two middle-aged men tried the smoothie samples. They sipped, frowned, and tossed the cups in the trash. Not fans apparently. "Parker Fitness Center, how may I help you?"

"Is this Willa Hart?" The woman's voice was young and familiar, yet I couldn't quite place it.

"Yes, this is she."

"Willa? It's Megan Hudson."

Savannah's teacher.

I stood, knocking the chair back several feet. A cold fear swept down my spine. "Is everything okay?"

"Oh, yes. I'm sorry. Savannah's just fine. I didn't mean to bother you at work; it's just that my class is out for recess and, well, I haven't shared this publicly yet . . . but I'm expecting."

I blinked, trying to clear the haze from my brain. "A baby?"

"Twins, actually." Her laugh was airy and light. "I'm due sometime in late April."

"Twins? Wow, congratulations." I'd known Megan since high school, but our interaction was limited to Savannah's weekly progress reports and my volunteer mornings at her school on Tuesdays.

"Thank you. I'm not sure what your plans are, Willa, but I know how hard it is to break into the system for Lenox Elementary and I just thought . . . well, with the news of Savannah's good health and all, you might like me to put your name in as my maternity sub. I've already checked with Principal Schultz and there's no policy against teaching in the same classroom as your child. I'm planning to go on early leave in February and need to give the district thirty days' notice . . ."

She went on but I was only able to comprehend every other word. I turned my back to the front door, trying to create a privacy bubble. In a lobby twice the size of my house, it wasn't easy.

My pulse thundered in my ears.

"And if all goes as planned, I'd love to job-share my classroom next year. Maybe teach just a couple days a week. You'd be a top candidate for the position if you took the sub job, and of course we could lesson plan together—that is, if you're even interested." She laughed again. "Sorry, I'm just excited."

"No, no . . . I understand why you would be." I bit my bottom lip. "When . . . uh . . . when would you need to give the district my name?"

"I'd need to put your name in before the start of Christmas break, and then you'd just need to make sure your teaching license is current before next year."

It wasn't, but I could take the test at any time. A scramble of dates filled my head. Three weeks. She'd need to give them my name in three weeks.

Why was I even asking her for a date?

Of course I couldn't take it. Teaching would take too much of my focus—too much time away from Savannah. But then again, subbing the remainder of this school year would put me in her classroom, and job-sharing next year would mean I'd see her in the halls and . . .

"Well, I need to think on it," I said, my voice wavering with indecision.

"Sure, sure, of course. I figured you'd need time to sort out your schedule."

And my head.

The scooting of chairs and chattering of children swirled in the background.

"Oh! My class is back. We'll catch up soon, then?"

"Yes. Thank you, Megan." I set the receiver down.

A melodious *Oooh* sounded behind me.

I whirled around to see Alex wagging her eyebrows. "Did you just get propositioned for a *job*? While you're at work? Scandalous."

This was bad. No, this was worse than bad.

The nape of my neck grew hot and sticky.

"Who's Megan?" she asked.

"No one."

She rolled the empty mop bucket in front of her and pointed the long wooden mop handle at her mouth. "Willa has a secret." She sang the words, actually sang them.

The girl was losing her mind.

"Stop." I waved my hand in the air, knowing full well that she would do no such thing without some kind of incentive—or in this case, without information. "I need a minute to think, Alex."

A head tilt, followed by batting eyelashes. "I'm a very, very good keeper of secrets."

I slapped a hand to my forehead and slowly slid it down my face. The only person in the world who would be worse to tell about this than Alex was my brother.

Regret sloshed in the pit of my belly at the thought of him.

"It's . . . an opportunity. That's all. And I don't think I'm interested."

Her eyebrows dipped. "What kind of opportunity?"

No. I would absolutely not discuss this with her. "I'm not really at liberty to say."

"So, it really *is* a job opportunity, then?" If I didn't know what I knew about Alex's less-than-ideal history, I would scold her for prying. But something about the way she asked—the openness in her face—made me want to reassure her that I had no intention of leaving. Not the fitness center, and not her.

"Yeah. But don't worry. I don't have plans to go anywhere."

The light in her eyes dimmed, which was the exact opposite of what I'd expected. "Worry? Why would I worry about you leaving? You don't belong here." She shot a look over her shoulder and glanced up the stairs to her half sister's office. "Why do you think Syd lets you work your weird hours—or trusts you to run this joint when she's out of town? Because she knows what everyone else knows . . . you're better than this place. If you have a better opportunity, you should take it."

Though her words were harsh and, well, Alex-like, the rare vote of confidence felt like a gift.

"Don't get all teary-eyed over it. I'm just being real."

"Exactly. You're just *being real.* A quality I hope you never lose."

A blush crept into her cheeks and she shrugged.

"Just . . . please don't say anything to anyone about this. Okay?" I needed her to understand that keeping this quiet was important to me, even if I couldn't explain why.

"About what?" She smiled over her shoulder and steered her mop bucket back down the hallway.

Chapter Twenty-Seven

For the second time in three weeks, I flipped to the last page of Rex's journal. There was no date, no pictures, no knickknacks taped to the inside. Just a final scripture verse: *We can make our plans, but the Lord determines our steps. Proverbs 16:9.*

I pressed a pink Post-it Note to this final page and copied the verse down for reference. The way I'd done countless times before.

Since my first pass through its weathered pages, something about the journal weighed heavy on my conscience. Like a bone-deep bruise that had faded on the surface, Rex's words seemed to ache from somewhere within me. His adventures, his stories, his Solomon-like wisdom were all beautifully strung and woven; they magnified a life lived to the fullest. So why then did I feel so unsettled?

Thoughts of Rex's journal stayed with me as I helped my mother prep for tomorrow's big feast. Sweet potato soufflé, green bean casserole, homemade rolls—Mom knew how to plan for Thanksgiving.

I checked the time, wiped my hands on a lace-trimmed dishrag, and then kissed the top of Savannah's head. Darting out the front door the second Patrick's car pulled into the shared driveway was pretty much the only way to avoid awkward small talk between my parents and my . . . friend.

I squeezed my mother's shoulder. "I'll come grab Savannah when we get back from the mountain. I promised she could help me bake a pie tonight."

"You two have been doing a lot of hiking lately." My mother's tone was forcibly light, a measurement of curiosity and concern.

I slipped on my coat and then pushed back the curtain on the living room window. No Patrick yet. "Yes." Eight trips to the same boulder on Cougar Mountain, to be exact. "And I really appreciate you watching Savannah."

"Of course." She tightened the straps on her apron. "I just never realized you enjoyed the outdoors so much."

I peeked again at the empty driveway. "Well, you know what they say about the benefits of fresh air." *Although fresh air is hardly the only benefit . . .*

The uncharacteristic pause in conversation had me glancing back over my shoulder. Everything about my mother's probing gaze led me to suspect that a safety lecture was near, only she said nothing more.

Patrick's car rolled into the driveway. With a quick good-bye, I let the curtain swoosh from my hand and then reached for the doorknob.

When I was three steps into the cold, she called my name.

I turned, fully expecting a talking-to on the dangers of hiking at dusk. Yet once again, my mother surprised me.

"Just . . . be careful, Willa."

It wasn't until I slipped into the passenger seat of Patrick's car that I realized her warning had nothing to do with hiking at all.

The sun was on its last blink, a showgirl's lash line of explosive colors: pinks, violets, and shimmery golds. It dipped under the tree line as we tromped our beaten path to the fork in the trail. The boulder marked not only a physical blockage but a mental one, too.

"We need to pick up the pace." It was the second time Patrick had mentioned our speed since we started the hike. Of course, he couldn't exactly re-create the sunset if he missed his chance at a shot tonight. His camera equipment was tucked safely inside his backpack—gear I'd organized and labeled for him just last night.

I pushed myself harder, lengthening my stride. "I never thanked you for what you did for Alex last night." Patrick had been so patient with her, showing her camera settings and allowing her to take a few practice shots so she could play with focus and aperture.

"I didn't know she was interested in photography until she started asking questions."

I stepped over a half-buried rock. "Alex will take an interest in anything or anyone who is willing to take an interest in her."

"Like you have."

I smiled. "And now you, too."

Patrick fell quiet again, much the way he'd started tonight's hike. The crunch of snow beneath our boots was the only sound to be heard. I didn't like it.

"How many sunsets have you photographed?" It seemed like an obvious question, one I should have asked him weeks ago, but the gear on his back made me curious about every sky he'd ever seen, every shot he'd ever taken.

"Not sure. Hundreds probably."

"And you really don't have a favorite?"

"Any sunset from the top of a mountain is . . ." He glanced down at me. "Special."

As we curved along the rock face, our arms swung in tandem. They found this rhythm often, though there hadn't been an accidental arm brushing since our first hike. Somehow he'd mastered the perfect calculation of distance: close enough to be of assistance, yet far enough away not to be touched.

His gaze swiped across my profile again. "You're too comfortable."

"What?" We stepped over a fallen tree limb that marked the last bend in the trail before the boulder.

"With this trail."

I twisted my mouth to the side. "Why do I get the feeling that you're not happy about that?"

"My *happiness* isn't why we do this."

"I know that."

He turned so quickly at the boulder I was forced to take a step back. I knew what was coming. *What's the chaos, Willa? Can you name the chaos, Willa? How long will you let the chaos live inside you, Willa?* No matter how he spun it, that elusive question remained unanswered.

"Do you?" he challenged.

He glanced over his shoulder at the path I'd never once stepped foot onto. At the skyline I'd never seen up close.

He was losing the light—losing his shot.

"Just go, Patrick. I'll wait here."

The disappointment in his eyes stilled my breath. "Is that really what you want? To stay right here—you're satisfied with *close enough*?"

He'd gone off script, strayed from our normal routine at the boulder.

"I—"

"Ten steps," he said.

"What?"

He pointed to the path. "You are standing ten steps away from a front-row seat of one of God's most awesome wonders. Are you really gonna miss it?"

His words shook me like a snow globe.

"Patrick—"

"If I could take these last steps for you, I would. But I can't, Willa." He moved toward me and clamped his hands onto my shoulders.

"Every day can be as different as every sunset." His voice was as strained as the expression on his face. "You told me that. *You.* And it's time you believed it. Not for Savannah or for your family or even for me. For yourself."

He waited three heartbeats, and then he turned away from the boulder to start up the unknown path.

Patrick was halfway around the curve when I took my first step forward.

"One!" I shouted after him.

When he spun around, I wished I could have been the one with the camera. I wished I could have captured the awe on his face. But even without a photograph, I knew I would never, ever forget it.

"Two!" He countered with a smile.

The buzzing in my core increased as I took my next step, as if my body had only now just caught up with my brain.

"Three." I looked away from Patrick to a small patch of fir trees on my left. They were the last obstruction to block my view of the abyss below—or the inclined trek ahead. The crescent-shaped pathway stretched between my boulder . . . and the unknown.

A sliver.

The clearing Patrick promised was only a sliver from where I stood, yet the cliffside on the left—the stark drop—was gaping.

My legs felt like a blend of rubber and liquid.

Gone were the swooping branches. Gone were the protective shadows.

This trail was fully exposed. To light. To dark. To death.

"Willa." Patrick had backtracked several paces, his voice urging. "Four. You're on four."

I blew out a hard breath, allowed the pounding in my chest to propel me. "Four."

By step six, I'd crossed the middle of the arc.

By seven, Patrick's hair was bathed in golden light.

By nine, a peek at the horizon wrenched a gasp from my throat.

And on ten . . . on ten, Patrick clasped my hand and pulled me to his chest.

Warmth spread through every hollow of my body as his arms encircled me.

"That was—you are—amazing." Pride swelled in his voice.

He stroked my back and pressed his lips to the crown of my forehead.

In a single heartbeat, the weeks of calculated distance vanished. Memories I'd stored away of woodsy cologne, shallow breaths across my cheek, fingertips grazing over bare skin, overwhelmed me. The pull, the rush, the chemical reaction that sparked in my blood at his nearness . . . all of it had been as real as *this* moment.

"We don't have much time."

Must he remind me of that every day?

Patrick gripped my shoulders and rotated me slowly away from his body.

And toward the sun.

"You have to see this," he whispered.

Hand to my heart, my breath hitched as I tried for words. Only there were no words.

Just this thought: *Patrick was right. The real thing is so much better.*

Patrick retrieved his camera from his backpack and was lost behind his lens, snapping pictures of a view I could hardly accept as reality.

My entire town was on display, like one of those winter villages people set up during the holidays. Jonny's Pizza, the community theater, the high school, McCade Medical Clinic, my church, my home. All of it was lit by a backdrop of colors that made me never want to blink again—a wash of orange with undertones of red and yellow and a smear of pink so bright it could be neon.

This. This was on the other side of my fear.

I tilted my chin skyward and let the tears come.

Not even the tingly rush of unease spreading through my core and into each one of my limbs could taint this new feeling burning inside me. This undeniable, uncontainable, soul-deep free fall.

How many paths had I avoided in life? How many times had I been content to stop at "close enough"—too afraid to push ahead? Too afraid to let go?

Too afraid to give up . . . control.

The series of clicks beside me paused. I turned slightly, expecting Patrick to remark on the glorious scenery before us. Only Patrick wasn't staring at the town or the sunset or the skyline.

He was staring at me. Not at a single part of me . . . at the whole of me. As if he could see the very truth I'd only just discovered—the chaos that lived and breathed and ruled inside me.

"Control." A single whispered word that held more power over me than I'd ever admitted before. "I can't let go of it or . . ."

He lowered the camera to the center of his chest. "Or what?"

"The people I love get hurt. I get hurt." Two years of therapy and I'd never been able to simplify it into one cohesive thought. Until now.

"The 'people you love' meaning Chad and Savannah?" Patrick stayed where he was, but again I felt his stare radiate through my entire body.

I nodded, a familiar guilt playing tug-of-war with my soul.

"You told me Chad died of a cerebral aneurysm; how could you have—?"

"I'd been so busy with my master's and lesson planning for my classroom and preparing for a new baby that my time and focus were divided. When I got the call he'd collapsed that Thursday morning . . . I felt like I must have missed something. Some sign, or warning or . . . *something.*" The exact way I'd felt the day Savannah was diagnosed with cancer. "If I'd just paid better attention—"

He stepped toward me. "No, Willa."

I lifted my tear-filled eyes to him.

"Not even the most dedicated wife or mother on the planet has the ability to control life and death. There was nothing you could have done to save Chad—and nothing you could have done to prevent Savannah's cancer." He gripped my shoulder. "I'm not only saying that as a physician, I'm saying that as a man who lives under the same rule and authority as you do. As we all do."

There were so many things that had attracted me to Patrick McCade—his adventurous spirit, his kind heart, his patient determination—only none of that compared to the freedom that lived inside him. A freedom I was just starting to understand for myself.

I took a deep breath and then released it slowly. "My brother's right. I've been trying to play God."

Patrick gave me a lopsided smile. "That's a pretty huge responsibility for one person."

"I've believed for so long that if I shrank my world to a manageable size, focused solely on the people I love, weighed out each and every decision carefully enough, that I could avoid being caught unprepared. Only, instead of lessening my anxiety, I've made it so much worse." I studied the tips of my boots. "I must sound crazy."

"No." He removed his glove and rubbed his thumb across my cheekbone. His touch was as cool as my wind-chapped face. "You sound like a woman who's learning to let go. That's not crazy, it's courageous."

His finger traced the curve of my jaw, an intoxicating touch that made my heart ache for more.

His hand slipped away, and I knew by the look in his eye, and the shift in his stance, and the bob of his throat, that the inevitable was coming. He was about to say it was time to leave.

Only I wasn't ready to leave the mountaintop.

I wasn't ready for him to pack his bag, or slip on his gloves, or remind me once again of the one thing we couldn't escape.

Time.

I peeled off my glove and took his hand. My warm skin melted against the cold of his callused palm.

"Just a little longer," I said on a billow of white breath.

The rigidity in his posture warned me that he would pull away, retreat back to the calculated distance that had become our norm. But then his arm went slack and his face softened into that open look of moments before.

"Just a little longer," he repeated.

He wove his fingers though mine and then stared out once again at the fleeting light of a dying day.

A day we'd conquered. Together.

Savannah ran across the driveway from my parents' house the instant Patrick opened my car door.

"We gonna make pie now?" she asked, taking the house keys from my hand and hopping up the porch steps two by two.

"Of course."

"Um." She twisted around and pointed. "What's that on your head?"

"Oh." I laughed and unfastened the headlamp Patrick had let me borrow. "My night eyes."

"Hm. Cool." She unlocked the door and shot inside the house. "I'll find the recipe!"

I was on the top step of the porch before I realized that Patrick wasn't following me.

"I have an early morning at the food bank." His explanation didn't quite fit with his lack of eye contact. "Weston's working the early shift with me."

"Oh, right." *Weston.*

"You finally ready to talk to him?"

I pressed my lips together, knowing full well that what I'd admitted on the mountain tonight would mean having a much overdue conversation with my brother. "Yes. It's time. It's been time for a while, actually." I took a step down the stairs. "Wait—I thought you stayed clear of family drama?"

He found my eyes again and ran a hand through his hair. "Lenox has a way of messing with my head."

Patrick didn't move, but suddenly he felt very far away.

Savannah called for me again and I glanced back at the open door.

"So . . . I guess I'll see you tomorrow, then? My parents are looking forward to having you over for Thanksgiving." I tucked my hair behind my ear. "So am I."

A change in Patrick's face made me take another step toward him. "Hey . . . are you alright?"

He tugged at the back of his neck. "Yeah."

"Okay," I said, even though I was sure he wasn't. "Well, good night."

But before I could turn back to the porch, Patrick strode toward me, erasing the distance between us.

With a hug that lifted my feet off the ground, he wrapped his arms around me and buried his face in the crook of my neck. He held me so closely, so securely, that his heartbeat vibrated against my rib cage. And when I exhaled, his hold tightened, as if he were afraid I'd be the first one to let go.

I wouldn't have been.

Slowly, he eased my body down and moved to frame my face between his palms.

In the half second before he blinked, the torment in his expression stole my breath. "Good night, Willa."

He dropped his hands and turned away before I could process what had just happened between us. *What had just happened?*

Dazed, I watched him slip into his car and drive away.

It wasn't until his taillights receded that I realized for the second time tonight, his actions hadn't matched his words.

I rubbed the chill from my arms and climbed the steps to my front door. Alone.

Chapter Twenty-Eight

One of the benefits of owning an antique store was a plethora of décor options for my mom's Thanksgiving table. She started hunting for her themed treasures at least six months in advance, usually longer. This year's theme could be coined "rustic farmhouse."

Everything in sight was some variety of shabby chic: candleholders, place settings, napkin rings, and a birdcage centerpiece filled with miniature white pumpkins.

The aroma wafting from the kitchen—my father's prized turkey and the far-from-random selection of steaming side dishes—sent a tingling of anticipation throughout the house.

Yet even with all those distractions, it was hard to keep my concentration off the obvious. Across from me sat an empty plate with a place card that read: *Dr. Patrick McCade.*

Weston and my father took the head and foot of the table, while Alex, Savannah, and I sat across from Georgia, Nan, and my mother.

Where is he?

Nobody had asked this question aloud—at least not in earshot of me—so to ask it now, while the rest of the guests seemed unconcerned by his absence, would create more drama than my curiosity was worth.

I checked my phone under the table again. My text to him was unanswered.

As we bowed our heads to pray, I felt my brother's gaze burning through the top of my head. Did he know why Patrick wasn't here? If he did or he didn't, it wasn't like he was about to offer that information to me, not when the only words we'd spoken to each other so far had been an awkward "Happy Thanksgiving."

Dishes passed right, as if in a traffic circle. Mounds of gourmet foods were piled high on my mom's new-to-her china. Alex's contribution to the meal, a whipped-cream fruit salad, was the only thing Savannah had asked for a double helping of.

"What a delightful spread," Nan said, looking around at everyone. "I am so very thankful to be joining such a wonderful family by way of this upcoming union." She touched Georgia's back and winked at Weston. "And," she continued, "I'm also blessed to have met you, Alex."

Alex dabbed her mouth with the corner of her linen napkin. "Oh . . . um . . . thank you." She took a small sip of her cranberry cider and then smiled. It was hard not to laugh at the extra effort she was taking to be polite today.

Georgia gestured with a forkful of turkey, her gaze fixed on Alex. "I was telling Willa earlier about a dilemma I'm having at the theater. She thought maybe you could help."

"Me?" Alex glanced at me and then back to Georgia.

"Yeah. I'm casting for the spring production soon and I'm realizing that all my strong talent graduated last year. With the wedding coming up . . . my ability to search through the masses has been limited. Willa thought maybe you'd be interested in trying out? I've heard you have a to-die-for voice."

The pink in Alex's cheeks bloomed bright. She gave me a sidelong glance and then set her salad fork next to her plate. "I'm not interested."

I knew she'd be a hard sell, but who said peer pressure couldn't be used for good? Alex needed to use her gift. She had too big a talent to go to waste. "Alex, I'd be happy to take you."

Her look could chill boiling water. "No, thank you."

Time to go back to Georgia. "What day are the auditions?"

"Two weeks from today. Six o'clock," she answered.

Alex picked up her knife and sawed grimly at her turkey, though it was so moist it could have been eaten with a spoon. The screech against the porcelain plate caught everybody's attention as if she'd just screamed through a megaphone. "And what day are you supposed to give Megan an answer about the *opportunity*?"

I gave her a quick shake of my head, hoping it would silence her. Yet there was only one meaning to the look she gave me now: payback.

"Megan . . . Hudson?" Weston drawled out.

"Hey, that's my teacher's name!" Savannah said, her mouth stuffed full of whipped cream and fruit.

I swallowed, wishing myself a place under this table instead of at it. "Hmm-mm."

Weston set his glass down and I could practically hear the questions pinging in his head. I would bet a million dollars that the only thing keeping him from asking was pride. The same thing that had kept me from pulling him aside to apologize to him the second he'd walked into my parents' house that day.

The exact same reason I hadn't dared to ask him about Patrick. My eyes flicked to the empty place setting once more.

"It's nothing."

"Sure sounded like something if you asked me. Nothings don't come with a deadline." Alex leaned back in her chair, showing me once again just how comfortable she could be in confrontation.

"Alex," I warned.

"You're not thinking of subbing again, are you, sweetie?" My mother asked from the other side of the table. This was how she posed every question: no before yes, the negative before the positive.

The apple hadn't fallen far from the tree.

"And why shouldn't she? She has a degree. She should use it." These surprising words came from my estranged brother—apparently not even pride could keep him from offering his opinion.

"Don't talk to your mother like that, Weston," Dad piped in.

"She already has a job," my mother rebutted, as if I weren't sitting three seats down from them. "And that takes up plenty of her time as it is."

Alex's head swung left to right, taking in the action around our Thanksgiving table like she was watching a tennis match.

"I always thought you'd be a wonderful teacher," Nan said.

"She wants to give you a teaching job?" Alex asked, her eyes widening. "Take it, Willa. An untrained monkey could do your job at the gym."

"Agreed," Weston said, raising his glass to Alex.

I swung my gaze back to the end of the table and stared straight into the eyes of my brother—the traitor. "Seriously? *You* were the one who got me the job at the fitness center, remember?"

"Only because I hoped it would knock some sense into you. Get you around people again." He nodded at Alex and she beamed. "I never thought you'd stay there forever. Nor should you."

The mashed potatoes in my stomach turned to cement.

"I'm pretty sure there are far better topics to discuss on Thanksgiving than my employment." Cheeks hot, I steered my gaze back to Georgia. "*Please*, tell us how wedding details are coming along?"

The room sighed with the change of conversation. Georgia, Nan, and my mother chatted about the final arrangements. The dress fitting was coming up in a matter of days.

The next hour consisted of nothing but polite talk around the dinner table, wrapping up with a domino challenge between Alex and Savannah.

"I'll take care of the dishes today, Mom. You outdid yourself again," I said, giving my mom a kiss on the cheek. "Go relax and catch up with Nan."

Lord knew my dad would be asleep in his chair in less than ten seconds.

I heard a throat clear as I left the room, but I didn't turn around. I needed a private second to check my phone. Nothing new from Patrick.

"He's at the food bank until four."

I whirled around to see Weston standing behind me with an armful of dishes.

"Who?" I asked innocently. Stupid, sure, but I wasn't going to give him the satisfaction of being right.

He laughed and shook his head. "The man you're about to text. The same man you kept imagining was sitting across from you at the table today."

Sometimes I really hated that he knew me so well.

I turned back to the sink. *Why hadn't Patrick told me he wasn't coming?*

Weston set the plates on the counter beside me, stacking them way too high. My mom would kill him if she saw this leaning tower of fine china.

A big splat of gravy smacked against the tile floor near my heel.

"I've got the dishes. I don't need you to help me," I said.

"You've made that abundantly clear."

So we're doing this now? Fine. I grabbed my mother's red-and-white-checked apron and threw it over my neck, covering the jade-blue sweater dress I wore over black leggings. I'd shopped for the outfit last week—for a certain holiday dinner that a certain young doctor was supposed to attend.

"Funny how that reasoning never stopped you before."

He dumped a fistful of silverware into the murky sink water, splashing my face. "Maybe I'm learning to butt out where I should."

That was impossible to imagine . . . but then again, I had never imagined myself hiking a mountain before last month, so? I opened the dishwasher and slid my mother's cookware between the prongs.

"Is there really an opening at Lenox Elementary?"

I straightened, my face twisting into a mock smile. "Is this an example of how you butt out?"

"Key words, Willa: *learning to*." He cocked his head to the side and air-quoted the words. "But since you mentioned it, is this job offer another example of how *you* hide things from the people who love you?"

My hands shot to my hips. "No." Maybe. Probably. Yes.

He slapped the leftover green bean casserole into a Tupperware container and squished it down with a wooden spoon.

"That's not the right lid for that," I said, watching green ooze squish out the sides.

"Yet it still works, see?" He held the Tupperware up like a trophy. "Perfection is overrated."

"So are brothers."

He laughed and then sighed the sigh synonymous with surrender. "I should've asked you first—at the cabin. I shouldn't have taken Savannah up the mountain without your permission. I'm sorry."

"And I'm sorry for freaking out on you the way I did. You were right, Wes. About so much."

He stared at me without blinking. "I can see it, you know?"

"What?"

"How hard you've been working. I was wrong to say you haven't changed. You're not the same woman you were three months ago. And not even close to the same woman you were a year ago."

"I'm trying, Wes. I promise I'm trying. And not just for Savannah, but for me, too."

He opened the fridge and tossed in the misshapen Tupperware while I turned back to the murky sink water and grabbed a handful of silverware.

A hard tug on my hair.

"Ouch." I rubbed the sting out of my scalp with my dry hand and splashed him with my fistful of spoons.

"If you were Georgia I'd actually be scared right now. She has a talent for spoon throwing." Weston's crooked grin favored his right dimple.

"I've seen it in action, remember?"

He dragged a finger through a mound of Nan's homemade whipped cream and popped it in his mouth, then leaned back against the counter. I opened the top rack of the dishwasher and reached for a soapy drinking glass.

"He cares about you, Willa."

The spasm in my lower stomach caused my grip to weaken. The drinking glass plunged back into the soapy water.

"He said that?"

Weston dipped his head and shot me a look that said, "I'm a guy, I don't speak relationship." "Maybe you ought to take him some pie— you know, since it's Thanksgiving and he's been serving the needy all day."

"Another prime butting-out moment, I see?"

He pulled an invisible zipper over his mouth and then quickly unzipped it. "How 'bout I finish these up and then challenge Alex, Georgia, and Savannah to a domino war so you can take off and do some goodwilling of your own."

"Goodwilling? Really?" I asked with an eye roll.

I untied my apron and grabbed the pie Savannah and I had made the night before. "Thanks for watching Savannah for me."

As I wrapped the pie tin with plastic wrap, Weston laughed. "Uh, you might want to fix your hair before you take off. There may or may not be a piece of stuffing in the back."

With a violent shake of my head, a lump of mashed breading fell to the ground.

Brothers. They really were overrated.

Chapter Twenty-Nine

There wasn't a soul in Lenox who hadn't driven by the McCade estate and wished for an invite to teatime. Their property was located five miles past the fire station on the west end of town. The lush acres of farmland blanketed with snow were nearly as breathtaking as their view of the Cascade mountain range, but it was the house itself that was so coveted. Like a castle transplanted straight from the highlands of Scotland, the custom build looked stunningly authentic.

I parked in the driveway and my stomach somersaulted.

Only a man like Patrick would miss Thanksgiving to serve the needs of the community. The same kind of man who'd hiked a trail with me day after day, week after week, sacrificing not only his time but his sanity as well.

And then there was last night. The way he'd touched my face, held my hands, hugged me like he didn't want to let go.

I reached for the pie in the front seat and stepped out of the car, scanning the property.

Two stone turrets stood like bookends at the front corners of the house. The covered porch led to glass doors etched with a landscape I'd never seen in Oregon. My legs shook as the wind sliced through me.

My thin black leggings were hardly winterworthy, but at least my long sweater and ankle boots made up for their thin fabric.

I knocked on the glass and clicked my heels up and down to keep warm. After a full minute of waiting, I tried the bell. *In a house this size it must be difficult to hear a knock, right?* If he was upstairs in the library or downstairs in the wine cellar or even in a back bedroom somewhere taking a shower . . .

I shook my head, erasing the last thought entirely.

Headlights cut across the driveway.

It didn't matter that I was temporarily blinded by the slash of light, there was no doubt that the figure emerging from the car was the man I was most thankful for on this holiday.

"Willa?" Patrick trotted up the porch steps, his gaze dragging from my heels to my head. "Is everything okay—?"

"Happy Thanksgiving." *Was it possible to sound more eager?*

There was a stunned grace to his features as he took me in. "Happy Thanksgiving to you, too." His studied the plate of buttery goodness in my arms.

"You brought me a . . . pie?"

I nodded. "Everyone needs pie on Thanksgiving."

He stared without blinking and then moved to unlock the door. "Would you like to come inside?"

Yes! "You don't have plans tonight?" Again with the eager.

He held the door open, allowing me access to step past him.

"No." Before I could analyze the slight pause in his response, he took the pie from my hands. "Let me set this on the counter and go change. Unless you want to smell gravy all night." He pulled out his shirt to reveal a few soiled spots in the fabric, but all I could focus on was the phrase *all night*. Really, someone needed to spray me down with cold water. *What is happening to me?*

"Give me just a few minutes," he continued. "Feel free to look around at my parents', uh . . . museum."

"Okay." Although *okay* was a far cry from the roller coaster of giddiness going on inside me.

I turned my back to the staircase he climbed, feeling about a breath away from hyperventilating.

The house was a thousand times more impressive inside than I'd imagined. Just from the foyer I could see that each room was decorated with expansive canvases, colorful tartans, dueling swords, and Celtic art.

I clamped my lips together to keep from gaping. Every room was elegantly designed, but the hallway between the kitchen and dining room was my favorite—an entire wall was dedicated to Patrick's sunsets.

My chest tightened and my heart swelled to two times larger than normal.

Footsteps sounded behind me. "Ah, so this was your plan, then? You wanted to see me with braces and tragically bad hair." He stood at my side in jeans and a snug black thermal shirt. "I think my mum had a thing for the Scottish highlander look. Sadly, all of us rebelled against the shoulder-length locks before our tenth birthday. Dad took each of us to the barber while my mum cried at home."

I laughed and studied the picture to my right—Patrick and his three older brothers.

"Well, I like the length of your hair now." *Geesh, why not just tell him he's a beautiful human being, too?* "Um . . ." I cleared my throat. "Tell me about your brothers?"

Patrick humored me as we moved down the wall at a snail's pace. He pointed to each one of his brothers' photos and gave me an abbreviated account of their lives: marriages, children, what kind of medicine they practiced.

"Do you miss them?"

His answer wasn't immediate, but it was careful. "I've trained myself not to dwell on what I've left behind. Instead, I do my best to focus on the opportunity and task right in front of me."

Despite the twist of pain his words caused me, I pressed on. "When's the last time you saw them before covering for your dad?"

"I visit when I can between assignments—schedule my layovers on the West Coast since that's where everybody lives. My parents usually drive or fly up, too. Although I suspect my parents will start traveling more and more once my dad retires in a few years."

"I sort of hope he never retires," I confessed. "He's one of my favorite people here."

"You've mentioned that a time or two." His voice was teasing, but I knew he agreed with me. Ivar McCade didn't have an enemy in this world, and I was willing to bet Patrick didn't either.

"It's just . . . he has this way of making someone feel important—valued. I think that's part of what makes him such a great doctor. He's willing to invest in people's lives, not just in a ten-minute office visit. I've met a lot of doctors over the last two years and the contrast is stark. Your dad has a special gift." A gift I could so easily see in Patrick, too.

He propped himself against the wall with his shoulder. "I'm sure Lenox will always be their home base; they love it here."

What must Patrick's family think of his drifter lifestyle?

He pushed off the wall before I could ask him anything more, and showed me a picture of his grandparents' home in Scotland before meandering into the kitchen.

A massive slab of black-speckled, emerald-gray granite took up the majority of the space. My pie sat in the center.

Save for a messy collection of mail at the edge of an L-shaped counter, the room was immaculately clean. It opened into a quaint living area that looked surprisingly intimate given the size of the house.

"This kitchen is . . ." I ran my hand over the cold stone, searching for the right adjective.

"A great place to store three months' worth of mail?" He pointed to the pile at the side of the fridge.

"Spoken like a true bachelor."

This earned me a cheeky grin.

"Gorgeous," I finally said.

Patrick's gaze drifted down the length of me before he averted his eyes to the pie. "Did you make this last night?"

"Yes."

My answer put a crease in the center of his brow, though I hadn't the foggiest idea why.

"Something wrong?" I asked.

He blinked and did a quick scan of the cupboards and drawers. "I have no clue where to find a pie server in this kitchen."

He gestured for me to sit on the stool at the corner of the island, placing his stool adjacent. Our kneecaps brushed as we sat and something inside me trembled.

I pushed the tin toward him. "The pie's all yours, so I say you should eat it straight out of the pan."

A glint of mischief sparked in his gaze. "Spoken like a true rebel . . . which you certainly are not."

"Hey—you didn't know me in high school. I had more than a few rebellious moments, believe me."

That glint again. "Willa the Rebel. I'm picturing her now."

"You can stop."

He laughed and a sensation like feathers swept down my spine.

Patrick flicked the end of a fork so it spun like a compass. When the piece of fine silverware finally slowed to a stop, the prongs pointed at my chest.

"That's a pretty fancy party trick."

He pointed to the fork. "If I'm throwing manners out the window tonight, then so are you. Dig in."

"Deal."

His fork sank into the pie. "Did you know apple pie is my favorite?"

I nodded. "You said so at Nan's house, that night when . . ." *I yelled at you for agreeing to a "setup" that never happened.*

It was hard to believe how many moments we'd shared since that night two months ago—the bravery tests, the dinners, the hikes up Cougar Mountain.

His brilliant blue eyes met mine. "I remember that night well."

"I really wish you didn't."

The lightness of his chuckle had me leaning toward him, my elbows braced on the smudge-free island.

"I believe your exact words to me were, 'Forget this night ever happened, forget me,'" he said.

A silent exchange passed between us. His gaze dipped to my lips and for a moment I was certain he would kiss me, would slide the apple pie down the counter and take my face in his hands the way he had last night.

Foolishly or not, stupidly or not, I wouldn't have stopped him if he had.

"But I don't think that's possible."

I blinked him back into focus. "What?"

"Forgetting you."

His face sobered as he shoved a forkful of pie into his mouth. Then his eyes grew wide. "Mm. Amazing." The mumbled word warmed me as he pointed to the pan and shook his head. "Best I've ever had."

I smiled at his enthusiasm and took a small bite of my own. He was right, this might just be the best pie I'd ever baked. And why wouldn't it be? Patrick hadn't only inspired me to deal with my fears, he'd inspired me to enjoy my life. My baking hobby didn't quite compare with his extracurricular activities, but I was grateful I could share it with him.

With him. With this man with a wanderlust spirit, a do-gooder's heart, and a nomad's soul.

A new boldness—an aftereffect of last night's victory—stirred inside me, pushing against my chest. "Do you ever wish you had a place to land between your adventures abroad?"

He took another bite of pie and then set down his fork, his face apologetic. "I don't play wishing games, Willa."

Of course he didn't. Wishing games fell into the same forbidden category as the what-if game he'd refused to play. But sometimes rules needed to be ignored. He'd been the one to teach me that.

"It's a holiday, and you skipped out on a riveting round of 'What are you most thankful for this year?' So technically, this is your makeup game." He didn't return my smile, but even so, my question needed an answer. I needed an answer. I needed to understand once and for all whether there was any possibility of an *us*.

"Can you . . ." I tried again. "Can you imagine it? Having a home base?"

The terrain I treaded now felt far more hazardous than the cliffside on Cougar Mountain. But whether it was the mountain's edge or a pile of burning coals, I'd walk whatever path I had to. I needed to hear it—from his mouth, in his own words.

Our knees bumped again, Patrick's unspoken boundaries fading as fast as my filter.

"I leave for the Pacific Islands next month."

A reminder I didn't need.

As the queen of deflection, I knew when someone was steering a conversation away from topics they weren't ready to discuss. From answers they weren't ready to divulge.

"That isn't an answer."

He gave a weighty sigh, then said, "No. I can't imagine it."

Apparently, we didn't only share the art of diversion, we also shared the same tells: no eye contact, a wavering tone, and an immediate swallow after the last spoken word.

The look on his face grounded me, but the slight heave of his chest and the tick of his jaw sent my pulse soaring. He'd told me once that risk was everywhere and in every decision we made.

The key was to make that risk count.

Suddenly I had every intention to do just that.

I licked my bottom lip and slid off the stool. Intoxicated by the way he drank me in, I moved toward him. With shaky hands and shaky breath, I touched my fingers against the hard planes of his solid chest. Under the pressure of my touch, his toned muscle tensed, but he didn't stop me. Not when I traced the contours of his shoulders. Not when I mapped the curved bones of his collar. Not when I followed the arc of his neck and skimmed my fingertips along the stubble of his jaw.

But as I brushed my thumb across the scar at his temple, a pleasurable pain shadowed his gaze.

"*Willa.*" My name was a quiet warning on his lips.

But I was done listening to warnings.

I memorized every inch of his face and the soft curls at the nape of his neck.

His tentative touch at my waist expelled a soft whimper through my lips.

And then Patrick's entire focus shifted to my mouth.

In half a heartbeat, he was up on his feet, the stool clattering to the floor.

Chapter Thirty

Patrick's hands dragged up the sides of my body until his fingers tangled in my hair. His hungry lips, charged with frustrated heat, found mine as the cold granite seeped through the thin fabric at the curve of my back.

Urging, desperate, and deliciously thorough, he kissed me deeper, the taste of cinnamon and clove dancing between us.

Eyes glazed and heady, he cradled my face and spoke against my mouth. "Willa."

My name sounded broken and breathy and a thousand times more beautiful than any poem I'd ever heard—a melody that awakened something far more powerful than need or desire, or even the two combined.

As our kiss continued, he wrapped my waist tightly in his arms and steered our steps into the living room. When we bumped against the sofa, the frenzied exploration of moments ago slowed into a steady simmer. I sunk into the pillows as he settled beside me, one arm braced above me.

"Beautiful." A sweet caress spoken into the arc of my neck. "All of you."

"I . . ." The burn at the base of my throat stole my voice as my fingertips grazed his chest and explored the grooves and dips in his shoulders. He breathed out, I breathed in, and our next kiss was everything the first was not. Sedated and unhurried.

It was the kind of kiss that could disintegrate doubt. Erase hurt. Erase time. Erase the worry of the unknown.

Patrick clutched the fabric at the curve of my waist, his fingertips searing my skin through the loose knit of my sweater.

Every lightly feathered kiss across my jawline brought back the mountaintop feeling of the night before, that same heart-pounding anticipation. That same weak-kneed exhilaration. As if gravity didn't exist.

As if fear didn't exist.

Words formed in my heart and then spilled out through my mouth. "I'm not afraid of this. I'm not afraid of *us*."

Patrick's lips stilled on my neck and the rise and fall of his chest beneath my hand went motionless. All at once, the warmth was gone.

Patrick twisted away from me.

He propped his elbows on his knees and scrubbed at his face with both hands. "This can't happen."

Only it had.

It *had* happened—my pulsing lips were proof enough.

I sat up and forced my breathing to regulate. Then I reached for him. "Patrick." The muscles across his back tensed the instant my fingers touched him.

He stood up and took three steps away from the sofa. Another hand swipe down his face. Harder this time. "We have to stop."

"We *did*. We did stop."

He pivoted and blew out a ragged breath. There was a chilling resoluteness in his eyes. "Not soon enough."

I went to him. "We'll know how to handle ourselves better next time—"

He held my shoulders. "Willa." The regret floating in his eyes stung me. "There was never supposed to be a *this* time. My attraction for you is too . . ."

I held my breath, waiting for him to acknowledge what I'd felt in the way he'd kissed me, held me, spoken to me—

"I should have ended it last night."

His sharp words seemed to puncture my lungs while a memory, one barely old enough to be boxed away, surfaced in the space between us.

The unexpected hug at my doorstep.

Spurs of rejection climbed my throat at the memory of his arms around my waist, his face tucked into the crook of my neck, his hands firm against my back. His "good night" was not intended as a "good night" at all. It was meant to be a good-bye.

The old Willa would have tacked this hurt to the walls of her self-preservation. She would have shrunk her newly expanded world and returned back to the carefully managed, tightly controlled avoidance of life and all its possible hurts.

But that woman hadn't hiked ten steps to freedom.

I raised my chin and stared at him. "Did the staff at the food bank ask you to work an extra shift today or did you volunteer?" My suspicion gained traction when he dropped his hands from my shoulders.

"Why does that matter?"

"Did you *volunteer*?"

His gaze dragged back to mine. "Yes."

The confession was as painful as it was promising.

I softened my voice. "Because showing up at Thanksgiving with people who care about you, people who want to invest in you . . . is the one risk you aren't willing to take, isn't it?"

The clench of his jaw was confirmation enough, but there was no joy in this discovery. No thrill in being right.

"I have commitments to keep. Organizations that count on me."

"And who—apart from God—do *you* count on?"

This time, the desire to touch him was too strong to ignore. I reached out and Patrick caught my hand midair, held my wrist with his forefinger and thumb. "I watched all three of my brothers trade their calling—their *passion*—for their comfortable lifestyles. Little by little: marriage, kids, office hours that end before dinnertime . . ." He released me. "I'm not the kind of man who settles."

I dug for truth under the sting of his words. "So, instead, you live for the short-term." And there it was, perched on a shelf in the corner of my mind. It was the mystery I'd sensed in Rex's scribbled journal entries yet couldn't seem to solve. Until now. The fragments flitted through my recollection like ribbons lost to a windstorm. "The way Rex did."

"Rex lived without compromise."

"But he didn't live without fear, Patrick. And neither do you."

His lips were pressed thin and his eyes were focused on something beyond me. Something I couldn't see even if I tried. I stepped into him.

"Rex was, without a doubt, a man who should be admired." I touched my heart, my bottom lashes wet with unshed tears. "I learned from him, too. His determination, his faith, his honesty, his willingness to go and be and do. But Patrick . . . Rex was *lonely*. He didn't always express it with words, but it's there—all over those journal pages. It's in his tone, it's in the way he spoke about people and relationships. It's even in the scriptures he meditated on."

No answer.

"You don't want to be tied down. I get it." I searched his face. "You want to go everywhere, experience everything, live a life with no regrets . . . and all of that is truly inspiring. But in the end, what will you have? In the end, what did Rex have? A long list of adventures and some amazing stories to tell?"

I pressed closer; the pulse point at his neck was my focal point as I splayed my fingers over his chest. "Who will share your heart, Patrick? Who will invest in your life? Who will know your hurts and your heartaches? Your passions and your dreams? Who will cheer you on when you succeed and hold you close when you fail? Life is a balance—one I'm only just figuring out for myself. But even though I've loved and lost . . ." A sob caught in my throat as I lifted my hand and brushed my thumb across his cheekbone. "I'd risk my heart again. For you."

His eyes closed for the briefest of seconds before he stepped to the side and severed our connection. And my heart.

"I told you my time in Lenox was limited from the very beginning, Willa."

"You're saying there's no option for us to try—"

"I'm saying I have obligations to keep."

Tears I could no longer hold back spilled down my cheeks. "I'm not asking you to break them."

"Then you don't know what you're asking. In my line of work, relationships don't last. They're not worth it."

I rocked back a step and then another, my strength dwindling as quickly as my courage. "You mean I'm not worth it."

"I didn't say that."

He didn't have to.

A thick, uncomfortable silence spanned between us before Patrick shoved a hand through his hair. The blue of his eyes darkened to an unfamiliar shade.

"You should get back to your family."

On numb legs I carried myself past the kitchen island, past the lonely apple pie, past the clutter of mail stamped with Patrick's temporary address.

He followed me into the entryway and opened the door. My invitation into his home and his life had been revoked.

"I think it's best we don't see each other again. Until the wedding." His parting words wove through my ribs the way grief weaves through a heart.

But I wasn't sorry I'd risked mine again.

I was only sorry that Patrick hadn't risked his.

Chapter Thirty-One

"An indecisive mind breeds minimal achievement."

—Rex Porter

After years of living at the speed of caution, my laundry list of Required Action Items was longer than I cared to count. So I didn't count. Instead, I'd spent the last three days prioritizing.

"Willa?" The receptionist at Valley View Veterinary Clinic smiled. "Dr. Davis said he'll meet you in the break room in a few minutes. He just finished up with his last client."

With the exception of a poodle who shared the same hairstyle as her owner, the waiting room was empty.

"Thank you, Marie."

I followed her down the hall and into the space Savannah affectionately called the Vending Machine Room.

The large panoramic window at the far end of the room displayed a town I knew as well as my own backyard. This vantage point of the valley wasn't nearly as spectacular as the one from Cougar Mountain, but I wasn't thinking about that right now.

I pursed my lips and scanned the streets of downtown.

Longtime residents worried that the recent hike in population and resources would compromise the heart and integrity Lenox was built on. But I knew the charm of my hometown could never be lost.

The same way I knew I could never be the woman Davis Carter needed.

"To what do I owe such a nice, unexpected visit?"

I pivoted and pushed the courage from the base of my belly into my throat. "Hi, Davis."

He hugged me, hands lingering at my sides.

"Please tell me you're not here to cancel on the holiday bazaar?"

If only that were the reason I was here.

"Wouldn't dream of it."

"Good," he said, offering me a dashing grin. "Best to keep your name off Santa's naughty list."

My give-it-all-I've-got chuckle failed. Miserably.

The warmth in his expression cooled. "Hey . . . is something wrong?"

I swallowed. So much for small talk.

"I was hoping we could talk?"

Despite the foreboding in his eyes, he gestured to the table and slid out a chair for me. "Okay, then let's talk."

I reached for a copy of *Dog Nation Magazine* and ran my finger down the rough edge of the spine. Maybe if I gave myself a paper cut the words would come out easier.

"What's on your mind?" Ankle crossed over knee, he appeared relaxed, although I didn't miss the steady tick of his thumb against his thigh.

"I haven't been fair to you."

"How so?" he asked.

I flicked the corner of the magazine with my thumbnail until he stilled my hand, forcing my gaze back to his.

I exhaled slowly. "You've been a good friend—a *faithful* friend who's given ten times what I've given back to you."

"That's not how I see it at all," he challenged.

"Davis." It wasn't perspective. It was fact. And he knew it.

Hope drained from his eyes. "But?"

"But . . ." I sighed. "That's all we'll ever be. Friends."

Two blinks and then, "The doctor?"

Patrick's face surfaced in my mind, and just like the other million and one times today, a ribbon of sadness curled around my heart.

"Is still leaving after Christmas," I finished.

He stared at our layered hands for several seconds. "I gave you too much space."

"No. You gave me exactly what I asked for. What I needed."

The irony wasn't lost on me. Davis had given me an abundance of time. And Patrick had given me none at all.

"You're the only woman I've cared about since Stephanie."

And though I understood his grief, I knew I wasn't his answer. "But I'm not the woman you deserve, Davis."

"I'm not so sure."

Three months ago I wasn't sure either.

But three months ago, I was content to wade in still water. Now I craved the pull of a rushing river.

"Someday you'll meet a woman who will see you for everything you are. She'll appreciate your kind heart and your sense of humor and your gentleness toward animals and people alike." I paused, my gaze shifting to the window behind him. "The kind of life partner who can visualize your future and love you enough to help you achieve it."

The concentrated lines etched into his handsome face began to soften. "That's what I want for you, too."

"What?"

"Love. The way you just described it."

I offered a timid smile to fight off tears.

Today had marked a new beginning. Choosing action over indecision and love over fear.

Yet none of that changed the fact that Patrick hadn't chosen me.

Chapter Thirty-Two

"What's that in your hand?" I asked.

Alex whirled around.

Much like her newest shade of hair—bing-cherry red—the neon flyer in her grip was impossible to hide. That didn't stop her from trying, though.

I reached around her and snatched the crinkly paper from behind her back.

"Hey!"

I rushed through the lobby of the fitness center, dodging her efforts to retrieve it. "Tryouts for the spring musical are—"

She ripped it from my hands and stuffed it in the nearby trash can.

"Next Thursday," I continued from memory.

Her cheeks were flushed and her mouth set in a tight line. "Somebody left that here."

"Oh?" My tone lifted an octave. "Somebody like . . . Preston Wilkerson?"

She shrugged. "I didn't see who."

Sure she didn't. "I hear he's Georgia's hope for a male lead."

"What?" She practically spit the word. "Why? He's a jock."

"Who says he can't be a theater geek, too?"

She narrowed her eyes into slits. "The laws of nature."

"Nope." I pulled a cleaning rag and glass cleaner from the cupboard below my desk. "People can be more than one thing."

"Maybe that's how you're a teacher and . . . a glorified window cleaner."

I tossed a second rag at her head. "And maybe it's how you're an incredibly talented singer, yet you spend your time hiding out in a fitness center."

She stuck out her tongue.

I faked an aim at her face, then squirted the glass doors.

"Geesh. You're sassy today," said Alex. "But I'll take sassy over Eeyore."

"Eeyore?"

"Um. Yeah." She gave me a sidelong glance while she wiped. "You've been moping around here like you lost your tail since Thanksgiving."

The circular motion of my hand slowed as her words struck home.

I hadn't lost my tail. Just my heart.

If only this streak-free formula could wipe away the smudges Patrick had left behind with his whispered words, sultry smiles, and hungry kisses.

". . . you decide?"

How long has she been talking? "Oh, what?"

The damp rag slapped her thigh. "I *said*"—she drew it out—"what are you going to do about the job? What did you decide?"

In fact, I'd actually done something about it already—taken the first step at least. Last night I'd called Megan Hudson after Savannah went to bed.

But maybe Alex didn't need to know that. Not yet anyway.

An idea pinged in my head. "I'm not sure if I'm going to take it."

"What?" Her arms became goal posts in the air. I hushed her.

"Are you *crazy*?" she asked.

"Some days." *Most days* was probably more like it.

"You can't not interview."

"That's a double negative." I moved to the next window, leaving her mouth agape.

She marched after me. "See? That right there is a very teacherly thing to say."

"It's been a long time since I was in a classroom, Alex. What if I forget how to do lesson plans? What if the kids hate me? What if the parents prefer Ms. Hudson's style over mine?" Playing the game of life with an angst-driven teenager was far more fun than I'd imagined.

"But it's what you do! You helped me understand that English paper a few weeks ago, and how to study for that history exam—which I passed, by the way. I bet when you stand in front of that classroom for the first time, you'll feel like you never left it. It will just be . . . natural, you know?"

"You're willing to *bet* me?" I couldn't help but seize the opportunity she'd just provided me.

"Uh . . ." She shrugged. "Well, I don't have any money, so—"

"It's a good thing I don't want your money."

Her eyebrows formed a deep V. "Then what do we bet?"

"How about, if I agree to interview for the position . . . you'll agree to audition for Georgia?"

The *whoosh* of air that left her lungs was audible. "I . . . I . . . uh . . ."

"It's always easier to be brave for someone else, isn't it?"

Story of my life.

She eyed me. "You'd really try for the position if I sing a stupid solo?"

I smiled. "I promise you I will."

After six full seconds ticked by without smiling or blinking, Alex gave me a single nod. "Fine. But don't even think about making me wear a dress."

I dropped my gaze to her combat boots. "Never in a million years."

"This has to be a mistake."

The outfit—if one could call this crushed red velvet minidress edged in white fur an outfit—lay strewn on my bed. I checked the bag again for the rest of the ensemble: the white poodle wig, the wire-rimmed glasses, the puffy baking hat, and the padded apron to tie around my waist.

None of it was there.

Instead, I'd been given half a dress, a pair of candy-cane-striped tights, and a Santa hat.

Oh, and lest I forget, a pair of patent leather knee-high boots. In red.

Unless Mrs. Claus had exchanged her grandmotherly ways to become a North Pole streetwalker, something had gone terribly awry at the costume rental shop.

"Mom, Uncle Wes is here!"

Savannah's announcement jump-started my panic. I checked the clock and combed my fingers through my hair. Maybe when I put it on it wouldn't look as . . . uh . . . incomplete as it did lying on my bed.

The boom of Weston's laugh from the other room hurried me along like a ticking second hand.

I tugged the stiff bodice over my head and secured the sewn-in black leather belt around my waist. To my relief, the dress was slightly longer than I'd visualized.

Even if *slightly longer* was only an inch—maybe two.

But showing a few candy stripes above the knee wasn't nearly as bad as showing stocking lines at midthigh.

"Hey, Willa—you do realize you were supposed to be gone five minutes ago, right?"

I took a last glance in the mirror on my closet doors and prepared to face the peanut gallery in the living room.

At first I thought the lack of immediate criticism when I exited my bedroom and beelined for the hall closet was a good sign. Maybe I'd overreacted. Maybe the outfit as a whole would simply blend in with the holiday fanfare and go unnoticed.

And then I saw my brother's face.

He was blinking, yet no words escaped him.

Savannah tilted her head to the side and began to count the horizontal lines that ran the length of my legs.

"Why do you look like you're going to a Halloween party at a frat house?" And there it was.

"I do not." Please, *please* let that be true.

"Can I feel your tights, Mommy?" Savannah hopped from the couch and ran her palm over the stockings.

"See?" Weston gestured to my daughter. "She just proved my point. That's what any frat boy would ask you, too."

"I didn't pick it out, okay. I think the costume shop messed up."

Weston laughed and crossed his arms over his chest. "Or perhaps Davis just played you like a fiddle." He huffed in mock appreciation. "At least he finally upped his game. Too bad he's too late."

My cheeks became stovetop burners.

Davis wouldn't do this on purpose. He wouldn't.

Then his words from the other night popped into my brain. *"Best to keep your name off Santa's naughty list."*

Wait—was I being punished for giving him the let's-just-be-friends talk?

My fingers tripped over the buttons on the long wool peacoat. "There is no game."

Weston leaned back into the sofa and shook his head slowly. "Dang. I kinda want to go to this thing now."

"But you said you didn't mind babysitting tonight." Savannah had been coughing most of the day; a cold virus was going around her class again.

"That was before I knew there'd be an English-language Spanish soap opera happening at the toy drive."

"What are you talking about?" I swung my purse over my shoulder and reached for the doorknob.

He lifted his hand in a mock salute. "Nothing. Don't worry about us. We'll just be over here playing Guess Who?"

"Weston." I tried again.

But he'd already opened the game box and was reminding Savannah of the rules.

I rolled my eyes and slammed the door on the way out.

Chapter Thirty-Three

At the community center, the Friday-night bingo paraphernalia had been stripped and replaced with Santa's Village. A line of adoring kids had already formed, and the photographer was setting up his tripod to capture the first of many Christmas card options for the season.

The charity's influence had grown beyond our city limits into bordering towns, inviting patrons who dropped off a toy to receive a free five-by-seven photo of their child with Santa. The drive had always been sponsored by a local business, and this year, that responsibility had fallen to Davis.

Davis. He was easy to locate.

If he hadn't already been sitting on his Santa throne with his snap-on beard, I'd have happily started the first public domestic disturbance between Mr. and Mrs. Claus.

My stride was quick, though I doubted that speed walking in this festive getup was the best way to prevent me from being seen.

I pushed open the white picket gate and entered the land of all things merry.

"Willa? I mean, Mrs. Claus?" Davis's eyes grew rounder the lower his gaze traveled down my stockings. "You look . . . uh . . ."

"PG-13?" I tried.

And then I considered him: stuffed potbelly, oversized hat, and a holly jolly grin. Why did he get to be the traditional Santa while I got stuck playing the naughty mistress of the North Pole?

"Seriously, Davis?" I waved a hand over the crushed-velvet catastrophe. "What happened at the rental shop?"

As if I'd just held him up at gunpoint, Davis lifted his white-gloved hands in the air. "I swear I didn't pick that out for you. The guy behind the counter asked me some questions and a few minutes later I was out the door with the costume bag."

I sighed through my teeth. "I'm supposed to be your nine-hundred-year-old wife. Not your nineteen-year-old girlfriend."

"Well . . . if it helps, I was right." His smile could have been decorated with gumdrops. "You are definitely the prettiest Mrs. Claus Lenox has ever seen."

Before I could turn away, Santa pushed his puffy self off his big red chair and caught my arm. "Hey," he said, his voice low and apologetic. "I'm sorry, Willa. I should have checked the bag."

So it wasn't revenge after all. Just really, really bad luck.

I let out a defeated sigh. "I'll try to forgive you before Christmas."

With a wink he pointed to the small fake kitchen table near us. "You should probably grab your tray of cookies to hand out to the children. The elves are opening the gate."

"I should cookie you," I mumbled under my breath as Davis returned to his throne.

"What's that you say, dear?"

"Nothing, Santa, darling."

A redheaded boy trotted up to Santa's lap, pulled his beard, and then rattled off a long list of toys he hoped he'd receive under his tree.

After the third hour of being gawked at by every parent standing in line, I was ready to pepper frosted sugar cookies at Davis's head.

Too bad I'd just run out.

I leaned over Santa's shoulder. "Where are the cookie refills?"

He patted his large belly. "Maybe I ate them all. You're such a good baker, Mrs. Claus."

A group of kids at the front gate laughed, but my humor had long ago been spent.

He turned his mouth to my ear. "There's some extra in the prep kitchen."

Of course there were—because the prep kitchen was on the opposite side of the building. Again with the luck today.

"Perfect."

"Hey, wait just a minute there, Mrs. Claus." His hand hooked around my oversized belt loop. "We need to get a picture to memorialize this event."

The photographer gave us a thumbs-up.

"Um . . . I'd rather not, Santa." *I'd actually like to forget this particular event ever happened.*

And then Santa morphed back into the man I'd known since high school. "I would really like to hang a picture up at the clinic, Willa. Sponsoring this event is important to the community."

One suck-it-up grin later and I was sitting on his lap, furiously yanking at my hemline.

"You look fine. Stop that," he said at my back.

I ignored him and continued the tug-of-war until I was 100 percent certain that nothing but candy cane tights would be revealed in this picture.

"Ready?" the photographer asked, his voice like the dull side of packing tape.

"Sure." But as I lifted my face to the camera lens, my stomach bottomed out.

Patrick stood just on the other side of the gate, wearing the same pained expression that haunted my dreams.

"Mrs. Claus?" the photographer called. "Can you *smile*?"

No. I really couldn't.

"Mrs. Claus?"

I tore my gaze from the only man who could cripple my resolve with a single glance and stared into the camera's big, glossy eyeball. The smile I slapped on my face more closely resembled a stray dog baring its teeth than a cherished holiday couple spreading holiday cheer.

I slid off Davis's thigh and reached for the empty cookie tray.

Out of breath, I escaped through the back gate, which slammed into my kneecap before I could clear it.

"*Ouch.*"

If I could have sprinted without fear of showing my backside, I would have. Even with my gimp knee.

The distance from the miniature North Pole village to the prep kitchen must have been miles, because by the time I pushed through the swinging door, my lungs were a breath away from collapse.

Cookies. Cookies. Find the cookies.

Easier thought than done.

Glittery snowflakes cut from white paper plates and an army of pipe-cleaner angels littered the countertops. Bags upon bags of miscellaneous winter crafts lay scattered on every surface.

Searching for white sugar cookies in this mess was like trying to find Where's Waldo? in Candy Land.

The rustling of plastic sacks drowned out the squeaky hinges on the kitchen door, but I didn't need to be alerted to his presence.

I could feel him.

My fingers paused and the Great Cookie Hunt plummeted to the bottom of my priority list.

I pivoted on the heel of my red boot.

Just like it had in his parents' kitchen, his jaw seemed to tick to the rhythm of my pulse. Only that night, I'd understood the reason for the heated intensity on his face. I'd tested his restraint, pushed his limits, and broken him down kiss by kiss.

But he had no right to wear that expression now—not when we hadn't seen each other for nine days.

Not when I'd left him alone the way he'd asked.

Not when he'd been the one to quit me.

His eyes fixated on the belt around my waist. "That's quite the costume."

I curtsied and held my chin up high.

"Thanks. I picked it out myself." I smoothed my damp palms over the thick bell skirt and wondered if my lie was as obvious to him as it sounded to me.

His face darkened.

"Why are you here?" I asked.

"I volunteered to load the toys out back."

Of course he had. Because assisting strangers was what Patrick did best. It was his friends that he dumped.

His stare intensified, but I refused to be the one who blinked first.

"Are you with him?"

"What?" My attempt at sass had sprung a momentary leak.

"Are. You. With. Davis?" He stretched out each letter, emphasized each syllable, lengthened each word.

With Davis.

A hot current zipped through my core. "If that's a serious question, then you don't know me at all."

"You were sitting on his lap."

"He's Santa Claus!" I threw my arms wide. "Everybody sits on his lap. If you're willing to wait in line I'm sure you can have a turn, too."

He heaved a long sigh and glanced up at the ceiling. Perhaps he was looking for a clean slate for this conversation. But unless he had a time machine, that was impossible.

"Weston mentioned Savannah has a cold."

Weston the traitor strikes again. "She's fine."

He leaned against the edge of the counter. "I'd be glad to check her out."

"She's already been seen."

Hurt flickered across his features. "You could have brought her to the clinic."

No, I couldn't have. "I really can't do this right now—"

He stepped toward me. "Are you going to interview for the teaching position?"

My mouth popped open. *Unbelievable.* "I'm not your little apprentice anymore, Patrick. *You* quit *me*, remember?" I pressed a hand to my chest. "I gave you my heart and you told me to go home. It doesn't get much clearer than that, so stop playing games."

"Willa, please—"

"No." The sound of my name on his lips was too much. "There's nothing more to be said. You've made your stance very, very clear."

Where are those dang cookies? I started the search again.

"I never wanted to hurt you." His voice sounded heavy, as if it took physical effort to lift the words from his chest and push them out of his mouth. "*Please,* believe that."

"What I believe shouldn't matter to you."

He smacked the counter with his hand. "Of course it matters to me! *You* matter to me."

Finally, I spotted them—the snowflake cookies camouflaged in the corner.

I gripped the plastic handles, placed my palm on the door, and glanced over my shoulder. "Not enough."

Chapter Thirty-Four

Weston stood at the back of the auditorium with Savannah perched on his shoulders. The sight still made me queasy, but some types of progress were easier than others. Right now, not wanting to punch my brother in the chest was progress enough.

"I'm shocked you got her here." Weston jerked his chin toward the stage. Alex was next in line. "I thought she was gonna claw your eyes out at the Thanksgiving table just for suggesting it."

"Everyone has a reason to be brave." Patrick's words rolled off my tongue like my own, and the thud of my heartbeat echoed in my chest.

"Guess so."

Weston cleared his throat.

He was dying to know how my phone call with Principal Schultz had gone earlier that day. He'd hinted at it twice since we'd arrived, but it was rare that I got the chance to hold something over him. He cleared his throat again, only this time the sound was better compared to the start of a race car engine than someone in need of a glass of water.

Several people twisted in their seats to stare at us.

I dropped my voice and kicked his shoe. "You're going to get us in trouble."

"Good thing I'm pretty tight with the theater owner."

I rolled my eyes at his smirk and he bumped my shoulder. "So? What happened? Tell me."

"It went well." Better than well.

He smashed me to his side. "I'm proud of you, Willa."

"There's still a few more details to be worked out—I don't have the job quite yet."

"I'm not worried," he said.

"I'm not either."

And for the first time in forever, that was the truth. I'd had several late-night conversations with Megan Hudson over the last week, and I was becoming more and more convinced that this rare opportunity wasn't coincidence, but part of God's divine plan.

Alex took a step toward the stage and adjusted the microphone.

I moved closer, clasping my hands at my chest. Her eyes roamed over a few scattered theater junkies sitting in the fold-up chairs and then parked on me.

"You can do this," I mouthed.

"Hi . . . uh, my name is Alex Reyes. I'll be singing 'Standing Tall.' It's an original song."

Georgia pointed to the pianist, and seconds later the auditorium was hushed by a pulsing bass note—a musical heartbeat.

And then Alex was singing—the lyrics heartfelt, honest, and somehow achingly familiar.

Alex was singing her story. The story of a lone building standing tall in a world of ruins. Everything crushed. Everything scattered. Everything lost. But still it stood. Brave and bold. Against what was and what would come.

The smoky rasp of her voice hypnotized every person in the room.

Weston leaned over my shoulder. "Uh . . . I think I should quit my day job and become her manager."

I flashed him a grin. He was right; Alex deserved every chance this world had to offer.

He lowered Savannah to her feet and she took my hand, mesmerized by the performance on stage. I closed my eyes to listen to the last few notes.

Perfection.

The final chords of the piano faded out and were replaced by an awed, stunned silence.

Like the slow leak of an inflated balloon, I exhaled.

Georgia got to her feet.

One by one, every student who'd stayed to hear the audition began clapping and cheering—all for this girl who had been given so little praise in her young life.

The second she was off the stage, I rushed her and threw my arms around her neck. She hugged me back, adrenaline humming off her skin.

"You were amazing, Alex."

I expected sarcasm and sass to follow my compliment, but instead her grip on me tightened. "Thank you. For believing I could do this."

My heart squeezed. "You're easy to believe in."

I may not have been expecting this girl with the hypercolor hair and the razor-sharp wit, but whether she liked it or not, I wasn't going to give her up. In such a short period of time, Alex had enriched my life, expanded my world, and challenged my perspective.

Just like someone else I'd known. Only I didn't get to hold on to him.

I pulled back and scanned her face. "You want a cupcake?"

She huffed. "I'm not five, Willa." Ah. There was the girl I knew.

I cocked an eyebrow. "Yet I know you're not about to turn me down."

"Nope." She reached for Savannah's hand and then froze.

Sydney stood at the back of the theater, propped against the wall. Her thin lips were pursed but her eyes shined with the same emotion I'd heard in Alex's voice.

"Syd?"

The woman didn't say a word. She didn't have to. She just took a step and Alex broke into a quick stride.

Hugging my chest, I watched these polar opposites embrace. My own eyes teared as Weston slung his arm over my shoulder.

He pulled me to his side and nodded toward them. "Maybe I should start calling you a miracle worker."

I shook my head as the half sisters actually communicated without their normal sarcasm and explosive arguments.

"I'm just grateful I've been able to be a good friend."

I swallowed back the tightness in my throat and tried not to think of Patrick's face. But the truth was impossible to ignore, no matter how much I wanted to. Patrick had been one of the best friends I'd ever had. And I missed him. Terribly.

"You're welcome to join us at the Frosting Palace, Sydney," I said as we approached the sweet reunion.

Sydney lifted her chin. "I think I can do that."

"You coming?" I asked Wes as Savannah pushed through the auditorium doors.

He shook his head and pointed toward Georgia in a way that suggested his night was already booked. A dull ache spread through my abdomen.

My suggestion for cupcakes hadn't only been motivated by Alex's killer vocals, but also by the growing void I hoped a strong dose of sugar might fill. At least for tonight.

The Frosting Palace was still the only place in Lenox that could celebrate a success and commiserate a heartbreak in equal measure.

Chapter Thirty-Five

Savannah flipped the shoebox lid to the side and pulled out another pair of white sparkly mini heels. "Ooh. I like these ones the best!"

Too bad I'd heard that same line seven times in the last thirty minutes. I was certain she'd tried on every pair that Bella Bridal had in her size.

I knelt to unbuckle her current selection and slip them on her feet.

"I'm afraid you've inherited my indecisiveness." Which had not been nearly as prominent as of late. My chest tingled as I thought back to Patrick's first life lesson—the night of the school auction just over two months ago. In some ways it felt like a decade had passed since then, but the memory was as fresh as yesterday.

I could still see the glint of mystery in his eyes after I'd read the note tucked into the fold of the program. *"Place a bet you know you can win. It makes the bets you lose a lot less defeating."*

Savannah touched my face. "Your smile is so pretty, Mom."

I kissed the inside of her palm as my mother and Nan got to their feet. A reverent hush fell over the mirrored room.

Georgia's gown swished as she took fluid, graceful steps to the platform. The combination of fabrics—silk, tulle, and lace—was stunning and sophisticated.

"You're like a real princess," Savannah breathed.

Georgia glowed, swaying gently in the trifold mirror. "I *feel* a bit like a princess."

"Exquisite!" Nan clasped her hands, her eyes glossy and bright.

"Truly, Georgia." I studied her delighted face. "It's the perfect dress. You're absolutely beautiful."

My mom dabbed at her eyes with a paisley hanky, the kind she sold in her store. "Weston's going to cry like a baby when he sees you."

The blushing bride bit her bottom lip, then glanced over her shoulder at me. "Would you mind helping me with the veil?"

I carried the delicate accessory up the two-step pedestal and secured it to her head. The sheer layers of her veil flowed flawlessly over her luminescent gown and the dark cascades of her hair. My mom was right; my brother was going to be a blubbering mess next weekend.

"I can't believe I'm getting married in seven days."

I wrapped an arm around her shoulders. "And I can't believe after twenty-seven years of putting up with Weston, I'm finally getting a sister."

Georgia laughed. "Yeah, you're seriously a saint, Willa."

"Nah. That title falls to you."

Savannah's newest pair of child-sized heels clicked against the wood-planked floors; her continuous twirls were making me dizzy.

Georgia grinned. "Guess I don't have to wonder if she loved the dress."

"Nope. The real issue now is if I'm going to be able to convince her to take it off."

I stepped down to allow my mom and Nan access to the bride, and began the process of Operation Shoe Cleanup. As I shoved the last box in place on the shelf, my attention was caught by a blur of plaid walking past the storefront window. I only knew one man who wore a flat cap in the dead of winter, and he wasn't Oregon-born.

"Savannah, stay with Grandma." I pushed out the door before I heard her reply.

My cotton sweater felt more like a piece of tissue paper as I slipped outside into the slicing wind and snow flurry. But I had to confirm my suspicion.

"Dr. McCade?" I jogged after him, snowflakes catching in my eyelashes.

His footsteps halted. "Willa?"

There was no mistaking his rich Scottish brogue.

"You're back in town." It wasn't a question exactly, but with it came a reality I couldn't ignore.

Time never waited for me.

Ivar McCade's smile was seasoned with kindness, his blue eyes almond-shaped and full of spirit—just like his Patrick's.

"Got in two nights ago—but you wouldn't know it by the sleep schedule the wife and I've been keeping. Jet lag is not a friendly sort."

I rubbed the chill from my arms. "No, I imagine it's not."

"It's been a blessing to have a son with so much experience crossing the international date line. He's given us some handy tricks."

"Oh, yes . . ." Because what else could I say? "That is great."

"I trust Savannah is well?"

"Yes, thank you. She loves school, and other than a couple cold viruses, her health has been stable. Her scans clear."

"Marvelous."

He ticked his head to the side, his gaze boring into mine. "My son's spoken well of you these past few months. Your brother, also. Think he's really enjoyed his time in Lenox."

He'd spoken to his parents about me? The last shred of my anger drowned in a sea of homesickness. Only it wasn't a place I longed for but a person.

He clamped a gloved hand to my bicep and squeezed. "You best get back inside, lass. Don't want you to—"

Panic gripped me as I forced the words from my throat, unwilling to sever the opportunity to speak the truth to a man I respected greatly. "He's a good man, your son. You should be very proud of him."

Ivar lowered his chin and searched my eyes. "We are. But I'll be sure to tell his mum you said so."

Sadness crept up my throat, a sense of finality settling in. "Yes, please do."

Ivar pointed to the bridal shop like a father sending his daughter to her room, then winked his good-bye.

A blistering cyclone of white curled around me and a fresh layer of snow melted into my scalp and dripped down my face and neck. But still I didn't move. Not even after I'd lost sight of Ivar's plaid cap and the feeling in my fingertips.

Ivar McCade was home.

And soon his son would be gone.

Chapter Thirty-Six

Ready or not?

It was the question I had asked myself a dozen times since I showered. And a dozen more since I parked. And a dozen more since I stepped into the hustle and bustle of wedding rehearsal pandemonium.

Savannah shoved past me, her basket of "practice petals" bumping against the poof of her "practice dress"—I wouldn't let her wear the real one until tomorrow. White ribbons waved behind her as she weaved through the bridal party toward the trio of groomsmen next to the auditorium doors.

Patrick was midsentence, shaking hands with Weston's best man, when Savannah tapped him on the leg, kicked out her heel, and flashed him her best ta-da smile.

I fumbled for the words to call her back, to remind her that it was rude to interrupt adult conversation . . . but then he dropped to his knee.

Savannah twirled.

Patrick grinned.

And my heart toppled over itself.

Ready or not had just been answered.

Despite my daughter's blatant compliment-fishing, genuine amusement shone on his face. That was, until I walked toward them.

The earth could have looped the sun in the amount of time it took for his six-foot frame to resume to full height. And even then, it wasn't long enough for me to form a coherent thought. For a man who climbed mountains, jumped off bridges, and swam through crocodile-infested waters, the vulnerability in his eyes unnerved me.

All we'd shared over the last three months lingered in the space between us. But this moment wasn't about who we'd been. It was about who we'd become.

Not everyone had the opportunity to spend a last week or a last day or even a last hour with the person they loved before they were gone.

Tonight I did.

I stretched out my hand to him the way I'd done so many times before. "It's good to see you."

The overactive nerves inside my body calmed the instant his hand clasped mine.

His thumb trailed over my skin in a slow arc. "It's really good to see you, too, Willa."

"I'm sorry." We spoke the apology in unison, our hands breaking apart.

Patrick shook his head. "Willa, I—"

"No, please, let me. I shouldn't have said what I did at Santa's Village. I was—"

"Angry," he finished. "Which is fair considering . . ."

Considering I fell in love with you. "I don't want to be angry anymore."

He studied me as if we were the only two people in this crowded lobby, and suddenly I felt the need to break the intimacy of the moment. My fingers closed around the strap of my purse.

I slipped it off my shoulder and unsnapped the closure in the middle. "Before I forget, I have something that belongs to you." I pulled

Rex's journal from my bag, its weight in my hand insignificant compared to the value inside. This journal represented more than a man's legacy; it represented a friendship that never would have begun without it. I placed the leather-bound book in Patrick's open palm. "Thank you for sharing Rex with me. I never told you how—"

A tug on my scarf pulled my attention. "When is it my turn to walk, Mom?"

My fidgety blonde, who shared her uncle's impatience, set her flower basket down at my feet, as if declaring a strike.

"In just a minute, sweetie. See that lady right over there—the one with the red hair talking to Auntie Georgia?"

She crossed her arms and huffed. "Yeah?"

"Well, it's her job to tell the bridal party when it's time to walk down the aisle."

"O-k-a-y." A whine stretched into a song.

Patrick caught my eye again. "At least you don't have to worry about stage fright."

"Nope. I think she'd do this every weekend if I let her."

"And that right there is the difference between boys and girls."

"What?" The tease in my voice felt surprisingly natural. "You mean Dr. Forge-the-Amazon doesn't like weddings?"

He laughed and my heart grew wings. I could have flown around the globe on a single breeze. *Oh, how I missed that sound.*

"There's only one thing to love about weddings."

"And what's that?"

Patrick opened his mouth but the tinkling of brass bracelets cut him off.

Georgia's wedding planner—a Californian with flame-red hair and about a hundred gold bangles too many—gestured to the taped *X*s on the carpet of the theater's lobby.

"Please find your assigned partner, and stand on your *X*. We're about to begin."

Georgia linked hands with Savannah and walked her back to her spot. Patrick and I were sandwiched between the two other bridal party couples.

He lowered his mouth to my ear. "Confession: I have no idea how to do this."

I eyed him. "You've never been in a wedding?"

The corner of his mouth tipped and immediately I glanced away. Touching him was hard enough. I couldn't look at him from so close a distance and be held responsible for my actions.

"How is that possible? What about all your brothers?" A rebellious button at the base of his navy polo shirt caught my eye. Half-in. Half-out. It was a 911 call I'd have to ignore.

I looped the end of my scarf around my fingers.

"One eloped in Vegas the second he passed his boards." He quirked an eyebrow. "I know, scandalous."

I stifled a laugh.

"One got married while I was in the middle of earthquake disaster relief in Haiti. And the last one didn't want to deal with a bridal party. It was a backyard affair with only close family and friends. Hey—speaking of which, have you seen your brother yet?"

"No. Why?"

"He came in two pounds over."

It took me a second to catch his meaning. *Oh, the bet.* "You're telling me he lost? He's actually wearing a kilt?"

Patrick shot me a disarming smile. "Not just any kilt. A McCade kilt."

And then the couple in front of us was on the move.

"Seems like now might be a good time for some how-to instruction?"

"It's easy." I linked my arm through his and my heart stuttered inside my chest. "Just walk slowly."

"Slowly," he repeated, watching my mouth.

"Yes. Slowly."

A shake of bangles from the wedding coordinator indicated it was our turn.

I tugged his arm to take the first step, and then we were walking, walking, walking.

The feel of him beside me made my stomach dip.

"How am I doing?"

"Shh," I teased. "You're not supposed to talk to me."

"But I've missed you."

I nearly stumbled, my heel catching on a seam in the runner, my heart catching on his words.

He tightened his hold on my arm as I pressed my lips together. I stared straight ahead, careful to avoid the gaze of the nosey kilt-wearing groom only a few paces away.

If Patrick thought I'd smile at his last sentiment, he'd thought wrong. I could be strong for an evening—do my best to keep my brave face intact for his final days in Lenox, but no amount of pretending could make my feelings for him disappear. Not even after he himself disappeared.

I counted the rows ahead.

Five . . . four . . . three . . .

"Did you hear me?" he asked.

How long is this aisle?

Two . . .

"I miss you, Willa." If a whisper could cut through bone, his had done just that.

One.

I dropped his arm, found my *X* on the left side of the stage, and pivoted into position, my mind and heart at war with each other. *Why would he say that? Didn't he understand how hard it was to be near him and not wish for—?* I took a deep breath, my smile locked in tight, my gaze fixed on the auditorium doors at the back of the theater.

The last couple in the bridal party found their places while my energetic daughter pranced and tossed handfuls of red petals.

Yet even when Georgia and Nan strolled toward the stage of the beloved community theater, and even after the pastor asked us to face the groom and his soon-to-be wife, I couldn't shake the whispered words from my heart.

Just like Patrick's gaze wouldn't be shaken from my face.

I'd never cared much for assigned seating at special events. Tonight, however, had given me an entirely new perspective on the issue. Segregation between the bridesmaids and groomsmen at the head table might be the only way I would survive the evening.

"Next, we'd love to toast our families," Georgia said. She glanced around the room, at all the smiling, hope-filled faces, and lifted her glass. "Thank you for all your prayers and encouragement over this last year. We've had a whole lot of change to work through—a lot of transition—but we both know that without your kindness and love, we wouldn't be here today." Palm to her chest. "So thank you all."

A round of clinks and then my brother pushed out his chair. I leaned forward, just enough to sneak a peek at Patrick, who sat two places down from Weston.

Yep. He was still watching me.

I offered him a shy smile and he returned it—only there wasn't a trace of timidity to be found on his face. Or in his eyes. I inched back again, exhaled, and tried my best to focus on the groom's speech.

"Couldn't agree more with my bride. Family plays a major role in each of our lives." Weston's attention swung from his audience to me.

I squirmed under his gaze.

"And because of that, I'd like to take a moment to recognize my sister."

In less than two seconds, my throat and mouth became as dry as parchment paper.

"There are a lot of seasons in life we get to plan for—college, marriage, children." He winked at Georgia and the crowd laughed.

He returned his focus. "But there are some seasons we never plan for. Seasons that take us by surprise and do their best to break our spirits, our hope, and our faith. As I've watched my sister"—he gestured to me—"wade through some of the toughest seasons a person should ever have to face—" Weston paused, released a slow breath, and then turned to me fully. "I can honestly say that I've never been more inspired by anyone in my life than I have by you."

I dabbed the corner of my eyes with the white linen napkin from my lap.

He lifted his glass high. "To you, Willa. For never giving up and for continuing to believe there are better seasons ahead than behind."

The muddle of murmurs and tinkling of glasses hid the sob that broke from my throat.

He pulled me to my feet a moment later and crushed me to his chest. "I love you."

"I love you, too." After a second to regain my composure, I whispered, "Even in a kilt."

He chuckled in my ear. "Georgia thinks it's pretty hot. Maybe I should pack it for Hawaii."

"Okay . . . that's really enough," I said, wiggling from his hold.

"Oh—wait." He turned back to the dinner party, holding me hostage to his side the way a python squeezes its prey. "I almost forgot! Please help me in congratulating my big sis on her brand-new position at Lenox Elementary School. Second grade will never be the same."

A loud round of claps and congratulations ensued while fire licked up my neck and face. I might be able to stand in front of a classroom full of children eight hours a day, but being the center of attention in a room full of adults might just cause me to implode.

I'd only heard the official word this morning, and the last thing I wanted to do was overshadow the wedding festivities with my news. But naturally, Weston had coaxed it out of me. And naturally, he'd not been able to keep quiet about it.

After a few pats on the back, I took my seat again.

Only this time, when I slipped into my chair, I didn't have to dodge Patrick's undeterred gaze.

Because he wasn't there.

Chapter Thirty-Seven

He hovered in the front of the restaurant as I cleared the last of the decorations from the tables. Although everything in me wanted to forget these frilly centerpieces and run to him—kiss away that haunted look on his face—I had to make peace with my new role.

A soon-to-be long-distance friend.

Controlling the cadence of my steps as I approached him, I reached for my coat on the rack by the door, but Patrick's hand was quicker.

Without a word, he held my coat open for me in invitation. I accepted.

Gathering my hair over one shoulder, I looped my scarf around my neck. "Thank you."

"Can I walk you to your car?" The gravelly undertone in his voice told me he was going to follow regardless of permission.

"Yes."

The blacktop shimmered under the light of the moon. No trace of snow or ice. Just tiny specks of salt that shone like diamonds in a black sea.

We'd walked together so many times over the last few months that we'd developed a cadence that allowed for our differing heights and strides, yet each step to my car felt out of sync. We were out of rhythm. Out of time.

I clicked the unlock button and the sound ricocheted through me like a gunshot.

He opened my door and clamped his hands to the top of the frame. "He's right, you know. Your brother. You're a . . . remarkable woman. An inspiration."

"Says the man who's helped save thousands of lives worldwide."

His knuckles faded from pink to white. "No. Says the man who's spent the last three months with you." The passion in his voice made my chest ache—a pulsing, throbbing, raging kind of ache I wished I could mute.

"I should have told you that sooner. I should have . . ." His words trailed into a soundless thought.

"Patrick." My fingertips burned to touch him, begged to soften the pain etched into each stressed line of his face. "It's okay." And for the first time, I believed it could be. Maybe not today. Maybe not tomorrow. But someday. "You've given me back a piece of myself I thought I'd lost. Your friendship has meant so much."

Patrick avoided my eyes; his Adam's apple rose and fell. "I hurt you."

I couldn't stand it another second. I touched my palm to his cheek and pushed my fingers through the russet locks of hair at his temple.

"Look at me," I whispered. "Patrick. Look at me."

The torment in his eyes was enough to make me double over, yet I stood strong. My mind and heart were finally working in tandem. I wouldn't allow the weeks we'd spent apart to erase the months we'd spent together. Wherever Patrick traveled, wherever he journeyed in this world, I needed him to remember—if nothing else—that his investment in me had been worth the risk.

"I don't regret you or the time we spent together." The truth of my words soothed the wound in my soul like a healing balm.

He placed his hand over mine. "I have something for you. A Christmas gift. Wait here."

He pushed himself back a step and jogged to his car just three spaces away from mine.

I watched him fade into the darkness and reappear a few seconds later.

He handed me an oversized envelope, my address printed on the front.

"You were going to send it?"

His eyes shifted to the weighted package in my hand. "I was hoping I'd be able to give it to you sometime this weekend . . . just wasn't sure."

Just wasn't sure if I'd let him.

I fumbled with the seal at the back, reached inside, and slid a rectangular object from the envelope.

Patrick stuffed his hands into the pockets of his jacket as I flipped it over. Tears sprang to my eyes before I had the chance to take a breath. Before I had a chance to remind my heart to keep beating.

Bathed in the bluish hue of the security light overhead was a picture of my freedom: head tipped to the heavens and my eyes closed in silent prayer, as a watercolor sunset radiated behind me. Peace. Joy. Love. Freedom. Patrick had captured every single one of those words in the blink of a shutter. That had been one of the most monumental moments of my life. A moment he'd shared with me.

My hand splayed over my mouth as tears streamed down my cheeks.

After a hiccup-turned-sob, Patrick touched the back of my head.

"You're starting to make me wish I'd mailed it . . ." The humor in his tone made me laugh through my sniffles.

As I lifted my head, a wet, sticky blink of running makeup stung my eyes. The twisted grin on Patrick's mouth confirmed what I imagined had happened to my face.

"You aren't supposed to make a girl ugly-cry when she has mascara on. That is really bad etiquette for gift giving."

That did it.

Patrick's choked laughter started out as a solo but soon became a duet. Our laughs were a release, a liberation of tension. The sound, bordering on full-scale hysteria, echoed in the open night air.

The instant one of us would start to quiet, the other would start up again. I unwrapped the scarf from my neck and swiped at my black-smeared cheeks. Patrick guided my hand and pointed out spots that I'd missed, which of course only began another round of tireless chortles.

After a few long sighs and sobering smiles, I held out the canvas picture.

And this time, I was determined to speak without tears and without a certifiable fit of giggles.

I looked between him and my new treasure. "This is easily the best gift I've ever been given."

Patrick's hand covered mine as he studied the piece of art. Several seconds passed before he spoke. "This one."

I wrinkled my face, confused.

"You asked if I had a favorite sunset and I told you I didn't. But that's not true anymore. This one's my favorite."

A surge of emotion rose in my throat again, and I knew Patrick could sense it. He always could. He leaned in and pressed his lips to my hairline and then backed away slowly.

The effort it took me to open my eyes was the same effort it took for me to accept what was coming in a matter of days. There were so many things I wanted to say, so many conversations I wanted to have, but none of them were suited for a parking lot.

I licked my bottom lip and stared down at my hands. "I wish I had something to give to you, something even half as special as this—"

"A dance," he said. "Tomorrow night. At the wedding."

"A dance?"

"Yes. That's the only thank-you I want."

A wavering sound came out of my throat. "Okay."

He flashed a grin that I could feel in my toes. "Okay. I'll see you tomorrow, then."

"Yes. Tomorrow," I confirmed, the words a chiming benediction as I climbed into my car and set the generous gift beside me.

He closed my door and then stared at me through the glass. He searched my face, from the top of my head to the underside of my jaw.

We'd shared many glances over the course of the night—some stolen, some freely exchanged. But Patrick wasn't looking at me; he was memorizing me.

My lungs burned for breath as I raised a shaky hand to the window and mouthed a good night.

Just a good night.

Not a good-bye.

Chapter Thirty-Eight

"So, this 'plus one' jazz comes with some great perks," Alex said, chowing down on the three-course reception dinner. She wiped her mouth on the linen napkin. "That was the first wedding I've been to in a theater. Looked like a friggin' winter palace in there. Never seen so many twinkle lights in all my life."

"That theater is a special place to Weston and Georgia—it's where they fell in love."

Everything about the ceremony had been flawless: the décor, the processional, the cheers for an encore after their first wedded kiss.

Alex slumped back against the tulle-wrapped chair. "Well, it was something. I even teared up."

The confession pulled me out of my melancholy. "You did?"

"Yeah. Weston's face when he saw Georgia . . ." She shook her head. "Thought that stuff only happened in sappy movies."

I picked at my dinner roll. "It happens in real life, too. Timing is everything." The words tangled into a knot in the pit of my stomach.

The reception was taking place in an upscale lodge just twenty minutes from downtown Lenox. I scanned the winter-wonderland-themed room and caught sight of Patrick. He was engaged in a lively conversation with a pocket of townsmen, and it was easy to imagine the peppering of questions he was receiving. Where was he going next? What kind of work was he doing? How long was this medical mission?

Would he ever come back?

He angled his head toward me and offered me a wink-smile combination that sent a fiery arrow straight through my heart.

Alex waved her hand in front of my face. "You know, your brother wasn't the only man staring at a woman during the ceremony."

My uneaten salmon suddenly called for an inspection.

Whatever Alex had seen in Patrick's face was one ten-thousandth of what I'd felt on that stage. Weston and Georgia's vows of undying love and commitment had been emotional enough without the added bonus of Patrick's presence.

I dropped my roll onto my plate and slid my chair back. "I should go check on Savannah."

"She's right there. With your dad." Alex pointed to the dance floor at the front of the room. "Looks like she's gettin' her groove on, too."

"Then I'm going to get some water."

"Uh." This time Alex pointed to my water glass. The one I hadn't touched all night. The one two inches from my plate.

"Fine." A weary sigh. "I'm going outside for some air."

"See? That wasn't so hard. I'd need a break, too, if Dr. Dreamboat had been staring at me like that all night." Legs crossed, her foot swung like a pendulum under the table.

I blinked twice. "Alex. You're not wearing your boots."

"Your observations skills really suck." She snagged the dinner roll off my plate. "You aren't gonna eat this, right?"

She was right. I should have noticed her dramatic wardrobe change way before now. "You look really beautiful."

"A little rummaging in Syd's closet and voilà." Her fingers imitated a bursting firework, and then, "But *my* getup is trash compared to what you're wearing. You look like you're about to audition as Audrey Hepburn. Except for the whole blond-hair thing."

I opened my mouth and immediately closed it again when Preston Wilkerson strolled up to our table. His Beach Boy hair and boy-next-door grin were quite possibly the sweetest combination of handsome I'd seen tonight—minus one tearful groom and one traveling doctor.

"Hey, Alex." Preston's tone was confident yet casual.

She eyed him like a stray dog. "Hey?"

He tapped his left foot—heel to toe, heel to toe, heel to toe. My jaw slacked. I'd known Preston since he was a toddler. The kid was a star baseball player, a debate class champion, and a theater buff. I'd never seen him nervous.

"I was wondering if you'd like to dance."

Her body jerked back as if electrocuted by his question. "With *you?*"

"Yeah," was his simple reply. "You look really pretty tonight."

Air escaped her open mouth—just air. No words.

Somebody should record this.

"She'd love to," I answered, pushing her shoulder.

Alex's swift glare could have drawn blood. "Weren't you needing to get some air, Willa? I think your brain is overheating."

"Nice try." I snatched the roll from her death grip and tossed it back on my plate. "Go dance." I leveled her with my best mom eyes. "Go."

Rolling her eyes as she stood, she twisted to face Preston. Her black A-line dress swished around her petite frame like ripples of water.

"I'm not a fan of hand holding," she said.

"Noted." His lips twitched.

"Or touching in general—unless absolutely necessary."

"Also noted." A slight shrug. "Who said slow dancing had to require touching anyway?"

Laughter burst from her throat—a beam of light in a dim room.

He crooked his elbow and offered to lead her to the dance floor. I held my breath, hoping she wouldn't completely flatten his attempt at chivalry.

But Alex never failed to surprise me.

In a very ungraceful fashion, she shoved her arm in his and tugged him to the dance floor.

A chuckle still on my lips, I lifted my hem and whirled toward the exit door.

"Escaping your brother's wedding is a punishable offense in some countries."

Patrick's voice reeled me in like bait dangling before a prize fish. Unlike a fish, however, I had zero desire to be thrown back after I was caught.

"And have you been to those countries?" I challenged.

"Maybe." That lazy grin of his could melt an igloo. "But that dress . . ." He gestured to the emerald bridesmaid dress—a strapless, heart-shaped bodice with draping fabric pinned to my left hip. ". . . would definitely be illegal in some of the places I've traveled."

Fine. If he was gonna play cheeky, then so was I. "Maybe I should have worn the Mrs. Claus costume instead?"

He groaned and swiped a hand down his face. "That costume should be burned."

"Can't disagree with you there."

"I'll add it to my list of things to do before I leave—right after transitioning the clinic back over to my father."

Before I leave.

These three words sucked the joy from my soul. Lighthearted banter could only last so long before the truth settled back in like a coming storm.

"Hey." He tilted my chin with the tip of his finger. "No frowning allowed on the dance floor."

"We're not on the dance floor."

"But we will be as soon as I collect on my thank-you gift."

I tried to salvage the remains of a smile I didn't quite trust.

Deciding it was too intimate a present to be displayed in my hall-way, I'd placed Patrick's photograph on my nightstand—the first thing I saw when I woke up. And the last thing I saw before I went to sleep.

He offered me his elbow. "Don't put it past me to beg. Because I will."

How I was able to burn with both unexpressed laughter and unshed tears, I didn't know. But one thing I did know: I was crazy about this man. There was no hiding it. No changing it. My feelings for him were as real as the breath in my lungs and the beat in my chest.

"You don't have to beg."

I linked my arm through his, and together we walked to the dance floor.

The wedding band had just started a new song. It was a slow melody I recognized, but the lyrics couldn't break though the haze of my thoughts. I was only focused on one thing, and it wasn't the music.

"So there's a lot to do at the clinic this week with your father?"

Patrick slid an arm around my waist and pulled me close—so close that I shuddered when his breath swept across my temple.

"Understatement. But I did let him know that if he ever needed a good office organizer, you were the woman to call."

"He knows I'd help him whenever and however I could. Anytime."

Patrick pulled back slightly, studied my face. "He does know that. You seem to have made quite the impression on the McCade family."

I remembered the conversation I'd had with Ivar on the wintry sidewalk just a few days ago. "He's played an important role in my journey." *Like you have.*

Patrick swayed and led us in a tight circle. Chest to chest, breath mingling with breath; his mouth was in dangerous proximity to my own.

"He's a good man." His voice was low, reflective.

"So are you." My soft-spoken words were saturated in honesty. "It may seem like your calling is so different from his—but I don't think that's true, Patrick. The *where* and *how* don't matter nearly as much as the *why*. And your *why*, your reason for serving others—whether that be in a small town, or a remote village, or a big city—is the same as his. Compassion is the trademark of a good heart."

A look of quiet intensity crossed his face, and goose bumps traveled up my arms. "Is that a Rexism?"

"You don't know? Guess the student just became the teacher."

Patrick's hand slipped away from my hip and pressed against my lower back. The scruff of his cheek brushed against the side of my face, and every bone in my body weakened.

One song faded into the next, in a continuous string of starts and stops, tempos and timing, rhythm and beats. Patrick guided me in twists and turns and spins and swings.

The music folded in on itself, building layer upon layer of melting notes and rising swells while a violent passion quaked within me. It was the kind of passion that birthed joy and sorrow, that clashed light and dark—the kind that moved and sang and lived.

Patrick slowed our steps and our movement matched the low purr of a reflective ballad. There was a sheen of sweat at the base of his throat where his pulse beat hard and steady. Our fingers intertwined, he brought our hands to his chest, and I nestled closer, resting my head against his shoulder and catching my breath.

"Maybe . . ." There was a slip in his voice, a slight release, as if someone had thrown open a gate and let his subconscious break free. "Maybe I could visit Lenox again this summer for a few weeks. Come and see you."

A few weeks. The words tumbled to and fro in my mind. Imagining Patrick's return was as easy as creating a countdown on our calendar. Only this countdown wouldn't end at his arrival, it would keep counting, a continuous cycle of comings and goings. A relationship with

Patrick would be an endless seesaw of emotions teetering between hope and heartache—a relationship with an indefinite time stamp.

"Internet can be spotty, and mail is slow, but maybe . . . maybe we could try. We could try to make this work. Make us work."

Three weeks ago, I'd begged Patrick for options—*any* option that would make the two of us work. Three weeks ago, I would have gladly settled for a long-distance romance that spanned oceans and continents and bad mail carriers. But this option was only half the answer to my whole heart's plea: to be with him.

"Patrick." He pulled me closer at the sorrowful sound of his name on my lips. "You told me yourself that relationships in your field don't work." I fingered a button near the collar of his dress shirt and then pressed my palm flat against his chest, over his heart. "Let's just enjoy the time you have left here."

"And what if that's not enough?" His fractured question matched my fractured heart.

Silence stretched between us until his arms slackened and his feet stilled. Everything around us dulled into a soundless, colorless haze. His eyes were my only anchor as I conjured up the last of my courage and said the words we needed to hear most. "It has to be."

Chapter Thirty-Nine

The familiar ping of my phone triggered a familiar pang in my chest. Three nights of midnight texting in a row had turned into something of a habit. Yet unlike my peppermint addiction, Patrick was a habit I didn't want to break.

I hadn't seen him since the reception, but we hadn't lacked for words. While he'd been buried under paperwork at the clinic, I'd been buried under the application requirements for renewing my teaching license. Another chime and I pushed out my chair, closed my laptop, and then reached for my phone on the back of the couch.

PATRICK: Are you still awake?

The same question that started each late-night edition of text threads.

ME: Lucky guess. How many cups tonight?

Patrick had been steadily increasing the number of cups of coffee he drank before the midnight hour.

PATRICK: . . .

I laughed at his attempt at a virtual drumroll.

ME: Don't leave me in suspense. I've been staring at a computer screen since Savannah left for her sleepover.

PATRICK: I need to see you.

My phone slipped from my hand and bounced off the couch cushion onto the floor. I leaned over my knees and reread the tiny screen, making no attempt to pick it up. *What does he mean?*

There was safety in texting—a clear boundary line I couldn't cross. No matter how severely I swooned over his written words, I couldn't do anything too rash. I couldn't do anything too reckless. Not that I hadn't fantasized about linking my arms around his neck and kissing him breathless. Not that I hadn't imagined locking him up so he missed his flight. Not that I hadn't researched the application process for a rushed passport and temporary work visa . . . because I had. I'd thought and cried and prayed a hundred times since Patrick last held me, but the burden of regret would always outweigh the pain of good-bye.

And I loved him too much to compromise the call on his life . . . or the call on mine. I might not ever understand God's timing, but faith wasn't a calculation. It was a trust fall.

PATRICK: Willa? I need to see you.

My fingertips tingled as I touched the text box and typed in a single word.

ME: Tonight?

PATRICK: I hope so. I'm at your front door.

His knock ricocheted through my nervous system.

Eyes wide and pulse like a jackhammer, I padded across the carpet in my bare feet.

I fumbled with the deadbolt, twisted the knob, and then opened the door.

Patrick stood on my doorstep: sexy rumpled hair, breath-catching smile, and the clearest set of blue eyes I'd ever seen. A hint of surprise lit his gaze as he took in my shower-damp head, my oversized T-shirt, and my favorite snowflake sleep shorts. A far cry from the bridesmaid dress I'd worn when I danced with him three nights ago.

Wind howled past him like a cold razor to my exposed skin.

"So I've been doing a lot of reading lately." Patrick reached inside his pocket and pulled out a stash of crinkly pink . . . *Post-it Notes?*

My pink Post-it Notes.

The pink Post-it Notes that I'd stuck all throughout Rex's journal.

"Oh!" I slapped my hand to my mouth. "I'm sorry, I should have checked it before I—"

Patrick stepped inside my house, tapped the door closed with his foot, and then moved toward me. "Twenty-seven. That's how many Post-it Notes you pressed between the folds of that old journal— and I've read them all at least three times today. Your thoughts, your reflections . . . a piece of your heart was written on every single one." His eyes stilled on my face. "And all I could think about as I read them was how lonely my life would be without you in it."

I'd backed up and up and up until there was no place left to go. My back was flush against the wall, and though he didn't touch me, his body was so close that my skin prickled with anticipation.

"Which made my decision very, very easy."

"What decision?" I asked on a single breath.

"My decision to partner with my father at the clinic."

"What?" I shook my head back and forth. "No, Patrick, you can't do that—"

"'We can make our plans, but the Lord determines our steps.'" There was a radiance to his smile that I recognized as he recited the verse I'd copied from the last page of Rex's journal. It was the same look he'd captured in the picture I now kept on my nightstand. "Falling in love with you was never in my plans, Willa Hart. But it happened. One brave step at a time." Pink Post-it Notes spiraled to the ground and scattered at my feet. He framed my face with his hands, his thumb wiping fresh tears from my cheeks. "I want to be here for your first day back in the classroom, and for Savannah's eighth birthday party, and for every single trek up Cougar Mountain. I don't want to be a man who's full of adventure and stories and not have you."

Achingly slow, Patrick leaned in, his warm breath on my face sending a chill up my spine. He kissed my bottom lip. And then my top lip. And then each corner after that, claiming my mouth the same way he had claimed my heart. With conviction and surrender.

"I love you," I whispered into his kiss. "I love you so much."

Patrick wrapped his arms around the small of my back and pressed me into his chest. We kissed until my lips felt swollen and hot and fully loved, and then he slid his hands down my bare arms and intertwined our fingers.

"I'd planned on getting a lot more talking in before that happened," he said, leading me to the sofa.

"I'm pretty happy with the order of events so far." I licked my lips instinctively and sat down on the middle cushion, angling my body for conversation—one I hoped would last all night with the amount of questions brewing in my mind.

Patrick laughed and pulled an afghan off the back of the side chair, draped it over my legs, and sank down beside me.

As if trying to remember the best parts of a good dream, I tried to replay the words he'd spoken to me when he first walked through my front door. And then I gave up. "Explain. Everything."

"Bossy." He tugged on a strand of my hair and then curled it around his finger. "My father has asked me every year since med school to consider taking over his practice when he was of retiring age, only that was the very last thing I thought I ever wanted to do." His lips quirked upward as he unwound the golden strand. "In fact, when I agreed to come here for the last few months so he could go back to Scotland with my mum, I made sure he understood that this arrangement was only temporary."

"But if you were so opposed to it before, aren't you worried that you're gonna make this decision and then regret it? Lenox is—"

"Where you are." He lifted my hand to his mouth and kissed it. "And no, I'm not worried. I just had the best trial run I could have asked for during the last three and a half months. Plus, partnering with my father for the next few years will give us plenty of time to travel in the summers." He leveled me with a stunning smile. "Us meaning—you, me, and Savannah. While you're both on summer break from school."

"Me, you, and Savannah?" Like an unforgettable song lyric, the words hummed through my entire being.

"I'm a part of several nonprofit organizations that need medical and nonmedical volunteers alike. We can find something that works for all of us."

The laugh that left my throat was a mix of shock and delight. "How long have you been considering this?"

"I'd say I've been fighting it since the night you made it to the top of Cougar Mountain, and then after the reception, I stayed up the entire night talking with my father. Between him, you, Rex, and God . . . I pretty much didn't have a chance."

As elated as his decision made me, it was still so hard for me to grasp. "And you're sure? You're really, really sure?"

"Maybe I need to help you understand."

In two swift movements, Patrick lifted me onto his lap. With the flat of his palm, he smoothed the blanket over my legs and lit a fire under my skin so hot that I wanted nothing more than to kick the afghan to the floor. But then Patrick's breath was on my neck, followed by a soft feathering of kisses. His lips inched their way along my jawline, my cheek, my chin—each tender kiss the equivalent of ten shots of espresso. My adrenaline went to war with my mind and if we didn't slow down soon . . .

I pushed against his chest.

"Patrick." But my voice was lost in our next kiss. I tried again. "Patrick."

A drugged-sounding "hmm" was his only reply.

I laughed and pulled back just enough to press two fingers to his lips. "So what does this mean for your assignment in the Pacific Islands?"

He kissed my fingertips and then shifted to tuck me into his side. "I still have to leave next week. I've already signed a contract with my agency."

"Okay." I nodded, trusting it would be exactly that. "I wouldn't want you to break your commitment."

"Four months. Four months and then I'll be here again. With you." He tipped his forehead to mine, and my heart lingered in the space between our breaths. "You can't even imagine how much I'm going to miss you."

"I think I have a pretty good idea."

"I love you." He spoke with such conviction that tears pooled in my eyes again.

"I love you, too."

I snuggled into the hollow of his side, pressing my head to his chest as his arm draped over my shoulder. For several quiet minutes, I listened to the calming beat of his heart, a sound as satisfying as an answer to prayer. Which was exactly what Patrick McCade had been to me.

"Patrick?"

"Hmm."

"What if you get bored—living in a small town most of the year? Doing normal stuff like grocery shopping and picking up dry cleaning and taking Savannah to the park on Saturday afternoons and—"

He kissed the side of my head. "I can think of plenty of nonboring activities for us to engage in."

His tone sent a fiery flush into my cheeks.

"I will never grow bored of you, Willa."

"Says the man who lives for his next big adventure."

"No, says the man who just found his best adventure yet."

Heart tumbling over itself, I nestled into my new favorite pillow. "How should we spend the next five days?"

"Together."

The only answer I needed.

Chapter Forty

When Christmas landed on day two of the five days I had left to spend with Patrick, time seemed to evaporate quicker than a snowflake caught in the center of a warm palm.

We'd spent every waking moment of those last five days together—cutting down a tree with Savannah, attending a special candlelight service at church, playing board games with both sets of parents, and laughing at my daughter's consumption of Scottish Christmas pudding in twenty-three seconds.

But with today being day five, and Patrick set to head to the airport in less than four hours, I was determined to make every minute count.

With my fingers laced with Patrick's, Savannah tugged on the hem of my coat, just ten steps outside the McCade home.

"Is Alex coming?" Her whisper-yell might as well have been nationally broadcast.

I shot her another reminder look and stealthily tapped my finger to my lips.

"Oh." She nodded and gave me a giant thumbs-up.

So much for secret keeping with a seven-year-old party addict.

Either Patrick was an Oscar-worthy actor or he was lost in a preflight oblivion again and had actually missed all two million of Savannah's verbal—and nonverbal—slips as to what was happening on the other side of his parents' front door.

His concern over leaving Savannah and me for the next four months felt bittersweet in a way that made my heart trip over itself.

"Hey." I squeezed his hand as we neared the massive entry. "I love you."

These were the only words with the power to snap him out of his distracted stupor.

He faced me. "I love you, too."

"You guys gonna kiss again?" Savannah asked before pumping the doorbell a half-dozen times in a row.

Patrick laughed. "That okay with you?"

Since the day we told Savannah about our relationship, Patrick had made it a point to answer every single one of her questions with patience. Whenever she asked and whatever she asked, much to my chagrin.

"Yep, you just might wanna do it fast since we're at the par—"

I rushed to cover her mouth.

The front door opened and Patrick's mom led us inside the darkened foyer. The back of my neck prickled with anticipation as she led us into the kitchen, to her son's fake good-bye dinner.

Only the second she flipped on the light, an overwhelming chorus of voices greeted us.

"Surprise!" Savannah threw up her arms and twirled in a circle.

Patrick's jaw slackened as he scanned the room full of townspeople—every one having been influenced by Patrick in some capacity over the last four months.

Everyone was there: from the staff at the clinic, to the families he'd seen and treated, to the guys he'd played basketball with in the wee hours of the morning at the fitness center.

"What *is* this?"

Before this moment, I'd believed it utterly impossible to surprise a man who thrived on fly-by-the-seat-of-your-pants scenarios. Yet his face said otherwise.

And me, the I-hate-surprises hypocrite that I was . . . I loved every single second of it. "This is your going-away-slash-welcome-to-Lenox party," I announced.

Ivar slapped his son's shoulder. "And a congratulations-on-your-new-job party, too. I always knew you'd come to your senses. You just needed a nice long visit." He winked at me. "And the acquaintance of a sweet lass."

"I'm . . . wow. Thank you." Patrick placed a hand on top of Savannah's head. "Thank you all for coming."

I stepped away from Patrick's side to make room for the guests and to help his mom with the extravagant refreshments on the kitchen island. An island I'd become well acquainted with.

Alex swiped a second cupcake from the platter in front of me. "I knew he'd decide to stay." She peeled the wrapper off in one swift tug and then took a bite that was pure frosting.

"You did, huh?"

She rolled her eyes and spoke through the sugary mass. "It was so obvious."

She tossed the bottom half of the cupcake in the trash can at the end of the counter.

"As obvious as you eating only the top halves of these cupcakes?"

"Life's too short to eat plain cake." She dusted the crumbs off her hands. "Anyway, I knew he would stay because that's, like, your thing."

"My *thing*? Are you going to personality-type me again—label me a *Classic Bore*?" My use of air quotes made her chuckle.

"No . . . I . . . uh . . . I may have been wrong about that."

My eyebrows shot up to my hairline. "I think I should get that on record."

"Never gonna happen." Her focus returned. "What I'm trying to say is that you have a way with people—something that makes them feel . . . like they belong. Just by knowing you." She shrugged and jerked her chin toward Patrick. "And even with all the crazy cool humanitarian stuff he does . . . I could still see it."

"See what?"

"That you gave him something he didn't have out there across the oceans. Somewhere to really belong."

Before she could push me away, I pulled her in for a two-second hug. "Are you sure you're only seventeen?"

At the sound of the front door opening, we broke apart.

"We didn't miss him, did we?"

It was Weston, hand in hand with his new bride.

I pushed forward to greet them. I hadn't been sure they'd get my message in time, or that even if they did, their plane would land in time to make Patrick's send-off.

A perfectly sun-kissed Georgia threw her arms around me. "I'm so glad you called us. We came straight from the airport." She pulled back slightly and arched a brow. "Looks like we have a lot to catch up on."

My smile said I agreed with her wholeheartedly. "Yes, we do."

Weston hugged Patrick, his back slap slightly harder than necessary. "I hear you've taken your groomsman duties pretty seriously." Weston's ability to be discreet was as effective as Savannah's ability to keep a secret.

Patrick reached for my hand and pulled me to his side, kissing me on the temple. "What can I say? I'm an overachiever."

For the next three hours, Patrick kept me close. The guests stayed until the punch had run out and all the cupcake tops had been eaten. Then, when Weston was busy giving Savannah her Hawaiian souvenirs, Patrick stole me away to a shadowed alcove under the stairs.

The sudden intimacy was my reality check. We no longer had days or hours. We had minutes. Minutes until his father would start up the car to drive him to the airport and drop him off for a flight that would take him thousands of miles away. For four months.

Good-bye was happening. Right now.

Patrick linked his hands around the back of my neck. "I can't believe you managed to put this together today—and right after Christmas, too."

"I wanted to show you how many people care about you here."

"One is all I would have needed." He kissed the arch of my brow and then the tip of my nose. "You're amazing."

"I think you're amazing."

"We could argue this all day and still, I would win," he said.

"Spoken like a man."

"In love." He stroked his thumbs down the sides of my neck. "Spoken like a man in love." And then he kissed me until I no longer cared about winning or losing or playing games of any kind at all.

The bang of the front door signaled the end to our kiss.

"It's time, Patrick," I said on a wavering breath.

He wrapped an arm around my waist and cinched me closer, lowering his mouth to my ear. "Just a little longer."

I pressed my head into his chest. "Just a little longer."

It was those words that would stay with me in the days and weeks and months ahead—those words that boosted my hope and soothed my heartache. They were the words that reminded me that winter only lasts for a season.

And this year, I was ready for spring.

Epilogue

My daughter was a die-hard sign carrier.

We had been standing in baggage claim for nearly seventeen minutes and not once had she lowered her carefully colored **WELCOME HOME** poster. And I knew she wouldn't, not until she saw her favorite overseas pen pal. Patrick had faithfully sent her a postcard each week he was gone—and all sixteen of them were taped to the back of her bedroom door.

At the sight of a new rush of people coming down the escalators, Savannah stood on her tiptoes, as if the neon sign with Patrick's name could somehow be missed.

"What if he forgets what we look like?"

"He won't, baby."

"Does he know you work at my school now—that people have to call you Miss Hart?"

"Yes," I laughed. "He knows."

A marching band, all wearing school uniforms that could double as bumblebee costumes, swarmed the carousel next to us searching for their luggage.

She rocked back on her heels, no longer able to see over the mass of yellow and black.

"Maybe I can bring him for my show-and-tell next week?"

"You'll have to ask him about—" My words were cut short.

Patrick.

Savannah tossed her sign to the ground and charged toward the foot of the escalators, her arms and legs pumping at the same speed as my heart. He lifted her into the air with ease and used one very tan arm to secure her to his side.

I paused as I watched her cling to him. She planted a hard smack of a kiss to his right cheek and giggled when he returned the gesture. It was a sight that made the last one hundred twenty-four days of his absence worth every single lovesick second.

Until this moment, I'd been certain that the man I'd committed to memory months ago would be the same man I would pick up at the airport.

But I was wrong.

This man's smile was brighter, his hair longer, his skin darker, his eyes . . .

His eyes were an endless layering of blues. As if every patch of sky he'd seen, and every span of ocean he'd crossed, had taken up residence there.

Patrick had told me once that it takes seeing the world though someone else's eyes to realize where you fit inside it . . . I hadn't understood it at the time.

But I did now. When our eyes met, I could see exactly where I fit.

And then the last few feet of the distance separating us was erased and our arms were tangled in a triangle-shaped hug.

Savannah patted the top of Patrick's head and then squirmed out of his hold.

"Well?" she demanded when her feet touched the floor. "Aren't you gonna kiss her?"

His smile sent a rush of heat to the center of my chest.

He pulled me closer. "I was sure planning on it."

Savannah clapped as he dipped me low and kissed me fully.

Unlike every kiss we'd shared in the past, this kiss wasn't tainted by a pending good-bye.

This kiss was a welcome home.

Acknowledgments

God: So thankful you are the author of my life.

My husband, Tim: Do you remember that time we moved three thousand miles cross-country exactly one week before I started writing *A Season to Love*? And do you remember how you made every single trip to the grocery store for three months straight so that I could hole up in my writing cave? And do you remember how you managed our household, worked a full-time job, and bought me case after case of La Croix Sparkling Water because you knew it made me the happiest girl ever—all so I could make my deadline? Well, I do. And I will never, EVER forget the ways you have loved me. You are my greatest blessing. I love you.

My boys: Your patience, understanding, and free back rubs are only a small part of why I think you two are the best kiddos in the world. I pray that someday I will be able to encourage you in your dreams the way you have encouraged me in mine.

My family: Mom, Dad, Ashley, Daniel, and the entire Deese tribe, thank you for your unwavering support. You are a huge part of my life story. I love each of you so very much.

Tammy Gray: THIS BOOK WOULD NOT EXIST WITHOUT YOU. Though I am sometimes (cough, cough) prone to exaggeration, the statement above is 100 percent accurate. If I could add up all the hours we've spent calling, texting, and e-mailing each other over the writing and revision process of *A Season to Love*, I would be looking at months. Your generosity, honesty, and die-hard spirit are the foundation of what has become an irreplaceable friendship. Thank you for telling me the hard stuff first so that I could believe the good stuff later. Thank you for saying, "Give me more Patrick!" ten dozen times in the first draft, and thank you for reminding me of my "why" on the days I wanted to turn off my laptop and bury it in the ground. So glad God set us up when he did.

Amy Matayo: Thank you to my "writer wife" for giving me some epic moments of comic relief during the writing of Willa's story. There is no text too random, no conversation too ridiculous, no topic too off-limits . . . and that's just the way we like it. I love our kind of crazy. Looking forward to many, many, many more years of friendship and fun.

Kristin Avila: Your titles have increased over the last few years—editor, writer, beta reader, office supply enthusiast—but I will always, *always* think of you first and foremost as my fabulously organized friend. There is little you haven't done for me, like when you showed up at RWA with all the things you knew I'd never think to pack (and you were right!), or when our flight was cancelled and you were willing to drive us eight hours if the airline couldn't rebook, or how even after I moved many states away, you still send me all the latest happenings in our industry along with reminder e-mails so I don't miss a deadline. Thank you a million times over.

My agent, Jessica Kirkland: Praise the Lord for unlimited mobile-to-mobile minutes. Our conversations are never short on words but always full on heart. Thank you for your wisdom, friendship, and authenticity. Looking forward to our next getaway weekend. (I'll bring the gluten-free cupcakes this time!)

My editor, Kristin Mehus-Roe: Thank you so much for your thoughtful corrections and feedback on *A Season to Love*. Your edits pushed this story to the next level and your overall care and concern for these characters shined through each and every comment. I hope our paths cross again.

Amy Hosford, Associate Publisher, Waterfall Press: Thank you for believing in *A Season to Love* (and in small-town romance) and for encouraging me to write from my heart. I'm so grateful to have found a home at Waterfall.

Waterfall Press: I LOVE being a part of your team! Thank you for caring as much about your authors as you do about the work they produce.

Beta readers: Amy Matayo, Ashley Brahms, Britni Nash, Carmen Hendewerk, Christa Allan, Conni Cossette, Jenny Jones, Joanie Schultz, Kacy Koffa, Kristin Avila, Lara Arkin, Nicki Davis, Rebekah Zollman, Renee Deese, Sarah Price, Tammy Gray. Thank you!!!

Jennifer and John Fromke: Thank you for answering my many obnoxious medical questions while on family vacation!

Melissa McClenathan: Thank you for replying to exactly 5,490 text messages on teacherly stuff and never once telling me to go find it on Google.

Real Life home group: For your many, many prayers and for your eagerness to befriend the "new girl." So blessed to have you in my life.

About the Author

Photo © 2014 Renee Deese, Renascent Photography

Nicole Deese is a lover of fiction and writes contemporary romance with an inspirational twist. She is the Kindle bestselling author of the Letting Go series and *A Cliché Christmas*, the first book in her new Love in Lenox series. She lives in northern Idaho with her husband and two sons.

To subscribe to Nicole's newsletter and stay current on all upcoming book projects, please visit www.nicoledeese.com.